The Journey from Heaven

William Essex

First published 2012

This edition published 2022 by
Climbing Tree Books Ltd.

Copyright © William Essex 2012, 2022

ISBN 978-1-909172-75-3

www.climbingtreebookstore.com

www.williamessex.com

Cover photo by Claire Wilson, LLE Photography

Cover design and typesetting by Grace Kennard

To Penny, who was there

Thanks, Colette

In The World That Is

"Prepare ourselves for what?" Ben says.

Hannah raises her hand.

"Tell us what to do," she says, her voice as fragile as the truth. "Realistically," she adds.

The consultant looks across the desk at the mother of his terminally ill patient. The mothers are always so much stronger.

"We can resume treatment if you wish," he tells her. "But it causes her discomfort. And I have to tell you that it may be better – for her – if we focus on making her comfortable." He looks at Ben. "I think you should prepare yourselves to say goodbye."

Ben is waiting for the man to start telling them about the small hope that still remains. That if only they – just – something, Megan may still pull through. There's a miracle cure that might just work. There's a miracle. But the man has stopped on the bit about saying goodbye. Ben doesn't get it. "When can we expect..." he begins.

"How long?" says Hannah.

In The Beginning

Where are the angels?

Where are you?

Startled, I–

I raise my head.

I am–

I am sitting at a plain wooden table in an empty stone room under a high arched window. The walls of this room are made of granite – beautiful – and the floor is bare wood – such colour.

Through the window the first sunlight has just touched a bell at the top of a high narrow tower.

The first sunlight.

Of this beautiful morning.

I can hear the monks singing their dawn prayers in the chapel.

I can hear–

There are voices passing in the corridor outside – voices – and faintly, the river in the distance.

Faintly, but it is the river.

In the distance.

So faintly. Faint sound. Distant.

It is beautiful.

If I was to stand up–

–I would see the trees, and above them–

–the road that skirts the southern edge of the valley.

If I was to leave this room–

–I would walk along to the open gallery–

–and look down–

–at the monks at prayer.

I could listen to the singing and feel the light radiating through the east window.

And the river in every sound.

There are people from the village in the body of the chapel.

In the high rooms around the monastery, there are solitary figures – not like me–

–but like me; no, not like me, but–

–solitary figures, open, aware, present.

I am a solitary figure in a high room.

I am–

Present.

"I am here," I say.

My words make sound in the room.

There is a small glass vase on the table, containing bluebells and rose campion picked by the girl from the village, and the devotional objects supplied by the monks. They are tolerant, and holy. The room is sprinkled with water that they have made holy, and there is a memory of incense in the air.

It is all for him.

In the corner of the room, there is a bed. The blanket has been taken away, and the thin mattress left bare.

This was his room. He is an old man now, close to death, and at the end, despite all he has done, he has found doubt.

Where are you?

It is a simple question, full of need.

And mine to answer.

•

As I leave the room, a voice says: "Chandrael?"

"Sahasrael, I am here."

I stand up from the table, feeling its surface under my fingers – my fingers – and it is as if, for a moment, I breathe the air, the pure, the beautiful air, such air.

The room is physical around me, the walls hard to the touch, the room a shape of flat surfaces and angles. The stone is beautiful, full of the labour of its making. The floor is under my feet.

I am standing on it, here, in this moment, in this place.

I am not ready for the touch of the closed door, not ready to work the curve of the latch, not ready, oh, not ready for the colour and sense of the wood against me – against me – and the tiny insects.

I lift the weight of the latch, the cold metal, and the weight of the door yields to me.

And so, called into nature by an old man's question, taken by surprise by my own presence in the living world, uncertain of everything beyond the need to answer, I pass silently along the unlit corridors, through the grey archways and under the blunted stone faces of saints, past the shelves and lecterns of old learning, to come out at last where the final corridor opens out onto the gallery, where the light populates the air.

I feel the living emotion swirl around me, and I laugh out loud, unheard, at the gifts I bring.

I am a child now, born anew into the world of physical things.

I am old beyond age.

Still unseen, invisible to their eyes, immaterial, I move past the bowed heads, and out into the day.

•

There is a garden here. The single twisted oak tree predates the walls enclosing the garden and even the monastery itself, although not the first settlement. It was planted by a man whose religion told him that his lost son would live again in the tree.

He sat on the stone where I am sitting now, grieving for his son, and decreed an end to wandering. His people colonised the hills and the plains and this opening valley, but now their stone circles and burial cairns are fenced off, their beliefs and purposes forgotten. A few bones and one complete skeleton remain in the museum, with the fragments of stone tools and the priceless bronze amulet, but the gored boy's remains have long since merged with the earth beneath the tree. He is at peace, and gone.

Is there nothing after all?

There are three monks in the garden today. Michael and Simon are young, new to the monastery. John, resting in his wheeled chair, wrapped in the infirmary's blanket, his face calmer than his mind, gently instructs Michael while Simon, nearby, picks the thin white roots of weeds from the earth around a line of green seedlings that waver in the wind. The day is passing around us. Hours have gone already.

I stand by the chair and rest my hand on John's shoulder.

He raises his head.

Michael glances up at him and then returns to his work.

John closes his eyes and his lips move, forming a prayer.

Sahasrael says, "What are you doing, Chandrael?"

"I shall answer him," I tell her.

In the living world, the words between us have no substance. They are whispers on the wind.

But Michael smiles as he works.

He will be wise.

The bell sounds. Their day is beginning its end. The edge of the light has moved slowly up the wall of the monastery and the garden has fallen into shadow. It is time for the prayers that will carry the monks into evening.

I step back as Michael and Simon help John to stand.

Tonight, at last, for the last time, I shall join them in their prayers.

•

There is the old woman knelt at the rail, dressed in black, her husband silent beside her, waiting to help her to her feet. There is the young couple, their baby between them, his hands clasping theirs together. The young mother's eyes are closed in prayer; tears run down her cheeks. The father tells himself that he must not cry.

There is the old man, gaunt, in too-big trousers a decade old and a jacket that he bought when his wife was alive, before he went to prison. He is emaciated and he grips his cap around the bent handle of his stick. This chapel is a place of fear for him, a place of shame, and he does not raise his eyes, does not raise his head, as he pauses in the aisle before taking his usual place in the shadowed corner.

Now, for an hour, he will pray silently for forgiveness. He will not sing; he will not give the responses; he will pray.

His victim takes her place behind him, her hand on his shoulder, waiting to forgive him. One day, when he understands, forgiveness will be her gift to him. Then he will accept the book from the young boy at the door. Then he will sing. And she will sing with him.

"We share the pain of their days, Chandrael. No more."

I pass through this congregation of the living and the dead, pass through the gate, pass between the monks and stand briefly at the altar. There is darkness outside now, but the candles give the old stone a tint of pale honey and their reflections are bright in the stained glass of the great window.

And then I take two steps back from the altar so that I am standing between the monks' stalls. They face inwards, so that I can turn first one way and then the other, studying the faces for the first and last time, saying my silent farewell.

In the beginning, after that first shared flight over the newborn land and its green ocean of trees, as we all travelled on to our places in the world that would be, I chose the river and the valley around it and the green horizons.

Sahasrael travelled on to enter the dreams and visions and the imaginations of artists, travelled on to become a guardian to the lost and near-lost and a guide to those freshly embarked upon a life's journey. I became one with the harmony of the river and the valley, then the circles and cairns of stone, then the walls and the rooms and their successive religions.

I became the spirit of the place, the quiet sense of peace, held to awareness only by the souls around me, and then by the questing presence of the tribe, then of the priests and their people, then of the monks and theirs.

Until now.

I am no longer the spirit of this place.

I see that John is watching me. I smile and he smiles in return. I am surprised that he should see me so quickly.

He sees me first as a young man with a rucksack, a tourist perhaps, who has come through the gate and approached the altar. Perhaps in a moment, he thinks, this young tourist might even try to take a photograph.

But now I see in his mind that he has begun to understand. The indulgent smile for the young man with the rucksack leaves his face. He glances to one side, at his fellow monks, and understands that he alone can see me.

In his eyes, as his mind opens, I take on the appearance that he had so hoped to see. The light flows through me. Bright wings spread about me. Before he can move, I answer his question.

WE ARE HERE. WE ARE WITH YOU.

I raise my right hand in a gesture of blessing.

He does not speak.

The thought forms in his mind that he should kneel.

But he can see in my face that there is no need.

"Is it my time?" he asks.

The other monks have understood that something unusual is happening. A space has cleared around Brother John. Two monks are on their knees.

BE AT PEACE, JOHN.

Now he kneels. I put my hands to his head and close my eyes to channel a blessing. I can hear his prayer. I feel the blessing move through me.

YOUR TIME IS COMING. WE ARE WITH YOU.

I know that the light concentrated around him has become visible to the other monks and to the congregation.

I have brought the angels to Brother John.

Later, he will preach.

His eyes are still closed and I acknowledge the greater presences in the light around him. They will stay with him now.

I vanish from his sight.

Every path has an end and every end is a beginning. We pass through experience to wisdom, and from wisdom to understanding. Beyond understanding, beyond our reach until we begin again, is acceptance. We are born and born again. We rise.

I walk away from the monastery towards the river. The long grass rustles against my legs. I can feel the cold wetness of the earth under my feet. A dew has fallen. The cold air moves against my face and I look upwards towards the bright stars lighting the Heavens. I raise my arms and feel the brush of subtle wings against my back. The monks' singing is carried upwards on the night air.

I am here, in nature; here, now, feeling the chill of the night.

The sky opens and I feel myself lifted through the monastery's evening to the greater truth beyond. I laugh out loud and my voice catches with ecstasy.

This is the place that John would call Heaven.

"Sahasrael, my sister."

"I am here."

"Let me see you."

There is a silence as long as a hesitation.

Then she steps into her own light and I see her.

She comes to me as she is seen in dreams, as a tall woman with long bright hair. In this form, she wears a long white shift-dress without shadows, and open sandals.

"You need to see me?"

Behind her there are arched stone columns, and in the shadows, an altar. But this is not the monastery; she stands against the background of a painting that hangs in the holiest place of another religion.

"You took away his doubt."

"I heard him."

"You heard one voice. Among the many."

"I wanted to help him."

She looks down at herself and then at me.

"We share the burden of their journey, Chandrael. No more."

As she speaks, her face becomes thinner than I saw it a moment ago, more focused.

Her body under the shift is wiry and thin now, her arms tanned. She is older and tougher and suddenly less familiar.

"Look around you."

I see rows of lockers, casual clothes hanging on hooks. There are open bags and more clothes on the benches. We are back in the living world again. This is a changing room, far removed from the monastery.

"It's a hospital."

"There is pain here. If you join us, you will know it."

Abruptly she pulls the shift off over her head and throws it into an open locker beside her. She is wearing a white sports bra and white running shorts.

"It is not the purpose of angels to prevent experience, Chandrael."

She takes a faded blue sweatshirt out of the locker.

"We do presence, and silence, and never leaving alone."

She pulls the sweatshirt down over her body and reaches up to loop her hair out at the neck, shaking it back into place.

"Their lives are their own. Not ours to change."

"Yes."

"Most of them don't even know we're here."

"I–"

"They don't want to know."

That is when the sudden question sounds clearly in the air between us.

"Will I live forever?"

It is a child's voice, touched with fear.

Sahasrael steadies herself against a locker as she works her feet into a pair of trainers.

"You hear her, Chandra," she says and we both smile at the spontaneous abbreviation of my name. "I will be waiting. Go into the world. Give her what she asks of you."

The space around us lightens.

"And no more."

I step forward.

In The World That Is

Will I live forever?

I step forward into a child's bedroom. There is a bed, painted white, with a dangling mobile of clowns. There is a rocking chair and a small chest of drawers. On the pink carpet a four-year-old girl is playing with a beanbag and a small plastic horse. She is murmuring their conversation to them, interspersed with instructions of her own.

She looks up. In her innocence, she can see me.

"Hello," she says. "What's your name?"

"Chandra," I tell her. "We are with you."

"Hello Chandler," she says. "Do you want to play?"

I kneel down and we play. Her name is Megan and her horse's name is Pugh. The beanbag is called Sleepy. As we play, I watch the tiny lingering fright of Megan's difficult birth and the hours of separation afterwards fade to a speck no larger than a star.

Sahasrael says silently: "We do not prevent experience, Chandra."

"I heard her," I say softly.

Megan sits back on her heels, satisfied with an arrangement of her dolls.

"There," she says.

She brushes her hands together as though clearing them of flour or dust after a job well done. Then she looks at me with the expression she uses for such small wishes as having a second story at bedtime or staying up until Daddy comes home.

"Will you tell me a story, Chandler?" she says.

"What would you like in your story?"

She settles against me, putting her thumb in her mouth. "Horses," she says indistinctly. "And magic."

I see the picture of horses and magic that forms in her mind and put my hand to her forehead to hold it there.

In the life she faces, we will need these horses again.

"I will tell you a story," I tell her. "It will be a story of horses. Some of them can fly."

In her mind the herd separates and a white foal is revealed. It trots to the fence where she is waiting and nuzzles her hand.

"Don't forget magic," she says around her thumb.

"In my story," I whisper, as the tears start in my eyes, "You and I will fly through a magic country where the birds are your friends and the stories never end."

I help her to climb from the fence onto the back of the foal's mother and then I mount my own winged horse, which is honey-coloured, with a long mane. I watch the story unfold in her mind, forming the words as the images come to her. Time stops in the small bedroom as we fly across gold horizons. Her breathing slows, although she does not sleep, and peace settles in her.

The story ends. Time begins again. She stirs. "Thank you," she says, removing her thumb from her mouth. The words come from a deep place.

"Megan," I whisper, bending forward to say the words that she will remember. "Your father knows many stories. Your mother will listen to them with you. Be with your parents now."

"Yes," she says. In her heart, in this instant, she understands.

A woman's voice calls. Megan scrambles to her feet.

"It's lunchtime," she says.

Then she stops. A look of perplexity crosses her face.

"Does Mummy know how to make your lunch?" she asks.

For a moment I see myself as she sees me. For Megan today I am a bright angel, like the angel in her picture book. For Megan, I have white, feathered wings.

"I shall leave you now," I tell her.

She frowns.

"Will you come back and play again?"

"Yes."

She leans forward on a child's impulse and kisses me on the nose. The kiss is wet. I raise my right hand again to touch my blessing to her forehead.

"Mummy's waiting."

As the room lightens around me, I hear her downstairs telling her mother that she has just been visited by an angel. "His name's Chandler, Mummy, just like Chandler's name."

"That's lovely darling, did you wash your hands?"

"Can Chandler come to play after playgroup, Mummy?"

"Of course, darling. I'll call his Mummy and we'll arrange a day."

"What do angels eat, Mummy?"

"I don't know, darling. What do you think?"

"Chandler didn't want any lunch."

I step through the door and away.

•

"What did you learn from that, Chandra?"

Sahasrael is waiting for me as I step down onto hard sand. I shield my eyes from the sudden bright sunshine.

"I hadn't expected such suffering."

Sahasrael looks away across the flat desert around us.

"It is enough to be with her. That is what she is asking you to do."

On the horizon, obscured by a haze in the air, is a settlement of tents and huts.

"You heard Megan as you heard John. But we do not prevent experience."

She turns and walks swiftly away towards the settlement. Taken by surprise, I stumble at first to follow her through the great heat of the desert.

"You talk about suffering," she calls over her shoulder. "On the scale of eternity, one life is just a moment."

"I know. But I can–"

"We are guardians of their souls, Chandrael. Not guardians of their lives."

We walk together, side by side, in silence.

The settlement is a refugee camp, set down in haste on the site of an abandoned village and intended to be temporary. Sahasrael and I stop at the end of an alleyway formed by sand-coloured tents. They are old, originally military issue, too heavy to be moved by the sluggish breeze that laps around us. The ground is hard-packed dust that coats the ankles of the relief workers as they pass us, listless and unseeing. At this time of day, most of the refugees stay in their shelters, exhausted by heat and fear and lack of food. There is noise here, but it is outweighed by the silence of those unable or too weak to move.

Now we are both light, with great wings.

"Oftentimes, we take the form of their deepest belief."

"This?"

"For many of them, yes."

I think of Megan in her small bedroom.

"But we don't show ourselves?"

"Let them decide whether they see us."

We walk into the camp.

Angels congregate unseen around the hospital tents, where nothing more can be done by the living for the living. The shaded space is hot and the flaps of the tents have been lifted to gather in the air.

Sahasrael steps away from me, and I follow her into the first of the tents. There are metal-framed beds in rows, some with stands beside them. There are trolleys to carry medical equipment and plastic cool-boxes to store supplies. There is no longer electricity, and little water. The whole camp is supposed to be a triage station, a temporary stop to prepare the weak for travel. But the war has come closer and the roads are mined now, and the helicopters are grounded.

"Just what we are asked to give, Chandra. No more."

She speaks from the air above a bed close to the table where the doctors meet. The air shimmers with heat and pain and despair. In the group around the bed, the bereaved husband-and-father cannot cry, but he lets the young aid worker hold him tight around the shoulders. It is as if she is crying for him; in his grief, he believes this and is comforted. The doctor moves the sheet to cover the faces of the mother and the young child. They have gone together, within a minute of each other. This is one of the quiet human miracles of this place.

The doctor raises her head and meets the gaze of the second aid worker standing at the end of the bed. She shakes her head slightly: not yet. Let the man grieve. The young doctors and nurses and aid workers are outnumbered by the scale of the disaster around them, but in the midst of their greater purpose, they can find time for small kindnesses.

Sahasrael stands in the air with the souls of the mother and the young child wrapped in soft wings. Her eyes are fixed on mine.

"Share it all," she says. "Feel it all," and I do.

The great, selfless commitment of the aid workers is heady and powerful in the air.

"I can do more."

"We can all do more."

I am drawn to a young woman who sits on a low stool beside a bed. She wears sand-coloured trousers and a sand-coloured shirt. Her dark hair has been cropped roughly short to get it out of the way; she cut it herself two weeks ago.

She is the youngest of the aid workers and has no medical qualifications, but she has been aggressive in taking on any task that will free the better-qualified to do their work. She has erected tents, carried supplies, dug latrines, cleared excrement, burned waste. She would have cleaned and prepared bodies, but without letting her suspect what they are doing, her colleagues have spared her this. They have come to believe that she is punishing herself for the tragedy around her. In her exhaustion, this is beginning to be true.

But her colleagues have noticed something else about Naseena. They have seen how she is welcomed by the residents of the camp. She is made welcome in the tents and the shelters and she plays readily with the children. When she plays, she shows no sign of her anguish. She shares her own vitality. She can laugh, and it seems that, briefly at least, she can re-animate listless children. She has made many friends among the refugee families.

And so, quietly, without her knowing what is being done for her, Naseena has been reassigned. She has become an unqualified, unofficial nurse of the living. And it has worked: in the days and weeks, she has regained her strength as she has given her love. She has discovered her true purpose in the camp. The children love her and the adults see the light in her face. She has organised games for small groups of children, and once, with her limited resources, even a party. Naseena has prayed for her children and the residents of the camp have begun to include her in their prayers. She has gained the respect of her fellow aid workers. The emotion of the camp focuses in her.

She sits now at the bedside of a twelve-year-old boy who has become her friend. She calls him Ali, which amuses his parents and he likes. He has helped her around the camp, following her, translating for her, sometimes explaining, sometimes saving her from inadvertently causing offence.

But now the happiness of their time together has turned to sadness. Naseena is filled with guilt and self-anger as well as premature grief for his condition. She believes, wrongly, that if she had not taken him around the camp, exposed him to so many potential sources of infection, his body would not now be coursing with blackness. She believes, out of her own rediscovered self-hatred, that the lesson of his death will be: do not bring the children together; do not let them play. Keep them separate from each other.

I sit on the edge of the bed so that I am facing Naseena in her chair. She reaches forward, and as her hand touches Ali's, I close my hand over both of theirs.

Ali's eyes open. "Nas," he murmurs. She moves forward in her chair. Now her other hand is on his chest.

"Hello Ali," she says. Then, after a moment, "You've been asleep."

"Dreams," he says faintly.

He can see me, but he thinks I am a doctor.

"Good dreams, I hope," she says automatically. There are tears in her eyes.

He turns his head so that he is looking at her. "My father," he says.

She misunderstands him. "They are coming," she says. "Your

parents are coming." They are not, and she panics: can she attract somebody's attention to fetch them?

Ali has not been there to stand in line for his father. It has been one of his duties and now his father will have to do it. This is the anxiety that has lodged in his mind.

"Tell my father I come back soon," he whispers, and falls asleep again.

Naseena is briefly surprised at Ali's failure to understand that he is dying. But then she thinks: better that he doesn't know.

She sits back and holds his hand again and closes her eyes. The tears run down her cheeks. She sees herself going to Ali's parents and telling them that the time is closer than they thought; that they should come now and be at his bedside. She sees Ali's father's face, which she has come to know well, soften in sorrow.

And then, at last, the force of the camp's emotion rises up in her. She opens her eyes, and if Ali had been awake he would have felt her hand tighten on his. "No," she says. Without thinking, she reaches out her free hand and places it on Ali's forehead.

No. Suddenly she knows that he need not die.

Give me a miracle, she prays.

Give me a miracle now.

I reach out my hand. The light flares within her and for a split second she sees the spark between her hand and Ali's forehead.

In the corner of her eye, she sees me. I am white to her.

But she turns her head and again she cannot see me. No matter; her attention stays on Ali. She can feel heat in both of her hands, one holding his hand and the other on his forehead. There is no time to think. A small voice of disbelief sounds at the edge of her mind but she silences it: she knows what is happening.

And then it is done. Suddenly she is gulping for breath, letting the tears come freely now. She lowers her head to the bed next to Ali, letting her hands fall into her lap. Suddenly she is weak. In her heart, the light gradually rekindles itself.

Across the tent, sitting at the table where she is writing up her record of the deceased mother and daughter, the young doctor is not sure what she has just seen. In her peripheral vision it was as though something short-circuited, although there has been no electricity here since the last of the back-up generators died. For a moment she watches Naseena, who has slumped forward on the bed, and diagnoses exhaustion. She shakes her head. Naseena won't slow down. She is almost a liability. But not quite. Not quite, the young doctor repeats to herself, sighing. She is fond of Naseena and knows her value.

The husband-and-father, who has been invited to sit but prefers to stand, knows what he has just seen. He is looking steadily across the tent at Naseena. Too late for his wife and daughter, he knows, but Ali's mother and father will have their happiness restored to them.

You are with us, he says silently. In his head, he voices a prayer. You are with us. Care for my family.

Within the hour, the whole camp will know. Naseena will be honoured.

Within twenty-four hours, Ali will have returned to his family. He, too, will be honoured.

Nothing will be said. But hope will return.

Sahasrael says, "Come away now, Chandra."

And we are gone.

•

We stand in a clean, dark room. The air is cool to the touch.

"Do you understand what just happened, Chandra?"

"I could do that for Megan."

But she is shaking her head.

"You gave Naseena what she asked for, Chandra."

"She didn't know I was there."

"In her soul, she knew. Not consciously."

There is a bed in this room, without a mattress. On the wall above the bed is a panel of controls, sockets, buttons, switches and unlit lights. A metal trolley, empty, stands by the bed. Against a wall, flanked by two hard plastic chairs, is another trolley on which there is a box-like machine with two small blank screens on the visible side. The room is deserted, although there are voices outside in the corridor and light shines through the cracks between the closed shutters.

Sahasrael stands with her face down, watching her fingers touch the plastic casing of the machine. She speaks slowly, in the manner of one choosing her words with care.

"What you have learned from that, Chandrael, is that we do not intervene. We do not interrupt their lives. We give what we are asked to give, and no more. Naseena called you for a single purpose. To help her heal her friend. She was never conscious of you."

"But I healed the boy."

"She healed the boy. You gave her what she needed to do it. She could have taken that from any one of us."

Then, in a gentler voice, she says, "The creation is only truly complete when it has been experienced. You know this. It can only truly be experienced by those who are discovering it for the first time."

She watches my reaction. "She will deny what she did. She will shut you out. Watch how she does it."

I am avoiding her eyes. "Yes," I say.

She laughs. "Go on then. See what you can do."

I am gone.

•

"Something happened. I know something happened."

Naseena Danti sits on the side of the fold-up bed that she and another woman use in shifts in a tent allocated to the female aid workers. The tent is as dark as it can be at this time of day, and Naseena is whispering aloud to herself. There is a man asleep on one of the other beds, lying on his side so that he has his back to her. Naseena is no longer troubled by this. It has been some time since any of them worried about segregated sleeping quarters.

I stand in front of her in the half-dark and raise my right hand to touch her forehead. She neither sees me nor feels my touch. The air in the tent now carries a scent of wood-smoke. It is a scent she likes. But she is not conscious of it.

Naseena rubs the heel of her hand across her eyes. She is fully dressed, but she has just woken up after maybe an hour's sleep and now she needs to wash. Always needs to wash, she reminds herself, and fights down the frustration. She cannot let herself be aware of her own discomforts.

When she opened the flap of the tent five minutes ago, confused, still half asleep, she found a small pile of gifts – a carved wooden figure, a necklace of pierced seeds, a zip-up pencil case containing dry leaves – all on an upturned plastic crate placed right in front of the opening. The petals of flowers, mostly blue but some red, some cut out of plastic, others made from torn-up paper, had been scattered on and around the crate.

"What?" Standing in the light of outside, eyes still mostly closed against the glare, Naseena had not immediately understood what she was seeing. She had crouched down, blinking, and picked up the necklace. "What is this?" she had whispered.

And then she had understood. Stepping back abruptly, she had stumbled back through the tent flap and come to rest on the bed again, sleep-musty, shocked. "No." What she had remembered could not have happened. It didn't make sense.

I speak to her, but she doesn't hear me.

"But something did happen," she whispers.

This time, she is not aware that she has spoken aloud. She can remember being with Ali, thinking him dying and anguished that she could not leave him to call his parents. Then she can remember – what?

It comes back to her as the memory of her body reacting to a physical shock. There was something between her and Ali like static electricity and she had received the shock. There had been a doctor … in white? … standing at the end … the end? … of the bed.

Hadn't there?

Then Maya – she definitely remembers the doctor who had been sitting at the table, Maya Brennan – then Maya had been touching her shoulder, whispering her name, and she had been asleep face down against Ali's hip. Only for a moment, surely, but she had been asleep. An electric shock. Knocked out.

But if that was Maya, who was the doctor at the end of the bed?

And then she remembers that when Maya woke her, Ali had been laughing at her. Lying in bed, giggling, laughing, childishly delighted that she had made a fool of herself. Laughing at her as though his strength had returned.

And now there is an upturned crate outside the door of the tent, bearing gifts. And when she first saw those gifts, a short moment ago, she had immediately known why they were there. She had known.

Just for a moment, she believes.

She scrambles out of the tent again, suddenly urgent. She steps past the small collection of gifts. Not possible. But she must be sure about Ali. She walks swiftly – the aid workers do not run, because that might cause alarm – towards the main hospital tent.

On the way, she is greeted in a manner that unsettles her again.

28

It is a short walk, not more than twenty metres, but in that distance: a man inclines his head to her; two women walking together stop and bow their heads as she passes; a group of men turn to watch her pass, openly but without threat. She becomes aware that she is also being watched from the tents. There are people coming to the dark openings as the news of her passing moves ahead of her.

A small boy runs up and touches her arm and then is scolded away by his mother.

Naseena lifts the net over the entrance to the medical tent, and steps inside.

•

"I can't make her hear me," I say.

Sahasrael is standing next to me outside the medical tent. The dust coats our ankles.

"She does not want to hear you."

"How can I get her attention?"

Sahasrael shrugs. "She is busy living, Chandra."

I turn away from her.

•

At first, as Naseena's eyes adjust, it seems that nothing has changed. Maya is sitting at the table, writing. One of the refugees – but not the same man, Naseena sees – is standing at Maya's shoulder. And Ali is still in his bed, asleep again – healthily asleep. She watches him for long enough to be sure.

Naseena experiences a curdled emotion that is somewhere between dismay and relief. She dreamed it all. But he is well.

"Hello." Maya sounds surprised. She lays down her pencil and pushes back her chair. "Back so soon? You're supposed to be sleeping."

"I came to ask if there's anything I can do." Naseena is suddenly conscious again that she has not washed. She cannot stop herself glancing towards Ali. "I haven't been able to sleep."

Maya is only nine years older than Naseena, but there are times when she feels like the girl's grandmother. She is the senior doctor in the camp, responsible for the wellbeing of staff as well as patients, and Naseena is not only the youngest among them, but eager to help in a way that makes her seem younger still.

So Maya stands up and comes across to take Naseena's elbow. Naseena seems embarrassed, not meeting her eyes and unable to stop glancing over to where Ali sleeps.

"He's fine," Maya says, and finally the two women's eyes meet. "He's fine. He's fast asleep."

They look at each other. "I'm so glad," says Naseena. "I was worried about him. I couldn't sleep," she continues, as if there is something here to be excused.

"He's as strong as a horse," says Maya. "He'll be fine now."

Naseena finds that she cannot even formulate, let alone ask, the question she has in her mind.

"You fainted," says Maya, smiling. She is suddenly brisk. "Come on, since you're here."

Then Naseena is sitting in the chair and Maya is crouched in front of her taking her pulse.

"I had a very extraordinary dream," says Naseena faintly. Sitting down like this and receiving Maya's attention has reminded her that she is exhausted.

"He'll be fine now," says Maya, cutting her off before she can say any more. "The fever's broken so he can sleep it off."

Naseena thinks: fever?

But Maya is her confident self now.

30

"I'm going to give you something. You really do need to sleep."
Maya smiles briefly. "Otherwise we'll be finding you a bed in here."

Naseena defies her own tiredness and Maya's competence to ask,
"What happened?"

"You fainted. Occupational hazard. Exhaustion. You just fainted."

Maya is not looking at Naseena.

Then she is.

"We're all tired," says Maya. "We've got to stay sane."

"I dreamed that–" Suddenly, Naseena is not sure what she
dreamed.

Maya does not respond to the unfinished sentence. She is busy
again, taking Naseena's pulse once more and looking down at her
watch. "Take these when you get back to the tent. Lie down, and if you
still can't get to sleep, pretend. Count down from a hundred. Count –
whatever. Animals. It'll come soon enough."

The pills come from a small – unsealed – plastic bottle in Maya's
pocket. Naseena receives them in a twist of paper torn from the
record book on the table.

"Thank you," she says, and Maya smiles quickly before turning
away. She has returned to her record-keeping before Naseena has
even left the table.

I'm such a fool, Naseena thinks, as she walks away from the
medical tent. I'm so tired I'm imagining miracles. Her mind curls
with embarrassment and she doesn't notice the small procession of
children that forms behind her and follows her back to the women's
tent.

My cry of despair is unheard in the world.

•

"You see how they shut us out?"

"Why are we here, if we do nothing?"

"They protect their – we do more than nothing, Chandrael."

"Megan hears me. She sees me, she–"

"She is young. And she has asked you to be with her. And you are not."

She sees my expression change. She takes my arm.

"I am sorry. But Naseena has a life to live. They all do. It is not our purpose to interrupt their lives."

Around us, the camp is silent in the heat. The sun has risen high in the sky and the tents conceal their own shadows.

"Sahasrael, I just want to help them."

She studies my face.

"They are not asking to meet you. Let them live their lives as new. Be with them if that is what they ask. Painful as that–"

"Even if–"

"Be with Megan now, Chandra."

And she is gone.

•

Hannah Rose saves up the tedious shopping for Megan's days at playgroup. Usually, this works perfectly well. But today, by pick-up time, she's totally frazzled. Traffic jam, no parking space, no change for the machine. No time for coffee. Then she picked the wrong queue at the check-out. Add the more-stressful-than-usual-because-she-was-late search for another parking space within walking distance of the playgroup itself, and she arrives at the big blue door too conscious of her irritation to be able to get rid of it.

But she's in time, just. They're all there, the familiar pick-up-time group: William who usually picks up Oliver because his wife works and he's self-employed; Sophie, who is Fergus's mum; Clemmie, who picks up the twins. And the new woman with the necklaces and the bangle earrings, Sarah something, mother of the little boy Chandler, Megan's new friend, and apparently two older boys as well.

Hannah thinks about inviting Chandler round to play at the weekend, a treat for Megan, but dismisses the idea. Maybe tomorrow, when she's in a better mood. Hannah leans against the wall next to William, who never speaks. Maybe tomorrow.

The idea with the big blue door is that after storytime, one of the children gets the task of walking down the corridor to let the parents in. One of the non-storytelling helpers has to sneak down and unlock the door during the story. On the days when it's Megan's turn, Hannah can see through the wired-glass panel that her daughter enjoys the tiny importance of opening the door.

It isn't as heavy as it looks, and there's an extra handle at child-height.

Hannah likes the way that, as soon as the door is opened, the parents all focus in so tightly on their own children, exclaiming at the day's painting or glued-paper model, crouched for the reunion.

Maybe the day's going to clear up now.

Hannah can't immediately see Megan. But Mrs Barnaby, the slightly scary matriarch of the playgroup, comes forward to meet her.

"Round here, Mrs Rose."

Megan is sitting at one of the painting tables, her head resting on her pooled arms. Hannah takes in immediately that her daughter has not joined the others for the story today. This is Megan in reluctant, tired mode.

"We've had a quiet day today," Mrs Barnaby is saying. "A bit of a sleep after snack time, and then a little painting. Shall we show Mummy your lovely picture, Megan?"

Hannah has gone down onto one knee next to her daughter. Megan, slower to react than usual, says, "Mummy!" and puts her arms round Hannah's neck. She holds on tight. Hannah had been braced to listen to a lively account of the morning's doings. But she's a mother; she adjusts quickly.

"Hello, darling, how are you? Have you had a nice day?"

If she's not careful they'll fall over.

Hannah slips her bag awkwardly onto the floor and gets herself squarely onto both knees, sitting down on her heels as she grasps Megan securely round the upper body and hoists her onto her lap. The little plastic chair tips over backwards. Megan clutches tightly around her mother's neck. Her eyes are focused on a point in the air behind Hannah's right shoulder.

Mrs Barnaby, a big woman in her fifties who has grown-up children of her own, crouches down alongside Hannah.

"She's been quite sleepy today, not really wanting to play," Mrs Barnaby says, in her parent-level voice. "We thought perhaps a bad night?"

Or something wrong at home? Hannah hears.

She shakes her head. "No, I don't think so," she says. "Nothing unusual."

Megan is still holding on tight. "Nothing's upset her here?"

Mrs Barnaby accepts this possibility with a slight nod.

"I did ask, actually," she says. "But none of us have noticed anything out of the ordinary. She's just been very quiet."

"What's up with you today, darling?" Hannah says to Megan, and Mrs Barnaby gets to her feet. The two women exchange a glance: if necessary, they'll talk another time. Mrs Barnaby leans forward and taps the edge of the painting laid out flat on the table, and is gone.

"Is that your picture, darling? Did you paint that? Wow."

Megan animates herself briefly. Still holding on round Hannah's neck, she reaches forward to pull the picture towards them. Then she puts her thumb in her mouth and snuggles back against Hannah's

34

neck. She glances briefly at the air behind her mother, and then closes her eyes.

Put her down for a rest this afternoon, Hannah thinks as she gazes at the damp painting. Brown stick-animals on a flat green field. A white – cloud? Blue sky and yellow sun.

This is the second time in a fortnight Megan has been unwell at the playgroup, Hannah thinks.

Third time, she suddenly remembers.

Keep her at home tomorrow?

The doctor?

Suddenly, unmistakably, Hannah inhales a scent that she associates with wild flowers.

It is begun.

Bright Messenger

I find Sahasrael on a rain-wet pavement, walking behind a fragile old woman who is unaware of her presence. The old woman's mind is full of small human practicalities: the early daffodils; the posting of that birthday card; her friend's wellbeing. There is also, later, the daily phonecall that will relieve her daughter of the need to worry about her. A chore, but it must be done.

She is walking the small dog who is now her only living companion.

Sahasrael says, "Let me show you something, Chandra."

The dog looks back at me without curiosity.

The old woman's mind has a background of memories. The days of her youth, her marriage, her active life. She was once a nurse. But she does not wish for the return of those times. Now she is content to feel the benevolence of the creation around her and she believes that sometimes her departed husband visits her. She speaks to him often, quietly, in their private moments, reassuring him that she is well and happy and telling him of their extended family of descendants. She is at peace with the late days of this life.

"Heel, Buster," she says. The dog, who knows the route of this walk, has already stopped beside her.

"Not here," Sahasrael says. "Not yet. Further down, away from the corner."

A hatchback car, driven fast by a young man, snaps around the corner and cuts through the air that the elderly woman would have occupied in crossing the road. She walks on. She will cross further down, where she can see both ways more clearly.

"You just prevented her death."

"She made her own decision where to cross the road."

"But she heard you."

"She did not hear me. Any more than she saw me. But I was with her."

We walk together behind the woman as she approaches the point where she will be safe to cross the road. She is still not conscious of our presence. Her name is Elspeth Carey and she is beautiful. Her aura is a steady blue.

"Think of what you did with Naseena," says Sahasrael. "They may not be conscious of our presence, but that does not mean we're not here."

We stand with Elspeth Carey and her dog, and then follow them across the road.

"If you really want to help them, Chandra, do not let them know it's you. Be an intuition, or a quiet word in the air, or a freak accident if you must, but for most of them..."

"...don't let them see an angel," I finish for her.

She laughs. "Do it in a way that they can explain rationally." The word amuses her. "They know better than to believe in us."

Her hand finds mine as we walk together.

"I've known their pain, Sahasrael. But never their lives. I never understood how isolated they are."

"And yet they are not."

"But the pain is real. And they don't know…"

"…that they are not alone. But that is their purpose, is it not?"

We are close now to Elspeth Carey's small bungalow.

"And ours is?"

"To watch over them while they live," says Sahasrael as we watch Elspeth Carey open her front door. "To be with them. To welcome them home."

"To give them what they need, surely?"

"Which is rarely an end to doubt. How can they discover what they already know?"

Sahasrael turns to face me.

"Tell me why you wanted Naseena to hear you."

I take a moment to choose my words.

"Because she cannot be–" Sahasrael begins.

"It's not just–" I begin.

We have spoken across each other.

"It's not just that I want to help her," I say after a moment, examining my own feeling as I speak. "I told you. I feel a connection, Sahasrael. It's open-ended. There's something that isn't finished."

"Does she want you to be with her at the end?"

"The end? She's not–"

"She cannot be part of Megan's life."

We stare at each other.

"You cannot see it, can you?" she says.

I return to the desert

•

Before I can find Naseena, I see the boy, Ali, out in the open, looking back at the rough shacks on this edge of the camp. He has wandered out into the desert, something he is forbidden to do and has never done before, and now he turns and looks at a scattering of trees and bushes some five hundred metres from the camp's real perimeter. He stands among the rocks that mark the edge of the southbound road, half-crouching to make himself harder to see from the camp.

Ali has in his mind the thought that perhaps there is water here. It is an excuse for his excursion, but he has convinced himself that it is a justification. He doesn't consider that others from the camp might have explored here before him, nor does it occur to him that these trees mark a point on the same dried-up riverbed that runs through the camp. There is no water here because there is no water in the camp.

Newly healthy after his confinement in the hospital tent and free of obligations for an hour, Ali for once lets his natural vitality get the better of the caution he has learned in the camp and walks towards the trees, keeping the rocks behind him. As he gets closer, he sees that the trees are further apart than he had expected. But there are bushes and there is cover.

"Their future is not ours to change," says Sahasrael.

"There is a river here," I tell her. "Perhaps it could flow again."

"No."

Ahead of us, a breeze rustles through the leaves. Ali does not notice it, but if he had, he would have thought it a miracle; such a cool breeze is seldom felt in this region.

"They won't need water," says Sahasrael.

That is when I see the future that awaits Ali in the trees.

The two soldiers are scouts for the rebel army from which the refugees are fleeing. They have seen Ali leave the camp full of Westerners and enemies and they have planned for his approach. Now they watch him from their concealment among the trees. The camp is on one of the likely routes for their army's advance towards the border, and they have never bypassed a settlement of westerners.

"What is this?"

The two soldiers laugh softly at the noise Ali makes as he explores. If he comes close enough, they will kidnap him. If he resists, they will kill him. If he submits – Ali will make a reluctant but eventually compliant soldier in their army. Nine months from now, in another war, he will step on a landmine and lose both his legs. Thinking him dead, his comrades will take his gun, his ammunition and his water. He will bleed to death in the sand.

And then I see the rest of it.

"Sahasrael, no!"

Within forty-eight hours from this moment, the advancing rebel army will launch its offensive northward to the border, to cut the country in two. By then, as the two soldiers have guessed, the camp will have been identified as a primary target for the offensive. If the rebel army can keep to its schedule, an advance group of soldiers will reach the camp on the morning of the seventh day from today.

Seven days.

The smiles fade from the two soldiers' faces as Ali approaches.

He comes to the edge of the dried-up riverbed. There is a thin trail of green vegetation marking where the last of the water still lingers under the surface of the ground. But he is looking at the fresh tyre-tracks in the not-quite-dry ground. He understands that a vehicle has parked here recently.

Sick with the dread that even now, in this danger, he will shut me out, I reach out and place my hand on Ali's shoulder.

"Go back to the camp and tell them about the tyre tracks."

He looks up.

"Can you see me, Ali?" I say, surprised.

He shields his eyes and does not speak. He stands very still, but there is no fear in his heart. I remember that he saw me once before, when he was sick in his bed. Then, he thought I was a doctor. Not this time.

"Come with me back to the camp," I say.

He sees me as a tall man, dressed like an aid worker, bright as the sunlight against the clear sky. His religion has a place for messengers. I reach out and he takes my hand. We walk back across the flat hard desert.

Ali understands what the tyre tracks mean for the camp. As we walk, I see the miracle form in his mind: all the Westerners and all his family and all his people spirited away in the trucks that used to come with supplies, before the war came so close. I see them all fled beyond the reach of the soldiers who made the tyre tracks, to the place across the border where the supplies are kept. I see the miracle and I feel the certainty in his heart: it shall be so. He knows this.

I stop and he looks up at me.

"Tell them they must leave now," I say.

He turns and runs away from me.

·

Again, the clean, dark room.

"Sahasrael, you knew."

"And you did not. Think on that, Chandrael. You didn't know."

"I got so close. How could I not–"

She waves away my question.

"The camp is a military target. The whole country is a war zone." Finally she looks up and meets my gaze. Her eyes are a liquid blue. "Death is where suffering ends. They are no longer alone. You should be happy for them."

"He has asked me for a miracle."

"Yes, and you let him see an angel."

"He didn't shut me out."

She rests both hands on the frame of the hospital bed. It is cold to her touch. I feel the chill that she feels.

"Chandra, there is life, and there is death, and we are outside both. It is so hard to be with them when their lives happen to them, but I am not a guardian of life. I must let them die."

The silence of the room is broken by the faint sounds of the hospital beyond. No light shines through the metal shutters covering the windows. It is night here.

"Sahasrael, he asked me for a miracle."

"It would be a quick death. For most of them. Hardly any suffering."

"Or they could live."

"Do you listen to me, Chandrael?"

And she is gone.

·

What a difference a good night's sleep makes.

Hannah Rose is feeling much happier today. Megan was still asleep when Ben left early with a bun, which she wrapped for him while he showered. She made coffee for him and went back to bed to watch as he drank it. He kissed her, thanked her and left.

Then, as though the click of the front door had woken her, Megan came running in with news of another of her dreams about horses. Lively as ever. Nothing wrong. They sat in bed while Hannah listened to the story. As has become usual recently, Chandler was involved, although the dumpy little boy from playgroup, delicious in his eye-magnifying spectacles and shorts, doesn't look like much of a rider in real life.

Hannah is beginning to understand that although the dream-Chandler may be a pure figment of Megan's imagination, not based on anybody, he's also here to stay for a while.

Then everything clicked with breakfast and getting into the car without forgetting anything. Then there was Mrs Barnaby picking up on some invisible cue and making a special fuss of seeing Megan again, which helped a lot. Hannah resolves to buy Mrs Barnaby something nice, soap or flowers or something, to hand over when the opportunity arises.

Then, just arriving at playgroup as Hannah said goodbye, there was Megan's flesh-and-blood friend Chandler, the real boy, coming in with his mum.

And the timing was just right and the words came naturally so now there's an arrangement with Chandler's mum that she'll come round for coffee one morning while the children are at playgroup. Sarah, Chandler's mum. Sarah, with the bangles, new-agey and bohemian, amused, different. Hannah thinks she will like Sarah.

Hannah is now browsing through the children's books at the town library. Supermarket next, and then fuel for the car, pick up Megan and home.

Hannah has chosen enough books for a fortnight. She's ready to leave.

On a sudden impulse, she goes instead to sit in one of the saggy comfortable armchairs among the adult bookstacks. She has never done this before, and as she settles herself, she smiles to think that even in her busy life, she can still sometimes act on impulse.

This is a relatively private corner of the open-plan space. She can be quiet here, alone with her thoughts. She'll skip the supermarket today, she decides.

She sees that she has settled in the reference section, next to shelves labelled "Religion and Spirituality A to M". She is amused at the notion of dividing up such a subject alphabetically. Then she is reminded once more of Megan's dream-friend. Hannah smiles. She imagines the dream-Chandler as a boy, Megan's age, friendly like the boy at playgroup but good at riding, agile, tanned, probably a real outdoor boy, with a penknife and good at fishing.

In her imagination the dream-Chandler glances up at her from the riverbank. He grins and reaches out his hand.

Chandler. C. He would fit right in ... this shelf ... here. Hannah is surprised at such a notion dropping into her mind and she smiles and shakes her head. But she's looking anyway. She reaches up and pulls down a book that must have strayed from the Art section. It is called "Symbolism of the Annunciation in Renaissance Painting" and it contains paintings of the scene where the angel appears to tell Mary that she's going to have a baby. The angel, as Hannah flicks through the images, is always carrying a flower stem.

They're lovely pictures, actually, Hannah thinks.

Although that's not the expression she'd have on her face if a man with wings flew in through the window and told her she was going to get pregnant without – Hannah gives a short, library-quiet laugh.

And wait a minute, aren't lilies supposed to symbolise death? Hannah starts reading. But no. Lilies, in these paintings, symbolise purity. Staying at home and not getting drunk at parties. Stupid of her.

I'd get daffodils or bluebells or something, Hannah thinks. Some cheap flower growing wild. And they'd be dead.

And the real miracle is the husband. Hannah smiles, thinking of her own Ben tucked up safely in his early-morning train while she gets Megan started. She is not aware that her eyes have closed. Darling, I'm pregnant, but I haven't been sleeping around.

How did they know the baby wasn't – the husband's? Her Ben would have to be part of it. Hannah is asleep now, and dreaming.

Sahasrael reaches forward and brushes a lock of hair back off

Hannah Rose's forehead.

"It's true, then," she says softly. "You've chosen it all."

I have watched from across the room and now I join her.

"You left me."

"I came here."

"In the desert," I say. "Why didn't I know?"

But Sahasrael just takes my hand.

"Not now, Chandra."

Together we watch Hannah sleep. She is dreaming now and the dream is insistent. It shows us her husband, Ben, knee-deep in water, splashing Hannah; then Ben running across flat sand, chased by laughing children; then Ben lying on a rug, shading his eyes as he looks up at Hannah.

"We are not participants in their lives, Chandrael."

"Although we can intervene."

"At best, we can help them with the choices they make."

"We can change things for the better."

"In small ways."

She is staring intently at Hannah.

"So quick and so easy," she says. "In a moment of happiness."

There is Megan, in her swimsuit, with shallow water fresh from a broken wave surging around her ankles. Megan shrieks with laughter, holding her elbows tight in to her chest against the cold.

"She is so happy in her life," I say.

"Happy in her moment."

The dream fades. But Sahasrael leans forward again.

"I hear you," she says to the sleeping woman. "It can be done."

She bends forward and picks up the book from Hannah's lap. Surprised, I realise that we have become visible in the room. We are angels in the form of Hannah's deepest belief, neat wings folded snugly against our backs. I look around. But nobody has yet seen us.

"If I took you to a destination, Chandra, would you travel to it?"

"Of course not. But–"

"If I showed you the path, would you search for it?"

"No, but–"

"Trust the journey, Chandra."

"But–"

"How could you know your own journey, before it's complete?"

"This is my journey?"

She is amused. "The question answers itself."

A man is watching us from the customer-service desk across the room. I see a confusion in his mind. Are we companions of the sleeping woman? Is she unwell? In any case, we are a disturbance and he will have to intervene.

I raise my hands to him and he takes this as a sign of apology. He looks down again at the print-out on the desk, reassured, without understanding why, that all is well. In his eyes, the white robes and the wings are some kind of out-of-season fancy dress. Couple of nutters, he thinks, embarrassing their sane friend.

Sahasrael returns the book to the shelf. "He is a rational man," she says softly.

We leave Hannah and walk through the room. Nobody looks up.

"For the camp, Chandrael, you argue against a quick death and no suffering."

"I argue for life."

Sahasrael looks back across the room. She shakes her head. "A quick death and no suffering," she says. "Such a small change."

She pulls open the door.

"Let's see what your visit to Ali has achieved."

The door swings shut behind us.

•

"The angel has spoken to me."

At first Naseena thinks that Ali is referring to Maya, who has just entered the room.

"What do you mean?"

"The angel." But then the bereaved husband-and-father, who went to find Naseena and brought her here to the boy, crouches down beside Ali. They talk rapidly in their own language and Naseena gives up trying to understand. It is a surprisingly drawn-out exchange. Maya has paused just inside the doorway.

The husband-and-father straightens up. "We must leave. I know this."

"How do you know this?"

"I know this."

"What's up?" Maya has been listening from the door. Now she joins them.

"We have to leave, apparently," Naseena tell her. She shrugs, embarrassed.

They are in the still-usable building known as the administration block, in the empty room that is the nearest thing the relief workers have to a communal refuge. The administration block was built as a schoolhouse by a long-departed charity, and this room was intended to be the children's dining room. There are still two trestle tables, and now there are plastic chairs. Wooden benches have been pushed to the walls. There is a serving hatch through to another empty room that is now used as an office. In that room they keep the communications equipment that still works; they are relying almost entirely on solar power now.

"Tell me, Ali," says Maya, crouching down to speak to him face to face. She takes Ali's wrist and Naseena understands that Maya has started to examine Ali while she talks to him.

"The angel has told me. We must go. There are soldiers. I have seen them."

"Where are the soldiers, Ali?" Maya briefly pulls down the lid of one of Ali's eyes.

"He has told me."

"What angel, Ali?" Naseena says softly.

"That's very interesting, Ali," says Maya, speaking over the gap where Ali would reply, and Naseena hears the diagnosis in her voice. Ali must be returned to bed.

And that is when Greg Doyle enters the room.

Greg is Maya's administrative counterpart in the camp, responsible for everything except the medical care. He is a heavy, noisy presence, tall and broad-shouldered, with long curly hair bleached by the sun and a blunt face whitened by sunblock. He is thirty-four, good with engines and broken things. The two women turn their faces to him.

"I was looking for you," he says to Maya, stamping his boots as though to clear them of mud. "People are packing up to leave."

"What do you mean, packing up?" Maya straightens up from the boy.

"They're leaving. Packing up to leave," Greg corrects himself. "There's a rumour going round the camp that we're about to be attacked."

He runs his hand back through his hair, clearing it from his forehead, and looks at Maya. He has clear blue eyes that rarely meet hers, and long eyelashes. "That's what they say," he adds.

He is good at keeping the camp running, but his confidence falters in her presence. She is the most beautiful woman he has ever seen.

Maya hardens her voice. "We're needed here, Greg."

His heart sags. Sooner rather than later, probably very soon, he's going to have to make the decision to pack up the camp and leave. Should have done it weeks ago. But Maya Brennan won't let him.

"Maybe somebody's got family on the other side, and they've heard something." He gestures to the serving hatch. "You have to admit the news is pretty bad." He stops, as though taking in the scene in front of him for the first time. "What's up?"

"You're not seriously suggesting that this camp would ever be attacked?" Maya begins. But Greg's question deflects her. She waves her hand to indicate Ali. "Some–" she can't find the word "–stuff about soldiers. Nonsense."

"Soldiers?" Now it's Greg's turn to crouch in front of Ali. "What soldiers? Tell me about the soldiers."

I could kick myself, Maya thinks.

But it is as if Ali is suddenly given courage. "I saw soldiers in the trees." He points. "Marks of wheels. Their trucks come."

"How many soldiers?" Greg asks.

Ali, who did not see the two soldiers in the trees, who has only mentioned soldiers to strengthen his case for departure, repeats, "Trucks. Marks on the ground."

Beside him, hand on his shoulder, the bereaved husband-and-father speaks softly. Greg, who has a working knowledge of the language, understands. "This one will believe," the man has said.

Greg looks up at him and then again at Ali. The expression on his face is a question in itself. What will I believe?

"The bright messenger told me," says Ali. "The angel."

Greg understands in an instant what has angered Maya.

But before he can speak, Maya herself reacts. "Are we going stark, staring mad?" she demands. She has enough self-control not to express her anger directly to the boy, but she says to Greg, "You know what they believe about–" She stops herself. Neither of them looks at Naseena. "Now he's going round telling stories about soldiers and angels. It's a fever, Greg. He's not as cured as we thought he was. We need to find him a bed and stop these people putting themselves into danger. They can't just–" Again, she runs out of words.

"We can't stop them leaving," says Naseena softly. She is looking at Ali. Neither Greg nor Maya hears her.

"The news is bad," repeats Greg. "Some of them do have family out there."

"And they're in touch with each other, are they?"

Greg sighs. "We can't stay here forever," he says.

He is studying Ali. Maya sees this.

"Greg," she says, turning and moving away from the group.

Greg comes to join her.

"You're not saying you believe him?"

Greg suddenly loses patience with her. "Maya. I know you don't have time for this. I know you're busy. But there is a shooting war fifty miles south of here. No more than that. It's turning really nasty. People are getting ready to leave. They know how dangerous it is. Probably better than we do."

He has surprised himself. He continues, his voice conciliatory.

"I listen to the radio. We're not so cut off that I don't talk to the people at Qasir. I know we've got to find a way of getting out of here, sooner not later. Now we've got a boy who says he's seen soldiers. What part of it don't you want me to believe, Maya?"

She stares at him. A second passes and then he raises his hand as if to take her by the arm and hold her in place. But before he can touch her, she pushes past him and walks straight out of the room without looking back.

"Ah, faff!" Greg runs his hand back through his hair.

Then he turns and sees that Naseena and the boy and the man who said he would believe are all staring at him.

"Okay," he says, sighing, meeting the man's eyes. "You'd better tell me all about it. Angel and all," he adds, crossing the room to join them.

We stand on a bridge over a wide river. It is still early morning in the city where Hannah's husband works. As the sun rises, glass buildings reflect the glittering water. Wind catches spray from the small waves and the air is fresh and cold. Fat barges, their hulls low in the water, glide below us.

"You understand that Greg and Maya are arguing about the angel, not about the danger?"

"How could she deny the danger just because Ali saw me?"

Sahasrael leans forward and drops a single lily on a long stem down into the water. We both watch as the lily curves into the current and is gone. She straightens up, brushing her hands together.

"It would be irrational to do what an angel tells them," she says.

Greg stands alone among the trees.

He has walked straight out here from the administration block and now he has seen the tyre tracks for himself. They're recent, although the desert beyond is still empty to the horizon. He has not stumbled across the two soldiers, who have shifted their position, but he has found evidence that people have concealed themselves here. He now believes Ali's story about soldiers.

He doesn't want to think about the angel.

Greg is angry with himself. He knows that the war has broken the country. He knows that the government has lost control and that what's left of the infrastructure is breaking down. He does not know, but he guesses, that the rebel armies have seen their chance and are preparing their final offensive.

He also understands, as Maya apparently does not, that a camp run by Westerners and sanctioned by the present, defeated, government will have little chance of surviving the chaos that will follow the war. Even if it is a hospital. With the journey to the border so dangerous now, and the one road almost certainly mined, the camp is an obvious refuge. When the rebel army comes, it will be an obvious target.

But in the face of Maya's confidence, he just can't make the decision to go. He knows how difficult it would be to get the refugees, even the able-bodied ones, out to the border. They would need trucks from Qasir, as many as possible, and fuel, and even then they wouldn't be able to evacuate the whole camp in one trip.

The convoys would be unarmed and vulnerable and, yes, he almost certainly would be leading them into a minefield. Back and forth across a minefield, in the face of a hostile army.

The minefield, Greg thinks. The minefield. He has no way of telling whether the one road really is mined, but in his heart, he knows that it is.

Standing in the shade of the trees, looking down at the tyre tracks, Greg now fastens on one certainty: the road is too risky. We would need to mark the trucks more clearly than ever, he thinks, so that they couldn't possibly be mistaken for military vehicles.

What about sheets? How about painting the trucks white, if we have any paint?

Is there any way we can find out if the road really is mined or not?

I can't risk the lives of a whole convoy.

But I have to know.

Greg shakes his head.

The road is too risky.

Maya has walked out from the camp and now stands in the open, hands thrust forward in the pockets of her jacket, watching Greg.

He turns his head, meaning to scan the horizon in both directions before returning to the camp, and sees her.

"Oh hi," he says, turning, surprised enough for it to come out natural-sounding.

She waits for him as he walks towards her.

"I'm sorry," she says softly, but he is not yet close enough to hear her and she does not repeat the apology.

"You know it's dangerous out here?" he calls as she comes closer. He always feels the same slight tension when he sees Maya, but this time, because he was taken by surprise, he seems to have jumped right past it.

"Dangerous for you too."

"Maya," he says, shaking his head. He reaches forward, and without thinking, touches her on the cheek.

It is a gesture of affection. It is also the first time he has ever touched her. She glances up and sees his face flinch as he realises what he has just done.

"Bad time to be eaten by an animal," she says, before he can spoil it by apologising. "We need you, Greg."

She is looking down as she speaks, and her headscarf conceals even her profile.

"Let's walk back," he says, his voice constricted again with shyness.

They walk in silence, heads down.

"I know we've got to leave sooner or later," she says eventually.

"I know it's a dangerous journey," he replies.

"We've got to be practical, Greg. If the situation is really so bad."

"I think it is. And–" he stops and waits for her to face him "–that's my own judgement. I listen to the radio. I talk to Qasir. I know the supply situation. But I make up my own mind."

Maya sighs and continues walking.

"We've got to talk about the practicalities," she says, and now he knows that she will not leave, even if he does decide to go.

She will stay here with the very sick, who cannot be moved.

He says, "I know it's almost as dangerous going, as staying."

Maya says nothing.

Greg's voice now carries a note of apology. "If we don't do something, these people are going to die here, Maya, sick or not." They walk in silence.

"We need to make a decision soon," says Greg after an interval.

"I know," says Maya.

Together, the decision still not made, they walk back into the camp.

Seven days from now, the first soldiers will enter the camp on foot. They will have a looted four-wheel-drive black Mercedes limousine driving slowly behind them. Its windows will have been shot out, there will be bullet-holes in its bodywork, and blood will have stained its leather seats. But its engine will still be running and its tyres remain unscathed.

Greg will emerge from a tent in his shorts, stripped down to show that he is unarmed, his hands raised, calling out, "Welcome". They will shoot him in the stomach and watch his agony until one of them grows impatient and shoots him twice in the head. No need to conserve ammunition now.

Then, spreading out and enjoying the terrified silence, they will machine-gun the closed tents nearest to them. After that, as the main army begins to arrive, they will herd the survivors out into the open, killing the wounded. Other groups of soldiers will spread out to other tents. They will separate the Westerners from the rest, and then they will kill the male relief workers and those of the refugees who are too weak to stand.

Over the course of the afternoon, they will kill the remaining refugees and the Western women.

Nine months from now, the atrocity at the camp will be cited as one of the justifications for the next war.

"At least they've forgotten the angel."

We are on the bridge again, and visible. Sahasrael wears a blue suit and a white blouse and carries a briefcase. I am once again the young man with the rucksack. Around us, the bridge is crowded with commuters hurrying towards the business district.

"Don't tell me that it can't be done."

Sahasrael looks out along the shining flat distance of the river.

"No," she says, "No, I won't tell you that."

Across the northern border, in the town of Qasir, at the headquarters of the relief effort for the region, contingency plans are already in place for an evacuation. Fuel has been reserved, available trucks have been identified and counted, and volunteer drivers have put their names forward.

If the decision is made to go, and if the first convoy from Qasir includes as many trucks as now looks likely, and if the trucks still in the camp can be refuelled and started once the convoy gets there, the projection is that three round trips, from Qasir to the camp and back, will be enough to evacuate Greg's estimate of the total population of the camp.

Allowing for packing, loading, refuelling, repairs and some driving at night, three round trips will take six days.

Six days.

But in Qasir, they are waiting for Greg to make the decision.

Even now, despite their constant attention to the available reports on what is happening, they do not realise the urgency of the situation.

This is a formality that they will observe until it is too late to save everybody: Greg is in place; Greg makes the decision.

"We have to get him through the minefield."

"And past Maya."

"If he could see the urgency..."

"If he could see the urgency, he would make his own decision. But even then, he would not call the convoy from Qasir while he believed there were mines on the road."

We have said all this. I spread my hands in despair.

"Sahasrael, help me!"

She ducks her head, surprised.

"You saved Elspeth Carey's life. She took her own decision, you told me, but without you, she would have died on that road. I gave Naseena a miracle. It was hers, but I gave it to her. We do presence, and silence, and never leaving alone. And yet Brother John called me into nature and I came to him. If he can change me, and if you can save a life, then we can do more here than just be with them while they die."

"And now you ask me to help you."

She is staring once again at the distance of the river.

"Sahasrael, please. We can do more. If Greg makes his decision to risk the minefield tonight, and if he leaves before dawn, the camp will be empty when the first soldiers arrive."

She pushes herself suddenly back from the guardrail.

"What I will do for you now, Chandra, is mend a radio."

She shows me what she means.

"Oh."

It is so simple, and the relief so great, that for a second I cannot speak.

"He is with people for an hour," she continues, "but then he will be on his own for the rest of the night."

"I shall go to him."

"Be with him. But do not show him an angel."

I am still shaking my head at the simplicity of her idea when Hannah's husband walks past us on the way to his office. Ben Rose.

It is a shock to recognise him, so different in his city clothes from

Hannah's dream of him in the library.

Sahasrael is watching me.

"Trust the journey, Chandra," I say, before she can say it. "Does he need me?"

But she doesn't reply.

No matter. I give a smile to a young, hurrying man in a dark suit, who is startled even to make eye contact. He is uneasy about a meeting later in the day, at which he must speak. Let it go well, I say silently. I exchange glances with a passing woman who decides: yes, I will have the baby. I raise my hand and bless the child within her.

All Is Well, I say to the child.

"Chandra," says Sahasrael, touching my arm. "That is enough."

But she is beginning to laugh with me. She settles her hand into the crook of my arm and we begin to walk, falling into a rhythm of walking, leaning into each other, heads close together.

But we are not following Ben Rose. Sahasrael has turned us to walk back in the direction from which Ben came.

"All paths cross, Chandra."

"Naseena?"

"Perhaps."

Now there is a man ahead of us, reading a poster that advertises an exhibition of sacred paintings. Sahasrael stops. He glances at us, and as he does so, she steps forward. Now we are standing next to him, as if to read the same poster. I catch his eye.

"Beautiful, isn't it?" he says. He addresses me, but I see in his mind that he wants to make contact with Sahasrael. He sees her as a beautiful woman, but also his instincts draw him to her. His wife is sick and he is afraid. He has come reluctantly to the city for a meeting with bankers. He is early.

"It is beautiful," I agree, nodding my head.

The painting in the poster shows a procession of men bearing gifts. They have followed a curving road down from the top left-hand corner of the picture and now they kneel in the foreground. The Mother sits in a cave mouth on the right, and the Child sits on her knee, his right hand raised. There are angels, and in the distance, a city.

"After Mantegna," Sahasrael says. "Do you know the picture?" She smiles in a way that takes the breath from him.

She asks because he does know the picture. Paintings such as this are a quiet love of his life, and she listens as he tells her of his gentle passion. He is a kind man and his wife loves him.

Sahasrael touches him on the arm. "Are you going to the exhibition?" she asks, and he decides that yes, he is going to the exhibition, right after the meeting. He tells her this, and decides that he will buy a gift in the gallery shop, if there is one, to take home to his wife.

"Good luck this morning," Sahasrael says as we part from him. He waves, forgetting that he has not told us of his morning.

Sahasrael watches him until he is out of sight.

"He didn't see an angel," she says.

"But he did see us."

"He was alone. He needed us."

"And his wife?"

"I think you might know them both, Chandra."

Before I can ask her what she means, she shakes her head.

"Go on. Be with Greg. I'll fix the radio."

She turns and walks back towards the bridge. I watch to see the moment at which, between one step and the next, she vanishes from sight and was never there.

In The World That Could Be

Greg Doyle stands on the edge of the desert, thirty metres to the north of the refugee camp's boundary. This is the opposite side of the camp from the trees where the soldiers watch, and it's further out than Greg's own safety regulations allow. He has walked out to the edge of the almost-certainly mined road to the border.

He stands with his hands in his pockets, looking straight out along the road. Around him, the flattened landscape of emptiness and distance has faded to black under the clear sky. Greg feels himself to be tiny in this emptiness, reduced to a speck of humanity by the great, overwhelming sky and the flatness that spreads so far around him.

Greg now knows that there are trucks being made ready for him in Qasir. There is a volunteer driver for every truck that will join the convoy. There are tears in Greg's eyes as he thinks of the volunteer drivers.

He has told Qasir that he believes the minefield to be real.

He has told them that the convoy must not set out from Qasir unless they can be sure that they will not be driving into a minefield.

And Greg has explained to Qasir the idea that has come to him: that he should first drive an empty truck north to the border, so that either he will be the only one to die, or they will know that the road is safe for the convoy.

He has not mentioned this to Maya.

When he suggested it on this evening's regular call to Qasir, his idea was greeted with silence.

I have to go, he tells himself. I can't let the convoy set out without knowing that the road is safe.

I have to drive the road.

It's my responsibility.

On the edge of Greg's mind is the conviction that he has only a very small chance of surviving the drive to the border. The road is mined. He is certain of this.

But if there is even the slightest chance that the road is clear, he has to know.

I stand beside Greg, unheard, unseen, unfelt, and together we watch the stars.

•

On the roof of a building in the regional capital, barely one hundred miles south of Greg Doyle's refugee camp, a journalist wearing a sky-blue flak jacket speaks into a hand-held microphone. He is a reporter for a satellite news channel. The team has the link up and running again, and this is going out live. Already it's being picked up worldwide.

"...rebel forces have launched an all-out attack on the regional capital, and we're getting reports that simultaneous offensives..."

Behind the journalist, no more than two hundred metres away, another rocket explodes against the wall of a building. It is the third explosion in the camera's viewfinder since the report began; the report was put live on air after the second, cutting across a pre-recorded story about ice-skating holidays in Alaska threatened by global warming. All day, it has been a slow-news day. Except, at last, for this shooting war. The journalist ducks but continues speaking. He can hear none of the anchor-woman's questions in his earpiece, and now the anchor-woman has stopped asking them.

The hacking sound of automatic-weapon fire punctuates the journalist's report. Behind him the town is burning. It makes fantastic television.

"I repeat, a major offensive is under way. We're getting reports that Tankiya has fallen to rebel forces, although as you can see behind me, there's still fierce fighting in the central–"

Another rocket explodes, closer this time, again right in the camera's viewfinder. Then a star-shell bursts in the distance over the journalist's shoulder and the screen blackens for a second before the camera compensates. The star-shell sinks down slowly like a dull firework onto the town, illuminating shadows and fire and buildings all made bone-yellow in its unnatural light.

"Wow," murmurs the producer, who is holding the camera. She frees a hand and rolls it in a 'keep going' signal to the journalist. He's barely more than a silhouette with the star-shell behind him, but that doesn't matter.

The journalist straightens up again. "We understand that rebel forces are also moving north towards the border in a bid to cut the country in two. These reports are unconfirmed as yet, but if they're true, it could mean that this blood-soaked war is entering a decisive phase."

The producer's earpiece is working. "Can you get him to start again from the top? We're pulling together an edit as we go."

The producer takes her face away from the camera, holding it as steady as she can, and mouths 'live' to the journalist, and then, 'again'. She rolls her hand in a wider circle that the journalist understands to mean, 'just keep going until I tell you to stop'.

Three rockets detonate simultaneously across the back of the picture and the producer breathes, 'Halleluiah'. The journalist, who takes a professional pride in being able to keep talking on any subject until he is told to stop, barely reacts. He is in full flow now, shouting over the noise.

"There's a battle raging across the town of Tankiya tonight, with house-to-house and indeed hand-to-hand fighting in the streets. Earlier this evening, rebel forces attacked in strength, using armoured vehicles, artillery and rocket fire. We understand that key government buildings have been occupied and half an hour ago, rebel spokesmen were claiming victory, although as you can see behind me–"

This time, the explosion is too close to be seen. But it's loud and as the camera swerves, the journalist can be seen ducking forward. He's up again, though, and the camera steadies. But the angle has changed; the producer is on her knees.

"Simultaneously with the attack on Tankiya, rebel forces are reported to have launched a major offensive to drive north to the border and cut the country in two."

The camera wavers as the producer stands.

"The reports are unconfirmed, but if they're true, they could mean that this terrible war–"

Something explodes. It's big. And it's close. Suddenly there's a bright glow, like an imminent sunrise, visible in the bottom of the picture, over the parapet of the building. The producer steps forward to get a better view.

"It looks like some kind of fuel dump has exploded below us," shouts the journalist, who is out of shot now. "As you can see, flames twenty, thirty feet high, illuminating a scene like something out of Dante's inferno. We're up here on top of the state news-agency building, and – look, over there – we can see tanks now, rebel forces are moving tanks into central..."

When this final part of the report is replayed separately in later bulletins, the journalist's voice will be muted and most of the screen will be darkened. In the lighted section, a circle down towards the bottom right of the picture, the viewer will see the tank appear from behind the distant building and turn on the spot towards the camera. The viewer will see the tank's main gun raise until it is pointing at the building directly under the camera.

There will be a white flash. Then the screen will go black.

•

Alone in the night, Greg has made a kind of peace with what he must do. He is calm. He has a clear duty to the people under his protection, and everything else comes second to that. This is what he signed up for. He must take the risk of driving to the border, just as soon as he can hand over his responsibilities in the camp.

The sky is vast above him. There are so many stars. Greg can hear animals and he is cold, but most of all he is conscious of the deep stillness above him.

He thinks of his parents, and decides that he will go back now, and write to them. The letter might survive, even if he does not. He will give it to Maya. Perhaps his father will understand. Greg stifles the emotion that rises up in him as he sees his parents' faces in his mind. He imagines them getting the news.

But he puts that away. He will write to them and explain the situation. They will understand that he has no choice but to do what he has to do.

At least, he thinks, he is single, and then he tries not to complete the thought. Small mercies: no dependents waiting for him back home. No children without a father if he–

Greg stares up at the night sky, looking for the constellations that he can remember his father identifying for him when he was a child.

Maybe I'll survive, he thinks.

But he stifles that thought too.

He turns and walks back into the camp.

•

Neither of them is injured, and one day, the journalist will write a book on the strength of this report from Tankiya. The camera is still working, although the producer dropped it when the shell hit and the live transmission cut back to the studio. There, the taken-by-surprise anchor-woman, hand to her earpiece, tells the world that they will reconnect to Tankiya as soon as possible, and in the meantime, let's go to Ben Kudney in our Brussels studio for a look at the political implications.

The link is still up to the control room. While the screen in front of the production team shows the dazed journalist crawling away from the smoking crater that has bitten out the edge of the roof, the producer's voice is saying, "We're okay, but we're under fire. This building's empty and they could walk in but they're shelling us. They don't know that they could just walk in." The hand-held has come unplugged and the microphone in the camera is taking the sound. The producer gets to her feet and walks to the edge of the crater. There is no time to get the journalist back on his feet and not much roof for him to stand on anyway, so she just keeps talking. "Are you getting this? The building was hit by a shell, the floor below us, I can see desks and that's a – hey, look at that filing cabinet!"

When this is played at the end-of-year awards, they will keep in the bit about the filing cabinet, and the embarrassed producer, who will then be dressed in a shimmering magenta off-the-shoulder long dress and the first of many pairs of seriously expensive shoes, will cover her mouth and nose with her hand as she laughs along with the audience. The filing cabinet will fall, in slow motion in the replay, out of the hole in the wall. And then the producer's voice will say, on the audio track, "They're entering the building – I can hear them on the stairs."

There is hysteria in the producer's voice now. The camera swerves and the audience will see the journalist, who will be dinner-jacketed for the awards, staring at the producer. There will be a stir of laughter across the audience at the expression on his face and on the stage the journalist will smile in rueful acknowledgement. Then, on the screen, his mouth will form a word that is beeped for the awards, more laughter, and he will say, "Where's the [beep] logo, they'll be up here in a minute?"

The producer will say, "Hold this!" and the journalist will take the camera and the audience will see the producer pulling two white vests from a rucksack, big loose tabards with the TV company's logo front and back. As she does this, the journalist pans around the roof while he retrieves and reattaches the hand-held microphone.

They didn't broadcast any of this at the time, in case it ended badly, but it was shown immediately after it concluded, as live, with the producer and the journalist both audibly cheering on a crowded landing, the screen full of soldiers' faces, also cheering, single shots into the ceiling, plaster falling, and then the journalist getting his hand-held microphone back, hugged by soldiers cramming themselves into the picture, and concluding his report, "And so, at the end of their successful battle for Tankiya, victorious rebel soldiers celebrate the fall of the state news building … "

The rest of the report is drowned out by cheering on screen and, at the awards, applause from the audience. Fade to black.

•

"The radio's working."

Sahasrael has returned to the bridge, where she now stands waiting for me. She leans forward over the guardrail, looking down at the river. The rail is made of dark metal, curved and smooth to the touch. It shines along its length. I stand beside her, feeling its cold beneath my fingers. The river is massive below us, a bulk of water that swells around the supporting legs of the bridge and moves slowly out towards the horizon. The water is a rich brown cut occasionally by the white wake of a boat pushing against the current.

"He won't see an angel," I say.

She shakes her head, as if that doesn't matter now.

"This one already believes," she says.

And she is gone.

A bird flies low and fast away from me along the length of the river, banking up finally and curving its flight towards the sun.

•

There are voices up ahead. Greg doesn't think he can talk to anybody just now. He turns sharp left between two buildings and walks silently. He will turn right in a moment and double back. The detour makes a pleasing shape in Greg's mind.

Behind the buildings a truck is parked. On impulse Greg hops up into the cab. He's still dressed for the day, and although it isn't exactly warmer in here, there isn't the same night chill. Greg really isn't ready for people yet and he decides that he will sit here for a few minutes.

This one has a radio. Greg can feel that the key of the truck has been pushed into the torn material of the driving seat. He fishes it out. Maybe there'll be a news bulletin to give him a reason for being here.

He turns on the radio.

"...are reported to have launched a major offensive to drive north to the border and cut the country..."

Greg shakes his head in disbelief: would you believe it? A news bulletin. It's a miracle that he can hear it at all on this broken old radio.

"...bloodstained war..."

Either the transmission's being jammed or this radio's useless. Greg leans forward and touches the dial.

"...exploded below us..."

Greg's touch is feather-light on the dial.

"...flames ... out of Dante's inferno ... rebel forces are moving tanks..."

That's it. Nothing but static now.

The thought enters Greg's mind that although he would be crazy to leave the camp before first light, he could certainly start the handover right now.

He stares at the windscreen, thinking: Dante's inferno; flames; rebel forces moving tanks. Then he remembers: bloodstained war; drive north to the border.

I am going as soon as I can.

With urgency displacing fear in his mind, Greg climbs down from the cab of the truck and goes to wake up his team.

•

Ben left early again. Woken by his departure, Hannah lies on her side, still cosy with sleep, studying the diagram of a flower on the mug of tea before her eyes. Stamen, sepals, pollen; she can remember the names, but she doesn't know which part is which. Pollen is obvious, but the rest – no. The flower has a beautiful, tiny heart.

Hannah closes her eyes.

"Mummy?"

Megan is standing in the doorway, barefoot in her pyjamas. She has brought Pugh.

"Hello, darling. What is it?"

Hannah is awake in an instant, coming up onto one elbow and ready to swing her legs out onto the floor.

"Can I sleep in your bed, Mummy?"

Megan isn't fully awake. She is rubbing her eyes with a fist, seemingly unaware, despite the brightness of the room through the curtains, that the day has begun.

"Of course, darling, come in here."

Hannah sweeps back the duvet, feeling the sudden cold, and Megan climbs in next to her, curling up instantly, still night-hot, thumb in her mouth, Pugh held up against her cheek. She settles back to sleep.

•

I sit in the cab of the truck beside Greg. It is one of the old trucks, one that Greg has decided is expendable, and this morning, the gearbox is fighting back and the engine is juddering so badly through the steering wheel that Greg remembers a ten-years-ago job working in a road crew, chipping out tarmac and stone with a jackhammer.

But the old truck does have a nearly full tank of diesel. And in the back, under the canvas, are families. Greg had expected to go alone, had intended to go alone, but when he emerged from the tent at first light, the handover complete, the truck had already been packed with people.

Word gets round in a camp like this, Greg had thought, sighing,

70

resigned to having to get these people out before he left.

"You can't come with me," he had told them, standing at the back of the truck. "It's too dangerous."

"Then we will walk," a voice had replied, and Greg, out in the open, had understood the futility of his position.

"I'm going to be driving through a minefield," he had protested.

And then the smiles had broken out. They were laughing at him.

What the heck, Greg had thought, turning away, his face lowered. I can't go. I can't endanger them. I'm defeated.

And then, crystal clear into his mind, out of nowhere, had come the conviction that he could go. They're in danger here, Greg had thought. They won't be any safer if I leave them behind.

I can take them.

And all is well.

They had cheered as Greg had turned, smiling and shaking his head, and walked towards the cab of the truck.

Now they have left the camp behind them and Greg is driving as smoothly as he can, given the distance they have to travel and the danger around them. This is open country, flat but for occasional scrub, and the road is clearly visible ahead: there are tyre tracks dried out from the last wet season, and in places even parallel lines of stones laid down as markers. This is a path for animals and people as well as for motor vehicles. In places, the road is raised; in places, dry, shallow ditches have been dug beside it. They have passed one deserted village and will soon pass another.

Greg is worried that the truck's dust will be visible for miles. But there's nothing he can do about that. He is crouched forward over the steering wheel, looking ahead for any disturbance in the packed ground that might betray a landmine. He knows that if there is a mine ahead, he will not be able to see it before it kills him and his passengers, but he looks all the same.

Behind the truck, high in the air, a wind blows, dispersing the dust before it can be seen by the approaching army.

•

Gently, Hannah eases herself up into a sitting position with her daughter asleep against her hip. She reaches out for the tea. It is cold, but out of habit, she holds the mug up in front of her face and blows on it as though to cool it down.

"...a story?" says Megan indistinctly.

Hannah sits still, mug raised. She's not in the mood for stories. Maybe Megan will go back to sleep.

But no. Megan moves against her – Hannah can tell that these are conscious movements – and worms herself into a more comfortable position for the story.

So Hannah begins, "Once upon a time," but nothing comes; her mind stays blank. She casts around for something that will serve as an adequate substitute for a story...

...and finds what she's looking for.

She's had the beginnings of this idea knocking around in her mind for several days now. It came to her in the library, on that good morning when she'd sat down among the reference books and fallen asleep and dreamed, but she hasn't said anything, or even properly thought it through.

She hasn't questioned her own odd wariness either; just a simple day out, overnight stay, see the rest of the family, but now, sitting up in bed with her daughter at peace beside her, she thinks: maybe I'm just afraid that Ben will say no.

And as she thinks that, she immediately thinks: if he doesn't want to come, we'll go without him. He's got no right to stop us.

It's just a brief flash of resentment, and she leaves it unexamined.

"I've got something better than a story," she says, putting the tea aside and burrowing down into the bed with her daughter. "I've got a plan."

She puts her fingertips to Megan's ribs and Megan giggles. "What's a plan, Mummy?"

•

"Sahasrael, what are you doing?"

"Hannah spoke to me. In the library, remember?"

"You're helping Hannah to save Megan? While I'm–"

"You saw the dream. To save Megan from suffering, yes."

"At the beach? I don't understand."

"Not now, Chandra. Trust the journey."

"What did you–"

"Trust the journey. Go back to the desert."

•

When the first mine detonates, Greg is thrown backwards and the truck judders to the left, towards a ditch – but the steering wheel turns of its own accord and the truck is back on the road. The mine exploded just in front of the truck but there is no damage. The wheels somehow straddle the crater and the truck pushes through the dust and debris to emerge unscathed on the other side.

"What the heck?" says Greg.

I am sitting in the passenger seat, whispering to Greg. "This old truck bumping along must have disturbed it enough to set it off early," I tell him silently. I can feel Sahasrael's gentle laughter.

Then all of the remaining mines detonate, along the whole length of the road. Greg, flinching back in his cab, his arms thrown up over his face, sees nothing of the dirt, stones and fire thrown harmlessly into the air. The truck rolls on as small debris rains down on the cab and the canvas roof.

"That first one must have detonated the rest," I whisper to him. "There won't be any more mines on this road."

As he sits in his cab, blinking, feeling his own heartbeat, Greg does not question the conviction that settles into his mind that the road is now safe.

The engine coughs once, twice, and then it runs smoothly. Greg recovers himself sufficiently to take hold of the steering wheel. "Even cured the engine," he says out loud, and then, as he stares ahead, the truck still rolling forward despite the absence of his foot on the accelerator, he realises what he is hearing.

His passengers are singing.

The Gift of a Decision

"Just as soon as you've finished your breakfast, we'll call them."

Megan is excited, inevitably, and Hannah, equally inevitably, is now worrying about the practicalities. This will be the middle weekend of Beatrice's holiday, and what if they've already made other plans? It's very short notice.

And such a long drive.

Am I being unrealistic? Hannah asks herself. Two hours. It's too far, surely?

Megan has shovelled in three rapid spoonfuls of cereal and has a fourth waiting for space in her mouth. Her head dips forward as she gulps down her breakfast.

"Darling, you'll choke. Slow down."

Hannah can hear the protest even though Megan's mouth is too full to speak it. "Okay," she says. "Stop hurrying. I'll call them now. No, really, darling, you don't have to finish your breakfast first. I'll call them."

Megan clears her mouth with a final, dramatic gulp. "Can we go swimming, Mummy?"

A shadow crosses Hannah's mind. Megan is a shallow-end swimmer at best.

"Of course, darling," she says, and busies herself finding her mobile.

I suppose I'll have to go in with her, she thinks, and deletes the thought of buying a new swimsuit at such short notice.

It'll be too cold. Or I could stand in the shallows.

A picture enters her mind: she sees herself standing on the edge of the sea, muffled up warm in her coat and scarf and the green woolly hat, a mug of coffee in her hands. Megan is jumping and squeaking and darting in and out of the surf. Hannah sees her sister Beatrice standing with her, similarly warm, sharing the moment.

Hannah experiences a moment's odd warmth towards her sister, whom she rarely ever sees.

Here's her mobile.

Somewhere she's got a phone number for the cottage.

But Luke always has his mobile with him, even if Beatrice doesn't.

She'll try Beatrice first and leave a message, then Luke.

If all else fails, she thinks, glancing across to see Megan's face, I'm sure I can find that number for the cottage.

It occurs to her that maybe she should call Ben first.

It occurs to her that no, she won't call Ben first.

•

Ten miles south of Qasir and forty miles north of the border, a convoy of trucks moves south at a steady speed on the metalled road. The mood has changed at Qasir, and a decision has been made to move the convoy forward. At the cost of fuel and volunteers' time, all the available trucks are now moving to a holding point just north of the border.

This will cut at least an hour from the journey time to the camp. There won't be enough trucks to evacuate the whole camp in a single run, but it is now obvious to everybody that time is running out. Nobody even knows yet whether the road is passable, but they do know that Greg Doyle is driving north to find out. If he can do that, the least they can do is meet him at the border.

The next decision will be an easy one.

If Greg's truck doesn't make it, that will mean the road is not passable.

There are ten trucks in the convoy, all that could be mustered in Qasir. One is a tanker full of diesel. It tows a generator. A second tanker contains water. Two trucks are hard-tops, packed with medical equipment. When they are emptied, they will serve as ambulances for the weakest of the refugees. Under the canvas of the remaining six trucks are crates of food. In one truck there is also a small box of tinsel and coloured paper that Naseena Danti will use to distract the children of the camp as they wait for evacuation. The relief workers will laugh at the apparent mistake of sending them such a useless box. But by then, in this changed future, they will have forgotten to be cynical.

Each cab contains a driver and a relief driver. All the relief drivers and four of the drivers are medically qualified. The remaining drivers are engineers. There were more than twice as many volunteers for this run as were needed, and the camp is getting all the doctors that Qasir can supply.

"We could have sent a full convoy south," said the director, back at Qasir, as he watched the convoy leave. Only the argument that the space would be needed for refugees had prevented the trucks filling up with volunteers before they left.

On every truck, both the driver and the relief driver have decided, independently of each other, that even if the decision is taken not to cross the border, because the road is too dangerous, they will try to convince their companion to go anyway.

Although Greg doesn't know it yet, he is already a hero to the people in Qasir.

•

Ben Rose sits alone at his desk, staring at the spreadsheet on the screen in front of him.

We can't all be creative, he tells himself. As an account manager, his career is much more secure. He's got the pension plan, the medical cover, the reliable tedium of his days.

And that's all bullshit. Life's a trap. He's held in place by the salary, which is just big enough for the mortgage, which buys the house, which brings in the bills.

Ben trained as a graphic designer. He's also an artist, or he was. With Hannah's encouragement, he has sold pictures off the walls of coffee shops, held exhibitions with other artists in church halls and occasionally at local art galleries, and he has drawn frames and worked out a rough storyline for a graphic novel of his own. But his dream of working in a small design house, making a living while developing his art, had to go on hold when he took this job. Just a temporary fix to get some money.

Now he's married, with a child.

He lowers his head to complete the drawing he has begun on last week's page of the burgundy-red, bonded-leather executive desk diary he pulled out of one of the designers' trash bins. He has drawn a tee-shirt: short-sleeved, round-necked, barely more than a wonky rectangle with extra lines. But now Ben adds shading: the tee-shirt is now three-dimensional. More shading: it's being worn by a woman, although too late now to make it skin-tight, comic-book style. Ben, concentrating now, adds the woman's legs. This is the oversized tee-shirt she wears to bed, he decides. About the coverage of a mini-skirt. A couple of lines to place the big, tousled hair he's going to give her, and then he starts in on the mouth, lips parted, and the eyes. How to get an expression of…

"Good to see you're busy, Ben."

THE BOSS IS: IN.

Shit.

Ben is embarrassed by the way he's taken by surprise, which makes him not react when Anthony leans forward to get a better look at the drawing. He leans back in his chair, getting back to cool as fast as he can.

"That's good. Really good."

Ben knows he can draw.

"Thanks," he says.

Anthony nods. Their eyes meet. Anthony walks on to his corner office. Ben stares at his screen.

"Fuck," he says softly.

•

Greg is navigating more by mathematics than geography now. He knows this road because he has driven it so often in the past, before the war came, and because he took the precaution of studying it on the map before he left this morning. He has the shape of the landscape in his head, and after so many months in-country, he's got to a point where the superficially featureless landscape offers up as many landmarks as the rolling green country of his homeland.

Greg's happy, and it's adding to his happiness that he's listening to the engine, watching the time, and second-guessing the evidence of his own eyes by calculating where they are as well as checking off the landmarks. Not only that: the old truck should be drinking the stuff, but it's not half as thirsty as he had expected. Which means he hasn't lost his touch with an engine. Another of this wonderful day's miracles.

Greg is aware that he is in an unusual state of elation and imagines somebody – Maya, perhaps – commenting that in this mood, he should be dancing rather than driving his truck. He keeps letting out bursts of laughter, partly because he can't help it and partly to release the pressure of his own happiness.

He never could dance, but right now he'd be happy to try.

Greg knows that neither he nor any of his passengers are going to die today. With that knowledge has come the understanding that he loves life. Something was knocked back into Greg as those mines exploded around him. He thinks of his father and his mother and the letter they will no longer have to read. [They will read it, because one day, Maya will show it to them.] Then Greg thinks of Maya and all his friends at the camp and his face breaks open in another wide, involuntary grin. A ball of happiness rises up in his chest. Without spelling it out so neatly to himself, Greg knows that by finding the courage to risk the minefield, he has passed a great test.

The truck is running smoothly and again Greg can hear singing behind him. The speedometer is holding steady and the fuel gauge still hasn't dropped below the three-quarter mark. He decides that he should be slowing down soon. The border, when it comes, will come quickly. The road will rise over three long, low hills, hardly more than rises in the ground, and then, suddenly, over the crest of the third hill, there it will be, still five miles ahead but clearly visible. The border. Even in the haze, the road on the other side, a dust-covered blacktop, will look like a clear line drawn to mark the crossing point.

Slow down because you'll be visible too, Greg thinks, particularly on a day like this. The border is usually manned. At 40 miles per hour, five miles, it will take precisely 7½ minutes of driving towards however many jumpy border guards there might be, before you can explain that you're harmless.

Play it safe, Greg decides. Stop before they can see the truck, just before, and walk up the road to take a look. Take anybody with you who wants to come, and let them decide. Better to drop them off five miles short, in the desert, than to take any risk now.

Greg is not laughing now. He is no longer smiling and nor is he mind-gaming with time and distance. His eyes are darting from side to side and he is making absolutely sure he knows exactly where he is. In five minutes, he will stop the truck, leaving the engine running, and unfold the map to double-check the landmarks. When he is sure, he will take the map round to the back and explain the problem to his passengers.

And they will just tell me to drive on and not worry. Greg shakes his head. Faith would be a fine thing.

He drives on, but more slowly. "Don't let this go wrong," he says softly. "Please don't let this go wrong."

Behind the truck, the dust of its passing rises and turns in a following wind, before spiralling up into the air and away into invisibility.

•

"What are you doing? What did Hannah ask you to do?"

"She did speak to me. And Megan's time is close."

"She could have so much."

"It's such a small change."

"No!"

Now, the girl has got both hands up tousling her hair. Ben has put down his pen and is using a pencil to make the outline of her body visible through the thin cotton of the tee-shirt. He smiles faintly. Then, economically, with just enough detail to give the idea, he places her in front of a bed, the head of it high and beginning to be ornate, as though it might develop into some kind of gothic four-poster, the bedclothes in a dishevelled heap on the floor.

"Hey, that's really cool."

This time it's the new girl. Some kind of general assistant to somebody. How long has she been there? She is standing looking down at his picture with a bundle of papers in her arms.

Ben sits back, letting his heartbeat subside as the girl studies the picture. In return, he studies her face in profile. Close up, she's maybe a bit older than he thought.

"Can you draw real people?"

"Oh yes," says Ben, and he flicks the page back briefly to show her his caricature of Anthony.

She doesn't say anything for a moment, just stares at the picture, and then says, "That's sooo cool."

"You want a portrait?" Ben says, not serious, leaning back, becoming aware of her. She is wearing a flimsy little blouse, no sleeves, and a short, flared skirt.

"You're really good," she says, still looking down at the girl in the long tee-shirt.

"Thanks," he says, sprawled in his chair, his arm hooked over the back. His hand is about six inches from her bare thigh.

Then, "Yeah," she says. "I do."

"Okay," says Ben.

"Okay," she says. "Yeah. I'd like that."

And then she grins at him, says, "Have a good weekend," and goes on her way.

I've just offered to draw her portrait, Ben thinks, watching the back of her skirt as she strides towards the door at the end of the room.

I must be at least a decade older than she is.

I'm married.

He looks down again at the drawn girl on the open page. She looks back up at him, sexy, sultry, and with the tip of her tongue, as he brings it into being with a touch of his pencil, flicking between her lips.

Don't be ridiculous, he thinks. She wouldn't go for–

And that's when Ben's mobile, set to silent in the office, buzzes on the desk to tell him that he has a text message from his wife.

•

I stumble into a sudden heavy world of wind and brightness and movement. I am physical, heavy, cold. I am present here, and visible.

I am standing on a stretch of rough grass above a sheltered beach and a windswept sea. Inland, in the distance, there is a line of white houses, each isolated within its own long, sloping garden. Sand-coloured paths have been worn from the gate at the end of each garden through the weathered, clumped-up grass.

"Megan, wait!"

The beach itself is still peaceful. The sky is still clear. But there is already a hard wind driving rough waves across the sea beyond the headland. My hair is whipped across my face by a sudden gust of wind. My feet are bare and cut by stones and sharp grass.

"Don't go!" I cry out. "Wait!"

In front of me there is the slope of earth and exposed rock that leads down onto the beach. I stop with the wet grass still beneath my feet.

It is early on Saturday morning here. Ben and Hannah drove down last night with Megan, to join Luke and Beatrice and the cousins for the middle weekend of their family holiday by the sea. The two husbands are still asleep in the rented white house. Coerced out by the children, the two mothers sit with towels, clothes and a picnic breakfast on a rug on the still-quiet beach half-way down to the sea. There was a stiff breeze when they left the house, but now they are recessed from the wind, enjoying each other's company as they always do, although they rarely seek it, and unaware of the storm gathering around them. They drink tea poured from a vacuum flask and I can feel their pleasure in the moment.

In the distance I can see that the four children, Megan and her three cousins, are already playing on the edge of the sea; they are knee-deep in the roughening water and the hems of their warm tops are already soaked and heavy. But they don't yet care. They are laughing, jumping the waves, diving through the water, splashing up fragments of light in the spray, half-falling, staggering to catch their balance again. Their bodies are tight, elbows in against the cold of the water and the violent approach of the breaking waves. One goes down, the boy, the youngest; and the two older girls, his sisters, instantly turn to bring him up again. Megan, older than the boy by two weeks, watches the rescue from the edge of the surf, her body jigging up and down against the cold. The two girls hold their brother's arms, bent over him in the shallowest water, brushing away the prospect of tears, making sure.

I scramble down the slope, physical, clumsy, and as I fall, the wind dies: the beach is still sheltered, even now, by the headland. At the bottom of the slope, the dry, heaped sand yields beneath my feet. It is difficult to walk. I have never known clumsiness.

Hannah and Beatrice didn't anticipate this early-morning excursion, and although they've willingly thrown buns and cocktail sausages and little boxes of fruit juice into the cool-bag, they're still newly hatched from their warm beds and wrapped in coats against the brisk air. Hannah has promised to walk down to the shoreline in a moment, so that the children can go into the water rather than playing on its edge. But they're safe enough, she tells herself, comfortable as she is in this rare moment with her sister. It was a long drive.

The two mothers are unaware of how immediately the sand slopes under the water where the children are. Their part of the beach is still sheltered from the wind and the sky above them is still clear.

I pass them, half-running now, heading for the sea. Hannah sees me out of the corner of her eye: to her, I am a young man in an open-necked shirt and jeans, rucksack on my back. Some kind of early-morning exercise fanatic.

I see that Sahasrael is also present here. She sits on a red tartan blanket on the hard flat sand nearer the sea, her arms clasped around her knees, holding herself tight and still, waiting for me. She is wearing a faded denim shirt and khaki trousers. Her feet are bare. The beach is otherwise empty. She is visible but far enough away from the two mothers, far enough out of their line of sight to the children, not to attract their attention. She raises her hand.

I am close enough now to get to Megan quickly. I stop.

"Why not now, Chandra?" she says.

I kneel beside her and put my hand on her shoulder. My body is out of breath and I cannot speak. But there is no pleasure now in the physical sensation. Sahasrael lays her cheek briefly on the back of my hand and then straightens.

"That could be her future," she says. "The sea. So cold and easy. So quick."

I watch Megan as she shrieks in advance of a tiny breaking wave in the surf, jumping it in triumph. The two older girls have lifted their small brother over the same wave. They applaud Megan for jumping it alone. She is so full of life.

"Let her die here, Chandra."

The two mothers are deep in their conversation now, laughing over memories that they have shared many times before. They are still not conscious of the danger. They are too far away from the sea.

I scramble to my feet. Sahasrael reaches up and catches my hand.

"You wanted to save her from suffering. Now you want to save her from an easy death."

Already, further out to sea, the waves are rolling in big enough to obscure the horizon. Later, in the world as it is now, the storm will hinder the search for the body.

"I can't take this away from her." I wave my free hand to show Sahasrael the beach and the sea and the sky and the Heaven behind it all.

"It's only death, Chandra."

But there are birds in the high blue sky and so much life in the sea and on the land.

"She will not drown here," I say.

And the world is changed.

I drop the rucksack on the sand and begin to unbutton my shirt.

"Do you not see the miracle of it all?" I ask her, as I fold my jeans to drop them on the blanket. "As I do? All this life?"

I am dressed in blue shorts now, as if I have been preparing to swim. Now there is a towel waiting for me on the sand. I begin to walk towards the water.

"Do you know your journey now?" Sahasrael calls after me.

"I choose life," I call back to her.

Hannah has taken another quick moment to help Beatrice unpack the picnic. Both of them, independently of each other, have popped chocolate bars into the cool bag at the last moment, and they are laughing at how similar they are.

The children are laughing too, splashing each other.

They do not notice as the sea draws back and gathers itself up into the freak wave that knocks all four of them off their feet.

I begin to run as the three older children fight the undertow, getting to their knees and falling again, getting to their knees and standing unsteadily, blinking water out of their eyes, without the breath to cry.

Unseen, the smallest girl, my own Megan Rose, slides down into the sea, drawn by the undertow, wrapped into a wave, scraped onto the sand and drawn back down again into the deeper water, where she begins to drown before she even understands that she is lost.

I reach the water as the oldest girl, Tanya, the first to recover, screams, "Where's Megan?"

And I dive into the cold oblivion, clear-eyed, as Megan's mother, Hannah, stumbles to her feet, dropping a pierced box of orange juice onto the blanket.

For a second I am fought by the water, the grey near-darkness swirling in front of my eyes, the harsh rushing of stones and sea filling my ears, and then I stand beyond nature and reach out my hand to Megan, whom the water gives up as my fingers touch hers. HOLD MY HAND, I say, and the small fingers close on my thumb. I bring her close to me and hold her against my chest. BE AT PEACE, I tell her, for she is afraid.

I turn and begin to walk out of the water, fighting it again as I become visible to the mothers and the children in the shallows. Megan is coughing; I feel her body begin to shiver. I pass her to her mother, who takes her and immediately turns away from me, hunched over her child. The family clusters around her and then, holding together, they all begin to walk back to their blanket where Megan will be made warm again.

Sahasrael hands me the towel. "Wait," she says. I hold the water on my body. My wet hair covers one side of my face. I shiver.

Hannah walks across the sand towards me. In her arms she holds Megan, wrapped now in towels and a blanket; she is a heavy burden on this yielding sand, but she is safe. Behind them, Beatrice and the children are packing up; they will retreat to the cottage now.

Hannah stops and stands facing me. She looks tired with the shock of what might have been.

"Thank you," she says.

And Megan says, in a soft voice, although she is unprompted, "Thank you."

Hannah's chin trembles. I hold out my hand and touch Megan's forehead and say, "Hey, thanks for swimming with me. You're a brave girl."

She knows me. But she is mute now with shock.

Hannah says, "If..." and cannot continue.

"Hey." I'm shaking my head. "You'd have got her. She wasn't far out. I was just lucky. Right place at the right time."

Hannah knows that this isn't true.

"Thank you," she says again. Again, she can't continue. She still hasn't properly looked at my face. Her eyes are full of tears.

"It's really okay," I say. "Really it is. Just watch out for this beach." I check my wrist although I'm not wearing a watch. "Don't swim before they put the flags out. Nine o'clock."

There is something about me that Hannah interprets as familiarity. But she is distracted by what I have just said. Flags. Nine o'clock. She says, "Would you like breakfast? Or coffee? Can I offer you anything?"

Sahasrael says over my shoulder, "It's okay. Really. Part of the service. Go and enjoy your holiday."

We watch Hannah and Megan rejoin their family for the return to the cottage.

"Do you understand what you've done?" says Sahasrael.

"I've saved her life. I've intervened."

She touches my arm but says nothing, her eyes averted.

"I understand," I tell her.

In half an hour, after the children and then Hannah and then Beatrice have told the story and told it again, Ben, accompanied by Luke, will return to the beach to look for me.

"When did you know?" I ask her.

She is still watching the sea.

"In the library. In the desert. Before. You argue for life. I could have known sooner."

I towel myself dry. Sahasrael picks up my rucksack and weighs it in her hands. As I button my shirt, she holds it out for me to shrug onto my shoulders. It is unexpectedly heavy. I turn, settling it into place. Our eyes meet, and spontaneously, unexpectedly, we laugh.

"I wanted to save her from suffering," she says. "For you."

"I know."

She takes my hand and we walk down to the edge of the surf. We stand together as the storm breaks against the coast. Rain gusts against my face. We share the miracle of the cold, the wet, the spray, the bullying of the wind. Waves throw themselves onto the beach then surge back down into the following sea.

"Chandrael," she begins.

"The creation is only truly complete when it has been experienced. You told me that."

She looks up at me then.

"I want to experience it," I tell her. I think of John, calling to me in his time of doubt. Of Naseena. Of Greg, alone in the night. "I want to live a life."

"To give up all that we know–"

"–to discover it again."

A broken wave surges up around our ankles, and as it recedes, we both feel the pull towards the sea.

"I want to see all this again, for the first time. Remember the trees? The first beginning?"

"There is pain in it, Chandrael. So much pain. Are you sure?"

"You'll be with me," I tell her. "This is our journey. We will always be together."

There are tears in her eyes then, or the spray of the sea, as she looks out at the sky.

She begins to speak, and stops.

Finally, she says, "Then come with me, my love."

And we are gone.

•

I step through a door. Sahasrael does not follow me.

The room is a kitchen. After the beach, it is silence. There are white-fronted cupboards and a silver-coloured fridge and a not-marble worktop. In the centre of the room is a round pine table with three matching chairs; a fourth is pushed to the wall and stacked with mail-order catalogues, magazines, old envelopes for lists. The room is otherwise superficially neat, as though an effort has been made, but there are crumbs and dust on the worktop and two breakfast plates and knives have been left unwashed by the sink.

"Why am I here?"

At the table a fifteen-year-old girl sits. Her head is down on her arms on the table-top. Her blonde hair shrouds her face. Her mind is an agony of weeping. She grieves already and she is full of fear and confusion. Once, when her mother was first ill, she thought for a brief moment how cool it would be to have a dead mother. Now the memory of this thought torments her.

"You are here because you are an angel, Chandrael, always. Megan is a human soul, and you can live a human life, but you are an angel. You are here because of what you are."

The girl's name is Bridget McCloud, and around her, holding her, there is a shimmering gold light that she cannot see. Her father sits beside her. His name is Ken McCloud and I recognise him: he is the man we met on the bridge, who likes Mantegna. His arm is across her shoulders; his other hand holds her hand on the tabletop.

"You are here because you are needed here, needed as what you are."

Ken McCloud is exhausted. His emotions seem to come at him from the far side of a long, deep emptiness. The surface of his mind teems with last-minute, absurd questions for his wife. Sally, do you want me to- Where did you put the- How do I work the- This is how his mind presents the knowledge that his wife really is finally dying. All the silly little things he could have asked her, just a few days ago. How the hell do I look after Bridget on my own? he thinks, and the deep chasm of his misery opens up to receive him.

Now I am also a shimmering gold presence, felt in the room yet invisible.

"My love, you are also here to understand the choice you have made."

I stand close behind Ken McCloud and put my hands to his head to channel the light. His eyes close and his head falls forward onto his daughter's shoulder. For a second, without realising it, he sleeps. In that second, I show him the river of life, broad and fast-flowing, reflecting silver in bright sunlight. Then he raises his head and closes his eyes to pray. Let me know what to do, he says. Let me be a good father to her; let me be the father that Sally would have wanted me to be. Misery splashes into him again. I hold him.

Upstairs, in the silent bedroom, Sally McCloud's time is close. The nurse sits close to the head of the bed now, leaning forward, listening. She touches a faint pulse. Shortly she will call the family, and then she will leave them in peace with Mrs McCloud while she calls the doctor.

On the table by the bed, with the water and the medicines and the record of Sally McCloud's decline, there is a postcard showing a painting from an exhibition, a religious painting in the style of Mantegna, with the words, "I hope you like this, my darling. All my love forever," scribbled in Ken McCloud's untidy handwriting.

For now, my place is downstairs. Ken McCloud is in darkness. I take my hands from his head and then I move forward through the chair, sitting down so that my body merges with his. Light merges with grief as my arm settles with his across his daughter's shoulders, and the darkness dissolves into weeping. His daughter, on hearing her father's tears, turns in her chair. "Oh Daddy." And then the two of them are holding each other, weeping together, releasing themselves. I merge with the light spreading through them, enclosing them within fragile wings.

"Mr McCloud." The nurse is waiting in the doorway. "I think you should come upstairs now. She's very peaceful."

Three days ago, the nurse – Mrs Benson, although somehow none of them can hold her name in their heads – had a sensible, coherent conversation with Sally McCloud. The patient had expressed anxiety about how her husband and daughter would cope with her death. Mrs Benson, who had experienced similar conversations before, had recognised this anxiety as the reason why Sally McCloud was still fighting her death. She had been able to provide reassurance, not that the impact would be lighter than Sally McCloud expected, nor that her family would recover easily from the blow, but that their enduring memory would be of the happy times, the joy of their lives together.

"You'll see, and if you want my personal belief, you really will see," Mrs Benson had said. "They'll always have you in their hearts, and they'll be happy again."

"Do you really believe that?" Sally McCloud had asked softly, her hand weak as a feather in Mrs Benson's hand.

"I do," Mrs Benson had said, leaning forward in her chair. "I truly do."

"I hope I can watch over them." Sally McCloud had closed her eyes then, believing, and Mrs Benson had prayed silently that her words might be true.

The prayer shimmers like music in the beautiful room, waiting.

"Yours to answer, Chandrael."

Ken McCloud comes through the door to the sight he never really believed he would see. His wife is curled up on her side, facing the edge of the bed; this is where Ken and Bridget now kneel. Ken pushes the bedside table out of the way, takes one of Sally's fragile hands and gives the other to Bridget. I kneel too, spreading myself over them both, holding them in the light.

Sally McCloud stirs in her final sleep. She can feel her family's presence and is comforted, although her body does not move.

It is time. She has been prepared for this moment by Mrs Benson. Her hair has been combed and there is blusher on her visible cheek. But these are her last breaths. She breathes in, audibly, and releases the breath. After a long pause, she breathes again.

"My darling, my sweetest darling," says Ken McCloud. "Goodbye, my love." His face screws up with weeping and he can barely see, but he brings Bridget forward to kiss her mother goodbye and then he leans forward to kiss her himself. "I love you, my darling," he whispers in her ear.

And then Sally McCloud takes a last breath, exhales, and is parted from her body.

"Oh," she says. "Oh Ken I love you."

She parts from herself, loosening out of the tight, foetal crouch of her body, and as she does so, the bright presences in the room yield to me and I reach forward to hold her in light. To her, as I spread my wings, I am pure brightness. "Oh my love," she cries out, as I draw her up. And then, as I raise her, still in her human form, to stand at the side of the bed, the limits of her human understanding fall away, and she sees truth. "Oh glory," she says. She closes her eyes.

I wait until presently she opens her eyes again and we see each other clear.

There is a light around her that I recognise.

"Welcome home," I say, surprised.

"You are not the first," Sahasrael says.

I reach out and take Sally McCloud's hands. We stand linked together as the light flows between us.

"Can I stay?" she asks. "Like this?"

"Yes," I say, answering the part of her that is still Sally McCloud.

"I have loved and I have been loved. At the end, I gave strength, and I released love. It is complete as I chose it to be."

"It is complete," I say softly.

She looks at me, surprise faintly in her eyes. "I gave," she says. "I received. I changed their lives."

Then she looks beyond me and speaks to Sahasrael. "You were mistaken," she says softly. "I would choose it again."

Sally McCloud turns to her life's family.

Ken McCloud is still kneeling. He is holding Bridget now. She is weeping. Mrs Benson has come back into the room and the doctor is behind her. Ken helps Bridget to her feet and they make way for the doctor. Sally McCloud crosses the room to join her husband and daughter. Unseen, she holds them in her arms.

"My sweet baby," Sally says. "My sweet baby, it doesn't matter, I don't mind, forgive yourself." Her head touches her daughter's head, briefly merging with it as she speaks.

Bridget McCloud stops crying. She tightens her hold on her father and he stands hugging her tightly.

"I'm here, baby, I'm here," Sally McCloud is saying.

While she is here, she will stay in her human understanding. The colours of her aura are orange shot through with turquoise and black.

I say, "Be with them now."

Sally glances at me but then returns her attention to her husband and daughter. The light in the room recedes. She will spend a further season in the human world.

I am gone from her sight until she calls me again.

One Big, Unequivocal Miracle

I find Sahasrael standing in the half-darkness of a long, narrow tent. In this place, ninety miles south of the refugee camp, it is almost dawn. But this is not a place of healing. There are bunk beds, plastic chairs, trestle tables spread with maps, crates of supplies and ammunition. Mats cover the dry earth floor. A diesel generator chugs out of sight and naked lightbulbs hang down above the tables. Oil lamps burn in the surrounding darkness.

"She would choose it again," I say.

Sahasrael appears older here, thinner. Flecks of dust float in the brightened air around her.

"I have been with her since the beginning," she says. "We came together when you settled into your valley. We shared the guardianship of so many, brought them into life and stayed with them, brought them home, and then..."

"She chose life."

"She was drawn to it. And I walked with her, beside her, unknown to her. She loved, but she also suffered. There was so much pain. I wanted you to know what you've chosen."

"You were mistaken. It was all love."

"When you ... came to me, first, out of the valley, the monastery, I thought–"

She closes her eyes.

"I thought that you wanted to be with them. Like me. You wanted to walk beside them. That much. I knew that you might want – more, but I didn't believe it. Because I wouldn't have–"

She stops and raises her face, her eyes still closed, as though feeling the warmth of a distant sun.

"Then you started – pushing. You wanted Naseena to see you, and you warned the boy, Ali, and then on the beach you–"

"I chose life."

She opens her eyes.

"Do you realise where you are, Chandrael?"

At one end of the tent there is a table spread with maps and documents held down with stones and the magazine of a Kalashnikov rifle. Men dressed in grey-and-ochre uniforms stand at the table. They are tired, gaunt, unshaven. But they do not doubt. One man is talking to the rest. His fist is clenched. He jabs at the map with a broken pencil.

"He is bringing forward the offensive."

"Yes, he is."

On one of the maps, hard pencil lines are drawn northwards. A thick pencil circle has been drawn around the position of the refugee camp.

The two soldiers watching the camp have reported the departure of Greg's truck. The man who is now talking has guessed that an evacuation is beginning.

"This is also life, Chandra. All this planning and determination.

All this hatred and darkness. All this, and then death. This is what you've chosen."

"But it doesn't have to be like this, Sahasrael. You know that. I want to give and receive. I want to change lives."

In the future as it is now, there will only be time for one convoy from Qasir to the camp and back. Greg and the volunteer drivers will return to the camp for a second time, but in this future, the soldiers will find him still arguing with Maya in the main hospital tent as his trucks are reloaded outside.

"Naseena will survive," Sahasrael is saying. "And Ali. The first convoy will take them."

There is activity in the tent now, and noise. The decision has been taken and the order given. The men are leaving to give their own orders.

"Hannah wanted more life," I say. "On the beach. Hannah thanked me for saving Megan. They both thanked me."

"Of course they did. But she spoke to me in the library. She brought Megan to the beach."

"These are lives. Individual experiences, each one opening up some new corner of the creation. And the longer they last, the more..."

I stop. An idea is forming in my head, so clear, so complete, that...

"...limits to what we can do, so this..." Sahasrael is saying.

"Trucks," I say, stopping her.

"Chandra, our task–"

"What if Greg had enough trucks to carry the entire population of the camp in a single convoy to the border?"

Sahasrael stares at me.

"What if – how about one big, unequivocal miracle? Just a simple one. We don't tell them what's happening. We don't show them any angels. We're just there. They can explain it afterwards however rationally they want."

"We can't–"

"We can. There are no limits to what we can do."

"But–"

"They'll find a rational explanation, if that's what's troubling you. It's what they do."

"But surely we accept now – surely we both know – surely we understand that this is life. This stubborn, resisting catastrophe all around us – this is life. This pain. And death is part of it. If you choose life–"

I open my arms wide. "Sahasrael, it's just trucks."

Again, she stares at me.

"And I'm asking you for help. Again."

Abruptly, briefly, she laughs out loud.

The man at the table looks up. He gestures, and another man slips outside to check around the tent for an intruder.

"There are no limits, Sahasrael. It's just trucks."

"We can't. It's too big."

"Yes we can. And it isn't too big. Remember the library? We stood right in front of them. The man at the desk, remember? Show them angels? Why not? They'll see what they choose to see."

She is shaking her head. "Chandra, they're not asking you to save them. They never were."

"Help me with this, Sahasrael, and then life. I want–"

"Stop."

She steps away from me. Raises her hand.

For a moment she stands in front of me with her hand raised and her head down.

Then she lowers her hand and looks up at me. Her eyes show the first glimmer of a smile.

"Will you ask me for a life of miracles?" she says.

And then she is gone.

I find her again in the empty hallway of Ken McCloud's house. The family is upstairs, gathered around the bed. The doctor and Mrs Benson are watching them.

I look down at Sahasrael from the landing outside the bedroom, and then I stand beside her in the hallway.

"We'll need drivers," I say to her.

She smiles faintly.

"If there are no limits to what we can do," she says, "I have a message to deliver."

For a moment her aura closes into a concentration of brightness, and then it spreads out once again through the hallway and beyond. She shakes her head briefly to loosen her hair. The air fills with a scent of apple trees and woodland.

Mrs Benson and the doctor descend the stairs. They do not see us. Sahasrael stands aside to let them pass into the kitchen. The doctor sits down at the table.

Sahasrael takes my hand, holding it as though to study my palm.

"I do remember our beginning," she says.

There is a flash of light where she stands and then she is herself again as I see her now, her eyes looking up into mine, still bright with eternity.

Before I can reply, I see that Mrs Benson is staring at us over the doctor's shoulder. I turn to face her.

Sahasrael also turns, and then raises her right hand in a blessing. Together we stand facing Mrs Benson, on whose face is shock and the beginning of joy. In her eyes, we are bright angels, radiant in light, come for the passing of Sally McCloud.

In my heart I feel Sahasrael's silent assurance to her: BE NOT AFRAID. YOUR PRAYER IS ANSWERED. YOU ARE

BELOVED OF HEAVEN.

Then we fade from her sight. Mrs Benson stands with her mouth open, hand on her heart.

The doctor asks her a question and when she doesn't answer, looks up at her. Then he looks over his shoulder to where we stand. He sees the empty hallway. He takes Mrs Benson's arm and stands up to help her sit down.

"That should make her day," says Sahasrael.

Suddenly she is giggling into her hand, like a child.

She steadies herself.

Then all of a sudden she turns to me, young again, and takes my hands.

"Come on, Chandra, let's give you your miracle. Then life."

"The trucks?"

She laughs. "The trucks. And let's find them some drivers."

In The World That Will Be

I stand at the edge of the desert. The sun is about to rise. Sahasrael stands near me.

For as far ahead as I can see, the flat landscape is broken by isolated bushes and stunted trees. The ground is hard here, and a dirt road defined only by tyre tracks leads out towards the desert and the camp and the expanding war beyond. The edge of the sun shows suddenly on the white horizon and its light brightens the drained colours of the early morning. There is now heat in the air.

Walking towards me across the desert, shimmering as if in a heat haze, is a figure. As I watch, another figure appears from another direction, and then another, and another. Gradually they gain substance. Gradually they draw close enough for me to see them clearly. Soon there are ten figures approaching me across the sand. We all wear the standard clothing of the relief effort – not uniform, but mostly sand-coloured shirts and trousers and boots. We all wear armbands showing a green symbol that is neither a crescent nor a cross, on a white background. We are all bare-headed in the desert sun.

The first to reach me has brown eyes and dark, shoulder-length hair. He laughs as we embrace. "You wanted drivers?" he says.

Together, we watch the sun rise on the day that will be my gift to Greg Doyle.

Sahasrael touches my arm. "Go to him, Chandra. We'll meet again at the border."

•

Hannah flicks off the television.

She is sitting on the saggy old sofa with Megan's head on her lap. Ben went out early. She doesn't know where.

Hannah is miserable. It's as if something has broken in her life. Maybe it was broken all along. They had driven back yesterday. Cut it short and come home. They had argued, and then Ben wouldn't speak to her. He hadn't really wanted to visit the cousins anyway, and now this.

After he'd left this morning, she had brought Megan down from her bedroom, with her duvet and pillow, made her a drink, and they had settled down to watch the children's art programme together.

She feels so terrible about it all.

If that man hadn't been there, going swimming so early and in such weather, Megan would have drowned and it would have been her fault. The knowledge goes round in her head and won't stop.

And then Ben blaming her, insisting on blaming her, going on blaming her even though she knew it was her fault, admitted it was her fault, insisted that yes, it was her fault, arguing, shouting, things that just made her so ... nothing.

It's as though something has broken so badly it can't be mended.

104

Ben won't want to mend it now and she can't do it without him. And Hannah can't trust herself as a parent. Ben can't trust her. Megan can't. Megan can't trust her own mother.

Megan is asleep. Hannah's plan to get together some coloured paper and card and actually make the mobile from today's programme on the kitchen table, with string, a couple of plastic coat hangers and craft glue will have to be postponed because Megan has fallen asleep and Hannah isn't even sure whether she was still awake for the bit about the mobile anyway.

What's the point? If she can't even notice that her daughter is asleep.

Out of habit, Hannah puts the remote down the back of the sofa where she will be able to find it but Ben won't be able to take it away and lose it, and closes her eyes. After the art programme there was the children's news broadcast, and with Megan asleep on her lap, Hannah had stayed in place to watch something about a war in Africa.

She should find out what time it is. If Megan sleeps any longer she won't sleep tonight, and Hannah needs to get something sorted out for lunch. They need to…

Behind Hannah, the curtains move slightly, although the windows are closed, and a cool breeze passes through the room. In the kitchen, the second hand on the big white clock stops moving. There is a scent of apples.

Hannah sleeps.

•

At the border, the rescue convoy from Qasir has stopped at the designated holding point. This is the wide tarmac space alongside the road where vehicles used to wait to make the southbound crossing. The guards' hut is empty now, its windows empty of glass and door hanging off its lower hinge, and but for the convoy, the tarmac space is empty. On the southern side of the border there is nothing.

The drivers and relief drivers have rigged up a makeshift shelter against the sun by roping a light tarpaulin between the two leading trucks, one parked on the edge of the tarmac holding area and the other in the empty road. Loosen two knots, and the tarpaulin is free. The remaining trucks of the convoy are parked where they stopped, back along the road. Nobody expects traffic in either direction, except for that one truck from the south, Greg's truck.

At one time or another, always singly, every person in the convoy has walked the short distance to where the made-up road turns to impacted ground at the national boundary, and stared towards the southern horizon.

Nobody is settled. Drivers and relief drivers are grouped around trucks, the engineers checking oil, water, fuel consumption, the security of their loads if they have them, anything else that might conceivably need to be checked. Some are comparing their findings, even discussing the handling characteristics of the trucks they have been driving. Soon, if the wait goes on, the relief workers will settle into their familiar time-passing routines. There will be a card game. Briefly, a kick-about with a football. But the heat will prevail. People will settle in their cabs to sleep, to read, or to listen to music. Some will head for the tarpaulin to discover that there is coffee, food and water.

But however effectively they occupy themselves, there will be frequent moments of stillness between them, as individuals and groups stop what they are doing and look towards the border.

They all know what it will mean if the games go on too long.

There is one odd thing. When they got here, there was a group of relief workers already waiting for them, just standing on the tarmac in the open, no vehicles in sight. And weirdly, not wearing hats despite the sun. The word had gone around that they were an advance party of some kind, although there had been no mention of an advance party before they left. When somebody had asked how they got here, somebody else had shrugged and assumed that they must have parked vehicles out of sight behind the buildings somewhere, out of the way of the convoy's arrival, and that too had gone around.

Nobody has seen the advance party since the convoy arrived; everybody assumes they're off talking to somebody else, or doing their own thing. Nobody really thinks about them now.

•

Hannah opens her eyes.

She has been asleep.

She is sitting on the sofa. Megan's head is in her lap. Megan is still asleep.

Hannah feels so very relaxed, so very warm, in the comfort of their old sofa. It's old enough that she has her own dent in the cushion. Ben's dent is next to her.

He'll come back when he's ready. And then they'll talk.

She has woken up naturally, peacefully, slowly. She has dreamed but does not remember the dream. The room is fresh and she can feel Megan's regular breathing under her hand.

She must have been asleep for hours.

"Come on, darling," she whispers, gently moving Megan so that she can ease herself out, pulling over the pillow to tuck under Megan's head, standing up. Just a few more minutes, but then she really must wake her up or she'll never get to sleep tonight.

Just a few more minutes. Hannah stands looking down at her daughter. Sleep, the great healer. Megan is still flushed, but it's not the same. She is flushed with Hannah's heat and the heat of the duvet, but she is sleeping easily, and with a mother's eye, Hannah can see that she is better than she was first thing.

An echo of her earlier misery enters Hannah's mind, but she pushes it back down.

I will never ever let you get into danger like that again, she says silently, still looking down at her daughter's sleeping face. I will always protect you. I'm sorry.

Hannah closes her eyes and a thread of prayer rises into the light over her head: give me the wisdom I need to care for my daughter.

Then she opens her eyes and walks into the kitchen and is surprised to see from the clock that no more than half an hour can have passed since she fell asleep. It is still morning.

I'll let her sleep for a bit longer, she thinks.

The thing to get, she decides, as she goes to the freezer to get one of the small round pizzas that Megan likes, is stuff like PVA glue and a proper supply of card, coloured paper and ribbons. I must get organised.

Hannah puts on the timer for the pizza, quickly lays the table, and goes to check on her daughter.

•

Under the tarpaulin, the nominated leader of the rescue convoy, a tired, grey-haired man in his early forties known to everybody as John Boy, has been using a satellite phone to talk to Qasir. First time he called, he just reported that they had arrived and that the border was deserted. He didn't think to mention the advance party. Then they ran through a news update. Pointless, but the duty voice at Qasir had gone into it and at least it passed time.

"Officially there's no change in the political situation. The government's still in place and the rebel offensive has stalled. That's officially. We've got all the permits agreed and I'm told that the field commanders know you're coming. So officially you're clear to go. But wait for our decision."

"Got that. Any other news?"

Nobody talks on-air about the US intelligence feed.

"You know they've left, don't you?"

"Yes." The US embassy and a last few civilians, oil workers, were evacuated days ago.

"Best estimate is still a week, based on geography, but like everybody else except the government, they're talking about the morale issue. Government troops are just going home."

In fact, there is already intelligence that a small force has separated from the rebels' northern army and is heading towards the camp, but the spy-satellite images are still being analysed, and the analysts have not yet connected the small force's direction of travel with the location of the camp.

John Boy comes away from that call relieved. If he still has a week, he'll have time for three, possibly four runs to get everybody out.

But we still don't know if the road is passable, he reminds himself.

Unless – until Greg gets through, we won't know if we're going to be driving the convoy into an ambush, or a minefield. Or going home.

John Boy is sitting on a small, folding canvas chair that he's brought down from his cab. The chair creaks under his weight. He brought it from Qasir for the wait here, because it's comfortable, and he'll probably leave it here because they're going to need all the space they can find in the trucks. He's a big, burly man with fair skin tanned to the colour of brick, and Greg Doyle is his friend. He is sitting forward with his elbows on his knees, his hands over his face, fighting down the conviction that Greg is already late. If he doesn't turn up soon, he is thinking, we will have to start talking about what we're going to do. Can we turn around without knowing whether he's dead or alive?

Will anybody come with me to find him?

There's a slight movement next to him and he raises his head to find one of the advance-party women crouching beside him. He'd forgotten about them. She lays her hand on his shoulder.

"Hello, John."

"Do you know Greg Doyle?" he asks her.

She smiles; yes, she does.

"If he doesn't get through, I won't know what to..." He can't complete the sentence. His face shows his anguish.

She nods, and then says, "I came to tell you that he is coming."

"What–"

He hears the shout. "It's him. He's made it. Greg's fucking made it."

John Boy bolts out into the sunshine.

At first he's just dazzled.

But as his eyes adjust to the brightness, shaded by his hand, he follows the pointing fingers of his companions.

And sees, there, in the distance, wavering in the heat haze but clearly identifiable, a single truck driving steadily towards him on the dirt road from the south.

•

Five minutes before his truck was first seen from the rescue convoy, Greg Doyle stood on the crest of a shallow hill, flanked by his passengers, and gazed at a scene he would remember for the rest of his life.

There.

Tiny but somehow clearly visible even at this distance.

There.

Seeming to glitter in the bright sunlight.

There.

A long line of trucks, stretching back from the border along the road from Qasir, back almost to the horizon, waiting for him to give it life.

"Oh, thank you," Greg breathes.

Then he turns, and runs back to his truck, calling for his passengers to get back on board.

•

"Sleep tight, my love."

Hannah leans forward to touch the back of Megan's head with a kiss. It's early for bedtime, but Megan doesn't know that.

Mother and daughter have been together upstairs for almost an hour now, going through the whole thing – bath, story, another story, sit with me Mummy – and now it is almost time to go back downstairs.

Ben is downstairs.

He was walking, he said. Just walking. Needed to clear his head.

Didn't need anything to eat because he'd had something on his walk.

She could smell the pub on him.

Hannah can't spin it out any longer. She steps out of her daughter's bedroom and goes downstairs.

•

His next call to Qasir takes John Boy about ten seconds.

Greg's arrived, bringing a whole bunch of refugees who will need onward transport, and the convoy is going South. Now.

John Boy throws the phone in through the open driver's window of the nearest truck.

"You'll get in and out once if you're very lucky," the voice from Qasir tells the empty cab. "There's an army heading straight for the camp. Don't go, John."

Greg's asleep already, in the cab of his own truck, on the passenger side. He'll count as the relief driver for this trip back to the camp, with one of the advance party driving, and then he'll take over for the return journey. His truck has been unloaded, refuelled and hurriedly checked over, and now it'll head out as the third truck in the convoy. John Boy's glad to have the extra capacity.

There's something on the edge of his mind, though, something odd that he's noticed, but somehow, he can't quite put his finger on it. He shakes his head. He's busy enough already. Ten trucks in his convoy, Greg's makes eleven, with a possible four at the camp, subject to getting them fixed. Enough to get it done in three trips?

Two of the advance party have volunteered to stay with the refugees Greg has brought back from the camp. Do they have transport? Again, that odd – it's gone again.

John Boy climbs up into his cab and starts the engine.

The convoy begins to move.

Watched by refugees whose eyes show no outward emotion, the long convoy of trucks rolls across the border and onto the southbound road.

•

Another Monday morning, fuck it. Ben is back in the office and he's pissed off. He didn't sleep well last night, after the tense evening with Hannah wanting to talk and him wanting to shut it all down. He has a right to be pissed off. He didn't sleep until five minutes before the alarm went off this morning. Hannah pretended to be still asleep while he was getting ready to go and then the fucking coffee shop at

the station was closed due to 'staff sickness'. And the train was short,
four carriages. At least he got a seat although he had to shove for it.

The weekend had been fucked up by that stupid, stupid, stupid
thing on Saturday morning.

Hannah letting Megan go for a swim in a storm.

Letting her almost–

If it hadn't been for some nut who also thought it was the perfect
day for a swim.

Not even watching Megan?

Not even close?

And now Megan coming down with another bloody cold.

"Ben?"

It's her. The girl.

"...hey," Ben says. "Good weekend?"

"Yeah. You?"

"Yeah."

She's waiting for him to say something. He can't quite–

"Do you still want to draw me? Do you remember?"

"Yeah. Of course I remember. If you'd like me to."

She doesn't reply.

"Look, I'd love to," Ben says, gaining reckless confidence, drawn to
fill her silence. He glances at Anthony's closed blinds and then at the
clock on his desktop. "How about lunch?" he says. "A sandwich, or
something. We can talk about it."

Suddenly she's grinning. "Yeah," she says. "Okay." Then she too
glances at Anthony's blinds. "I'd like that," she says.

She turns, and he watches her go.

•

I ride in the second truck with two men, each of whom assumes the other knows me. I am once again the young man Hannah saw on the beach, visible, dressed in the standard clothing of the relief effort and with the rucksack between my feet. There is room for the three of us in the wide cab, and possibly a fourth, but as the convoy moves further into the desert, we fall silent. Greg Doyle has driven this road and it is therefore likely to be safe, but still, the tension of the journey holds us.

The miles pass more quickly than expected, without incident, and the thought begins to circulate that perhaps, if there's no problem when they get there and they can do a fast-enough turnaround, they could make the first return trip now rather than waiting until the morning. They might cross the border after dark, but with luck, they'd be out of the danger zone well before sunset. In the first cab, John Boy says, "Any delay, mind. Anything. And we wait until tomorrow." He starts to think about setting a latest possible departure time for the first return trip.

As the convoy draws near to the camp I see that the tents are closed and nobody is out in the open. White and off-white sheets have been added to the symbols and multilingual signs declaring the camp's neutrality and lack of weapons. We are approaching from the safe direction, and we are expected, but the sand cloud indicates that this is a much bigger convoy than the eleven trucks planned and Greg's safety procedures are clear and unambiguous. Anybody could cut around and approach from the north.

The convoy stops at the camp's marked perimeter and engines judder into a sudden, incongruous silence. For a moment, there is no movement. Then a man steps out through the flap of the nearest tent. He wears a vest and shorts and his hands are open at his sides. He is bareheaded. This too is the procedure as set out by Greg. I step down from the truck, as others do the same, and we walk towards him, several of us with arms open in a gesture of welcome. His face breaks open and he gives a cry of relief as he sees people he recognises. He begins to cry, and as he does so, John Boy reaches him and encloses him in a big, rough hug.

There are others coming forward from the trucks now, and behind the man, the flap of the hospital tent has been lifted. Ali is looking out at us. He is without fear and I see Naseena come out from the darkness to stand beside him. The flaps of other tents open now, and light floods into them as figures emerge.

Another relief worker, another man, comes forward to clasp my hand, his fear evaporated. I give him the knowledge of what the convoy brings. His eyes widen.

"What are we waiting for?" He swings round and gestures at the tent behind him. "It's okay. Come on out. We've got supplies to unpack."

Then, as the tents empty and we are suddenly surrounded by people, he starts giving orders to all of us. "Medical supplies up there, back in close as you can. That generator. We need it right now, right there. How easily accessible is the food? We need a couple of trucks opened up now..."

I turn away from him and see Greg Doyle looking in amazement at Maya Brennan. She is crying. As I watch, she takes hold of Greg's shirt. "You big idiot," she says. "Driving into– You big, bloody idiot." She pulls herself forward so that she is both hugging him and crying into his shirt.

As I turn away, I come face to face with the bereaved husband-and-father. His clear eyes look straight into mine. Neither of us speaks. BE AT PEACE, I tell him. He nods his head. He knows who we are.

•

Megan is drawing at the kitchen table. Hannah is sitting opposite her, also drawing. It's the middle of Monday. Megan slept through the night despite the early bedtime and was sluggish this morning. Nothing specific, but earlier, Hannah rang the playgroup to say she'd caught a chill and wouldn't be in today. She's sure that Mrs Barnaby could hear the waver in her voice. Deal with that tomorrow. She doesn't want to have sympathy pushed at her today.

They read a story and watched a film and didn't go outside. The house is a cocoon. The lunch things have been cleared away to the side next to the breakfast things; washing up can wait for once. Hannah is feeling sluggish too. Some days, you do. It's normal. They have drawn each other, and now Megan is drawing Ben. Hannah has been instructed to draw horses, but she's putting in the grass and the sky first. In a moment, she will invite Megan to add the horses for her. They will agree that Megan's horses are better than hers.

Megan finishes. "There," she says, putting the cap on her felt-tip without having to be told.

"May I see?"

Megan slides over the picture, and despite the weight in her heart, Hannah feels a sudden twist of tenderness. Ben has brown squiggled hair and round blue eyes with barely any white and black dots for pupils. He is wearing blue eyeliner and it would have taken him a lot of lipstick to get his mouth that shape and colour.

But it's a lovely picture, and somehow, it is Ben.

"Let's see." Megan holds out her hand.

So Hannah passes over her own unfinished – barely started – picture.

"Mummy!" says Megan.

"But you're better at horses, darling. Why don't you draw my horses while I ring Daddy and tell him about your lovely picture?"

Hannah goes out of the kitchen to make the call before she can change her mind.

116

She hears him pick up, and all the tenderness invoked by Megan's picture is suddenly replaced by nervousness.

"Oh Ben, it's me. Sorry, I – that was quick."

"–"

"Look, I don't want to disturb you, but–"

"–"

"–I just wanted to say I'm sorry."

She hears the tone of his voice change, and that gives her courage.

"It's just that we've got so much together, and I know it was terrible, and I'm sorry, but I don't want one horrible weekend–"

"–"

"Ben, can we just–"

"–"

"Tonight, we could just talk, maybe, and–"

Hannah talks, and then listens, and then talks again. She finishes the call.

She goes back into the kitchen and Megan looks up from her work on the horses.

"What did Daddy say about my picture?" she asks.

"He said he's looking forward to seeing it tonight, darling," lies Hannah.

"I'm going to put it in my bedroom so he can see it when he comes in," says Megan, and she goes on talking as Hannah sits down again at the table, wondering why the conversation with Ben has not made her feel better.

•

"So," says Ben. "What kind of portrait do you want?"

"This is really kind of you."

"No, I'd love to do it."

They are in a crowded, tiny coffee shop down the street from the office. On impulse, Ben has offered to pay for her salad and bottle of water, and now they are sitting side by side on two stools in the corner, facing the window over a long black surface that is barely wider than a plank.

Ben is ... not quite sure what he thinks is happening. He offered to pay for her lunch, okay, but that's just normal between colleagues. Nothing special going on.

This is a portrait, he reminds himself. Not like I'm even thinking about anything else.

Intermittently, their bodies brush against each other.

"I'd like the whole of me, if that's okay," she says, looking at him as though it might not be.

"Okay," says Ben. "Standing up?"

She raises her eyebrows as though this is an odd idea.

"Possibly..."

"And how big?" says Ben, thinking: *not standing up.*

"Picture-sized," she says, as if it doesn't matter, and shows him a roughly A3 size with her hands. The way she does it, it's wider than it is tall, landscape rather than portrait, Ben thinks.

"I'll need to get a drawing pad," he says, "and some materials."

She looks at him.

"We'll have to do it in a lunch-break," he tells her, thinking: *we could look for an empty office, or she could sit at my desk.*

"I know where we can do it," she says.

"Okay," says Ben, surprised.

"I've got the key to a friend's flat," she says. She points out of the window. "Up there. Five minutes from the office."

"Okay," says Ben again, automatically. A friend's flat. She's got all this worked out, he thinks, and tries to ignore the sudden dismay sinking down into his gut.

"If that's all right," she says, looking at him obliquely.

"No, yeah, that's fine," says Ben, and then, as she slides off her stool, he adds, "When do you want to do it? Tomorrow?"

She is looking down at her empty salad box, her hair curtaining her face. It's the wrong question again, somehow.

But then she says, "Tomorrow? Yeah. Sure." She's standing up ready to leave and he thinks he's offended her somehow. But she's saying, "No. Stay. Finish your lunch. I've got to get back."

She puts her hand on his thigh and says, "Thanks for lunch, right?"

Then she doesn't look back as she moves through the crowd and lets herself out into the world again.

Ben watches her go, thinking: oh, shit.

·

Maya has not left Greg's side. They are not holding hands but their forearms touch. Around them, the camp is full of haste and activity, but they are too intent on each other, silent as they are, to be aware of this.

"You were so lucky," says Maya. She now knows about the defective mines setting themselves off around Greg as he drove past. One mine obviously so sensitive that it was detonated by Greg's approach and the rest going off in a chain reaction.

"It was a miracle," says Greg, whose expression suggests a sun rising behind his eyes.

"Don't be silly," she replies, but gently. He'll get over it soon.

Maya sees me walking towards them from a distance. She steps forward, away from Greg, as if she is protecting him from a stranger by diverting me. She extends her arm. Briefly we clasp hands. "All these trucks," she says. "Most of them look new. Have we got money from somewhere?' She is suspicious, although she is not sure why. In this moment she believes that she has met me once before, back at Qasir.

I shake my head. "It's an emergency. You need them." Our eyes meet. "You need to get everybody out as soon as possible. You're going to need every one of them."

Her first instinct is to challenge me. "Have you got paperwork on any of this?"

Stupid question, she thinks, as she says it. But she has patients too weak to travel. She's not going anywhere.

"Let's wait until we've got all this stuff unloaded and then we can talk."

She sees the sense in that. We separate, and as she walks away from me, I call after her, "We've got doctors in the team." She raises her hand without looking back at me. Greg has moved on and she goes to confer with the doctors she knows.

I see Naseena and Ali standing in the back of a truck. They are already handing down flat loaves of unleavened bread to a crowd of refugees, from a plastic crate. Behind them are more crates containing more food to meet immediate need, and behind those crates, there are yet more crates.

"Could you do it again?" I say, silently, to Naseena, and she does not hear me.

Ali sees me and waves before going back to his work.

•

Ben decides on pastels. And an A3 pad of good, thick paper. Art board? She wants it wider than tall, so ... no, just an A3 pad. Just do it landscape A3.

She will want a likeness, but he's guessing closer to comic-book photo-realism than something schmaltzy to put in a frame. He will have about an hour to do it, assume less. Maybe he could finish it later.

120

Landscape. Pose her sitting back on an armchair, or maybe lying on a sofa, if there is one?

How about on a bed?

Ben doesn't want to think about that.

His mobile rings, juddering on the desk.

Startled out of his reverie, he snatches it up and has it to his ear before thinking to look at the caller ID.

"Hello!" he says, hearing the urgency still in his voice.

"—"

"Oh. Hi. I'm sorry, no, I was busy with something."

"—"

"You're not, no, not at all."

"—"

Ben hunches forward over the phone.

"I am too," he says softly.

"—"

"I know, neither do I."

"—"

"Of course we can."

Ben listens, and then speaks, and then listens again. He finishes the call.

What the fuck am I doing?

Ben decides that he will not spend tomorrow lunchtime in a stranger's flat drawing a portrait of a young woman he hardly knows. He will call her, maybe even just email her, and then quickly sketch her in the office instead.

Buried in the forgotten heart of Ben's imagination is the life he expected to lead. He sees it as an office in a wide, open attic, all light wood and window lights, his wife at another desk, working as his partner, meeting his eye, and designers who work in a team in his practice. They go out for lunch together on Friday, a regular thing, and there is laughter, creativity, always progress in the office. His wife will be proud of him.

Hannah, Ben thinks. My wife's name is Hannah. This is my wife, Hannah. He imagines the others in his imaginary office talking about how he and Hannah are always laughing together.

I can still buy the pastels, Ben thinks.

Maybe I could draw Hannah.

•

It is time to speak to Maya Brennan in the company of the other leaders of the camp.

Now that the first rush of unloading is complete and the distribution is under way, this is the first opportunity for the two groups, camp and convoy, to meet and start planning their next move together.

I stand with John Boy and two members of the advance party. John Boy has played no part in the unloading, instead going straight to work on the camp's four trucks, which are now refuelled and sufficiently fixed to be added to the convoy for the return journey.

Yes, John Boy has agreed. We will go now. If we can keep the talking and the celebration to a minimum, we'll have ample time to get to the border before dark.

We stand in the shade of one of the two trucks from Qasir that are intended to serve as ambulances. It is emptied now, and there would be space for us all to climb up inside. Such is the activity in the camp that there are few other places where we could be assured of privacy.

"Where do you get your information?" Maya Brennan knows that Qasir is well-connected. She is feeling disorientated with the speed of what is happening around her.

I shrug. "Does it matter? They'll be here in three days."

Greg says, "We're not going to be doing this again, are we? Another supply run? There's no chance."

Another man who has not yet spoken says, "That looks like a hell of a lot of capacity out there. Maybe we should concentrate on loading now and talk later. If we're still short of space," he adds, seeing that John Boy is frowning.

John Boy is frowning because fifteen trucks – his ten, plus the camp's five – isn't his idea of a hell of a lot of capacity. Something about this whole trip has been bothering him ever since they crossed the border, but he still can't quite put his finger on it. He opens his mouth to say – what? The thought comes to him that anything he says will only prolong the debate. We can either talk or get on with it, he decides, and shakes his head.

I am watching Maya. She is thinking of her patients.

"Okay, let's start getting the able-bodied onto the trucks," she says. "Is the road still safe?"

It's a question asked at random to keep the initiative. She doesn't want to give Greg time to think.

Shouldn't have said "able-bodied", she thinks. Don't tip him off.

I nod. It is safe. For a moment she wonders how I could be so sure, but she doesn't voice the question.

"Okay, that's a decision, I think," she says, hurrying the meeting to its conclusion. "We need people on trucks, and trucks ready to go. Let's get to it."

But Greg isn't so easily deflected. As the meeting breaks up, he catches her arm. "Maya, once this convoy goes, it won't be coming back."

She pulls her arm free. "I know that."

He gestures to the ambulance. "There's space. You can bring them with you."

This makes her suddenly angry. "I can't leave them, Greg. I've got patients who can't travel. I'm not leaving them."

"Then I'll stay with you."

This shocks her. She covers it with anger. "Your convoy needs you, Greg. If you're stupid enough to drive through a minefield, I can certainly stay with my patients. But your convoy needs you."

He's not fooled. In that moment, each of them precisely understands the other. Their hands touch. But neither speaks.

She has known all along that she will stay behind, in a skeleton camp, with whatever medical supplies can be left, to care for those who cannot travel.

But she absolutely will not let Greg stay with her. It's too dangerous.

She is further annoyed to see that all of a sudden, Greg isn't even looking at her. He is staring at the weird guy from Qasir, who is smiling back at Greg like somebody who's found the happy pills and taken them all.

"Was there something else?" she says to me.

I can't help smiling at her. "Three days from now you'll both be in Qasir," I tell her. "You'll all be safe."

Maya's immediate thought is: you're new out here, aren't you? Which of course is as ridiculous as it gets: the guy has just driven in on the convoy from Qasir.

"Glad you think so," she replies, embarrassed, and because she is embarrassed, she turns on her heel and walks away.

Greg stares at me for a moment longer, and then runs after her.

•

Ben, laptop and new diary under his arm, passes the entrance to the coffee shop where he had lunch with the girl. I'll sit her down at my desk tomorrow and do a quick drawing, he thinks. I'll tell her I'm too busy for lunch.

That was crazy. What was I thinking?

This is his route to the station every evening, but Ben isn't going that far yet. There's an art-supply store just up ahead that he always passes, and tonight, he's going to go inside for the first time. The windows are full of painting-by-numbers sets, boxes of pastels and crayons, easels, plastic palettes and pose-able wooden figures in various sizes; the back of the display is a collage of posters showing the portraits, landscapes, still-lifes you could paint, draw or colour in with the shop's supplies.

But this isn't about what he can see. Ben has developed a relationship with the shop. Every time he passes it, he's reminded that he's not an artist any more. For Ben, the shop is a test that he failed years ago. Here is everything he would have needed for the life he's failing to live.

Now Ben has spoken to Hannah and heard her voice and all that has suddenly blown away. Ben feels released. I could draw Hannah, he thinks. I could draw Megan.

Ben's new mood takes him all the way to the shop itself. He stops outside. At the back of the window display, holding the posters, is a peg-board that obscures his view of whatever it is that he would be buying if he knew what he wanted. Pastels, was it? I've got pencils, Ben thinks suddenly; I can draw with pencils. In fact, what could I possibly need in here that I couldn't order up from stationery? Standing outside the shop in his grey-nerd suit and tie, holding a laptop and a desk diary for fuck's sake, Ben suddenly loses his nerve.

A man about Ben's age, wearing jeans and an open-necked shirt, a rucksack on his back, stands for a second next to Ben at the window, then steps forward and opens the door of the shop. He steps inside and then stops, holding the door open, looking back at Ben.

"You coming in?"

It's instinctive for Ben to step forward and take the door with his free hand. "Thanks," he says.

"Part of the service," the man says over his shoulder, as he moves forward away from Ben into the shop. He has broad shoulders and Ben registers that his curling blond hair falls down over his collar.

Ben releases the door and it swings gently shut behind him.

The shop is bigger inside than he had expected, and more professional, less hobby-artist than the window. There are display shelves of paper, various sizes of sketch pad, watercolour paper, stretched canvases slotted like books into tall shelves; slanting trays of pencils, pens – an abundance of brushes, palettes and racks of paints in numbered colour order. Ahead is a counter and behind the counter sits a woman wearing an indigo-coloured loose-knit cardigan and a band that holds back her hair. She is reading. She looks up and gives Ben a slow, languid smile. "Hello," she says. She glances at the other man and returns to her book.

The smile from the woman puts Ben at his ease. He comes forward and says, "Do you mind if I put these here?"

"Sure," she says.

So he leaves the laptop and the diary on the counter and returns to the display.

He wants to draw. So he will need paper and pencils. Oil pastels? A pad small enough to carry everywhere. A pencil sharpener. An eraser.

"These are useful." The man with the rucksack is standing next to him offering him a pen. Brown ink, fine tip. "Sketching in the lines, you know?"

Ben assumes that the man is connected to the shop. But he's relaxed now, and he finds himself replying like talking about his dreams is easy after all.

"I want to get back into the habit," he says. "Make it easy for myself, you know? Get the skill back."

"It's like music," the man says. "Easy not to practise."

"That's right," Ben says.

They stand together in silence for an easy moment and then Ben picks up a pencil and lightly tests it on a pad left for the purpose on the display. It's right; he feels it straight away. He tries the brown pen; that's good too.

"Try this." The man offers him a drawing pad, more like a book, bound in something that looks like leather but isn't. It's about A4 size, the size of a desk diary. "It's perforated; you can take out the ones you like and frame them."

"Yeah, that's good," says Ben. "Thanks," he says to the man, who grins and passes him two more pencils and another pen.

"Starter kit," the man says. "You'll do well with that collection."

Ben uses the brown pen to add a curved line to the scribbles he has made on the test pad. He adds another line, and another, and the man sees it: a pair of eyes under heavy, scribbled eyebrows.

"Back in the habit already," the man says.

•

I catch up with Maya as she walks alone towards the main hospital tent. The loading is almost complete, and people are telling her that there's still space in the ambulance trucks. That isn't the point and it's beginning to irritate her. There may be space, which seems unlikely anyway, but the point is, space or no space, some of her patients just can't travel. They're too sick.

Maya's fear has become an unexamined melancholy that sings in the back of her head. As long as she doesn't confront it, she will not give in to it. She covers it by silently repeating phrases that have become a mantra to her: don't you see that I can't leave my patients?

As long as there are sick people in my hospital, I can't leave them.

Surely the soldiers won't – she blanks that one. Don't you see that I can't leave my patients?

As we begin to walk together, Ali runs up to us and takes my hand and hers. He walks between us.

"Where's Naseena, Ali?" Maya asks.

"Helping angels," he says, with an inflection in his voice that suggests she should know this.

We walk on in silence.

They do know not to talk religion with these people, Maya thinks. Don't they?

They could cause such offence.

Ali begins to skip as he walks. Maya remembers his sudden, swift recovery. She stops and crouches down. "How are you doing, Ali?" There, in the sun, she holds him close to her and looks into his eyes. "How do you feel?"

He laughs, and that is enough of an answer. She straightens up, suddenly conscious that after the convoy has left, she may never see him again. He runs away, waving his hand to me. I return the wave and he grins over his shoulder. Idly, Maya wonders how he knows me.

"He was really sick the other day," she tells me.

"You're a good doctor," I tell her.

"No, really, we weren't expecting him to make it."

We are close to the tent now. "Are you a qualified doctor?" she asks me.

"Just a messenger," I tell her, as we step out of the bright sunlight into the relative darkness of the tent.

I hear Maya Brennan's intake of breath as her eyes begin to adjust. To her, it seems that just for a moment there are shards of multi-coloured light everywhere between the beds, standing vertical, shimmering. But what she sees does not fit into her understanding, and a moment later the tent is clear of light, calm, quiet, as she knows it to be.

"Are you all right?" I say.

"Yeah. Sure. Sorry." Optical illusion. She has her hand to her eyes. Migraine? Please not now. She lowers her hand.

"Takes me a moment to adjust, that's all." She smiles at me to show that she is all right.

"Okay, I'd better leave you, then."

It is appropriate that she should believe herself alone when she discovers that there is no longer disease in any of the hospital tents. That even the weakest of her patients have recovered sufficient strength to convince her that they are able to travel.

Later, as the convoy of many shining trucks rolls out on its single run from the camp to Qasir, leaving behind only emptiness for the soldiers to find, Maya Brennan will wrestle with her own experience of the impossible. She will fight it with denial at first, calling up her own self-doubt, doubting her equipment, her diagnostic skills, her own senses.

For a long time, she will refuse to discuss the events of today, sometimes even shutting her eyes and shaking her head, using anger to block any speculation. "We were just lucky, that's all," she will say. "Very, very lucky."

Maya will never use the word 'miracle' to describe what happened today, because she is a rational adult. She will always believe that there is a rational explanation just beyond her reach, waiting for her to see it.

But in time, the hard edges of her convictions will soften, and in her heart, she will accept that in medicine as in life, sometimes, that which is given strays far beyond that which is sought.

In The World That Is

Ben dozes on his evening train. He is tired now, and his spirit has faltered. He is watching the warehouses, silos and blank concrete spaces of the city's endless edge. In time, there will be fields and a horizon, but the train is crowded and hot, and Ben is cramped in his seat.

What is the use of dreams? Ben asks himself. What are dreams anyway? They're just a fucking waste of time.

I lay subtle hands on his heart and the surface of his mind clears again.

There is time, I tell him silently.

Always there is now, and now is always a beginning.

I could start again, Ben thinks. Just go home and buy some flowers and talk to her and start again. Tell her how I feel about her. Tell her what I need, just simply, so she understands. Not make an argument out of it.

Leave the job. Do what I really want to do.

Take that risk.

In his mind I am a whiteness that he cannot see.

I am here, I tell him silently. Dream now, Ben.

But Ben has started thinking of Hannah, imagining her at restaurant table in candlelight, wearing a low-cut red dress and a necklace he has not yet found to buy her. There are tall fluted glasses and a white tablecloth and white napkins and he is holding his wife's frail hand in his own. Her eyes are full of tears and he wants her to know that he still loves her. In this imagining his words flow so clearly and her understanding of him is deep and secure.

Ben's eyes fill with tears. The way he feels now, even his dreams turn against him. It is as if they remind him of failures that have not happened yet.

He lays his head back and closes his eyes. Fuck this, he thinks.

He does not expect to sleep, does not intend to sleep, but I am with him now.

I wait for his dream and then weave myself into it, taking what it brings and turning it towards the light. Ben is standing in a dark room. But now the door stands ajar. He is looking out at a garden. A straight gravel path leads to a gate in a white-painted fence. The flowerbeds contain bare earth. Beyond the fence there is a clear space and then trees.

I walk from the edge of the clearing to the garden gate. I stand aside from the path, holding the gate open.

Ben sees the young man standing at the gate. He is wearing jeans and a blue-checked shirt. He is smiling. The young man carries a rucksack on his back. He is holding the gate open, waiting for Ben. In the dream, Ben knows me.

The young man speaks. YOU'RE NEEDED OUT HERE, I am saying, laughter in my voice. COME OUT AND PLAY, BEN. I am half-turned, ready to walk with him into the forest.

Ben opens his eyes. "Shit," he says, and the woman sitting opposite him in the train looks up at him. Ben is blinking, as though woken from sleep. "Sorry," he says to her, and she goes back to her book. Ben misses the tight disapproving look she purses up for him to see.

"Wow," he says.

•

"That was fun."

"They're safe now, aren't they?"

"Yes, they're safe."

The convoy has reached Qasir and relief workers are struggling to cope with the multitude of refugees. Fifteen trucks, no more, stand parked on the tarmac, their engines ticking as they cool in the night. The advance party, gone now, has been forgotten in the chaos of arrival.

"They believe what they want to believe," says Sahasrael. "Regardless."

"We take the form of their deepest belief?"

"We take the form they give us."

We walk for a while in the starlit darkness.

"Naseena would like Megan," I say.

"Yes, and what of your life, Chandrael? What life do you choose?"

I see Ali, grown to adulthood, standing in a hospital room next to the bed of his father, feeling for a pulse. Ali reaches forward to touch his father's eyelids, which are already closed, and then he stands for a moment by the bed. He is the doctor and he must complete the formalities of death, but as he understood long ago, it is fitting that there should be a moment of farewell.

I see Maya and I see Greg, together and separately, arguing, agreeing. I see a child, and then another.

I see an old man, alone, add a last stone to a pile of stones. But the old man wears his bereavement lightly now. He has told nobody why he has piled up these stones and he has accepted no help. He is an elder now, and his people tolerate his quirks.

Further away, in the world that could be, I see Hannah alone at a café table. Then I see Hannah and Ben together: they hold hands; they clutch to each other; they cry together.

I see my own life, as it could be.

And then I see a young man that I have not seen before, in a place that Hannah and Ben will come to know, in darkness.

Sahasrael laughs, seeing what I see. "You are what you are. Even in the choosing, you reach out."

"I can help him."

"Show him an angel, Chandra."

"He'll deny it."

"Not the third time. He'll see what he needs to see."

We are laughing together now.

"Go on, Chandra. Let's weave this life of yours."

And I am gone.

•

Ben steps off the train onto the familiar platform and breathes the air. Around him and ahead of him, men and woman in coats carrying briefcases and bags are hurrying to the bridge over the track to the ticket office and the car park. Ben walks slowly, overtaken all around.

"Wow," Ben says. He is still thinking of the man in the forest, in that dream on the train. He was wearing a rucksack. We were going hiking, Ben thinks.

That was kind of weird.

I walk with him through the barrier, past the ticket office and out to the car park. Doors are slamming and engines starting. Ben steps to one side of the exit, although the crowd has dispersed already and there is nobody behind him. "Wow," Ben repeats. He is aware that he feels much calmer than he is used to feeling. He watches for a while as the car park empties, and reflects that it will all happen again when the next train arrives. The last taxi pulls away from the rank, leaving a short queue.

The newsagent is closed, but the usual woman is still sitting on her folding chair among the racks of buckets that make up the flower stall. She's done well today, Ben thinks, standing over what little stock she has left. The woman doesn't stand up; she waits for him to make his choice.

He nearly picks a single red rose on a long stem, but a sudden vision of himself as she probably sees him – yet another man in a suit making a quick, predictable choice – persuades him to take his time.

Ben points, and she tells him that he's chosen carnations. "And a couple of those," Ben adds. The only thing he knows about carnations is that they're ordinary. She tells him that he's chosen alstroemeria, which pleases him because he's never heard of them. Conscious of his own patience, he watches her wrap the flowers, and thinks about the quick, neat way she repeats movements for him that she probably repeats dozens of times every day. She wears a quilted fleece waistcoat and a worn leather pouch at her waist for the money.

Fleetingly, Ben feels a sense of connection to the woman who runs the flower stall. I have stepped out of the herd that passes in front of you every day, he thinks, pleased with himself that he is seeing her – actually looking at her as opposed to taking her for granted as part of the station's familiar background – for the first time.

People know you, he thinks, not sure what this means but registering the tortoiseshell clasp with which she has caught back her faded-blonde hair, the grey strands that escape at the nape of her neck.

For somebody, these are familiar details, he thinks.

She straightens up and tells him what he owes her. They exchange money, and as she presents him with his bunch of carnations and alstroemeria, their eyes meet.

"I hope she likes them," she says.

Their eyes have met for less than a second, but for Ben, it is as if she has seen inside him and understood.

"I hope so too," he says

At the exit, he looks back and sees that she has watched him leave.

"Good luck," she says.

•

I come to a long twilit room, clean and still. It is night here and I can hear the soft regular noises of machines around the beds and the quiet voices of nurses in the corridor behind me.

Some of the beds are shrouded, although most of the curtains are pushed open on their rails. Behind the beds are plugs, lights, buttons, mechanisms for treating the body. Every bed is occupied by a child whose condition is stable but who cannot be moved from this ward. Beside the beds are armchairs, most of them low, upholstered and comfortable. These are occupied by mothers or fathers.

The walls of the room are painted a shade of yellow that will pick up the morning light. There are big pastel-coloured painted teddy bears and balloons on the walls, flowers with primary-coloured petals and blobby hearts. Around the room are child-sized chairs and low work-tables scattered with paper, crayons and toys.

The staff here do not wear uniforms to their work. Some of them are nurses of the hospital and some of them are volunteers trained and provided by a religious order that has begun a charity to provide care. There are counsellors and other willing helpers nearby. Parents are allowed to spend the nights on the ward, in the armchairs or in any spare beds that can be found. There is a television, magazines and comics, electronic games, donated films and storybooks.

I raise my arms and the wakeful children sleep; the restless parents sleep.

In a small room along the entrance corridor, behind a closed door, a young man cries silently. He is the young man that I have not seen before, the young man in darkness, whose need cannot be denied, who denies his need. He is the hospice's visiting chaplain for his religion and all religions and no religion, and earlier in the night, he said goodbye to another child.

In a drawer of the desk in front of him is a file of papers. Each sheet gives the admission details of a child he has accompanied through the last moments of life.

On top of the file, closed in the drawer, is the holy book of his religion.

The young man has not slept. He is awake, but his room is in darkness; he wants to conceal his wakefulness from the nurses. They have left him alone to rest, but he cannot do that. He wants to know, how could this be allowed to happen?

I stand inside the closed door of the room. Two children come to me, standing within my arms so that if he chooses, the young man may see that they have my protection. We stand in silence. Now I am light. My wings spread to cover the wall behind me.

Then the silence is not silence and in the brightened air the children and I can hear Sahasrael's delighted laughter. "Yes," she says, unheard in the room. "Yes."

The young man becomes aware that the quality of the darkness in the room has changed. His desk is sideways-on to the door; he has only to turn to see us.

But he does not do so.

His faith is strong but he denies it. He is angry.

"Richard," I say.

He does not turn his head.

"Look at us," says the child who died tonight.

Richard Hailey covers his eyes with his hands. He has heard nothing.

•

Ben took Hannah by surprise that night.

He was late. Not very late but late enough for Megan to be in bed, asleep already, and just late enough for Hannah to have given up on him and eaten her own supper. The pub again, probably.

By stopping at the art shop he had only missed two rush-hour trains, ten minutes apart, and then had to wait fifteen minutes for the next, but she had given up on him more due to self-analysis than reason.

His lateness was enough to bring the darkness back.

She shouldn't have called him at the office this afternoon. She just made it worse by interrupting his work. Megan nearly died. All because of her carelessness. Her stupidity. It was all her fault. Megan nearly died.

By the time Ben comes home, Hannah has brooded herself into a misery.

She hears his key in the lock and freezes in place at the kitchen table, feeling the flush rising in her face.

She tracks him through the house by the sound of his movement. Coat off. Keys on the table. Wait in the hallway. Go through into the living room. Stop.

Come into the kitchen.

She doesn't look up and he doesn't speak. He stands in the

doorway.

"I'm sorry," he says. "I was ... held up." He hesitates because the mood of the room, Hannah's mood, is like a drench of cold air to his spirit. He has been thinking about how he went into the art shop, went inside and talked as if he was that kind of person, wanting to find the words to tell Hannah about the change that has befallen him.

Now, in this familiar kitchen, so full of how it was when he left this morning, so full of everything between them – Saturday, Megan, so full of everything that has been wrong – he falters.

She has still not looked at him.

In a single swift movement he brings the flowers back from in front of him to behind him and lays them down in the hall, along the wall, where she will not see them and he can dispose of them later.

"Your supper's in the oven," she says. "I've eaten. I didn't know when you were coming home."

If you were coming home.

She wants to hide.

She feels the tears start as she hears him move about the kitchen, setting his place at the table, retrieving his plate of dried sausages and congealed vegetables from the oven. She forgot to cover it.

"I'm sorry," she says. "I don't know how I could have done that." She means the beach, but the mistake with his supper finally breaks her. She is dissolving into tears, hunched in her place, silent.

He feels her sudden, complete subsidence into despair and softens despite himself.

By a lucky instinct he has laid his place next to her rather than facing her. He puts his hand on her arm and then takes it away. She can see through her tears that he is looking down at his plate.

"I was angry," he says.

"Yes. But." I deserved it, she almost says.

"I didn't want to hurt you," he says. "I'm sorry. I was shocked."

She is drying her tears now. "Letting her play so close to the sea like that," she says. "It's just, I can't bear to think about it."

At last he turns in his chair and looks at her. His eyes are clear.

"I don't want to lose you," he says.

He has spoken without thinking. She realises that he is also close to tears.

For a moment she stares at him in astonishment.

Then, two clumsy adults, they are trying to hold each other across the two chairs, trying to embrace.

"I was so angry. I'm sorry. It was just a mistake. I know it was just a mistake."

He's saying things and she's saying sorry and she's telling him not to say anything more, he doesn't need to, and she's sorry. Then he just pushes the plate away and his chair goes over backwards – they freeze, but there's no noise from upstairs – and then they're on the sofa, her mostly on his lap, and he's telling her that anybody can make mistakes and he's sorry and they just need to promise each other they'll be careful.

Then she detects the change in him and realises that he wants to. She brings her head back and they look into each other's eyes for a second.

Yes.

They go upstairs.

After that, comfy and undone in their night things, they sit on the sofa while he eats the fresh supper she makes for him and she watches him eat. The flowers are in a vase now, on the low table in front of them.

When he has finished his supper, he lays the plate aside and she settles her head down on his lap in the same way that Megan was settled down this morning. His warm hand finds her breast while she pulls Megan's downstairs blanket over her and dozes.

After that, for a while, as she lies safe under his hand, he flicks through the channels and finally watches most of an old fantasy movie on Freeview.

•

There is silence in Qasir. Fifteen trucks, desert-stained, their engine blocks still ticking as the last heat of the journey goes out of them, stand unloaded and empty on the concrete space. The air is cooler today than any of them have known it this season, and the night sky is misted with faint, high cloud. Around the camp, the new arrivals settle into huts and tents.

There are too many of them.

Fifteen trucks could not possibly have brought this many refugees out in one trip.

But they're here.

Greg and Maya have joined the meeting. They sit together but at right angles to each other, around the corner of the table, and they avoid each other's eyes. Greg's face is alight and Maya is angry, although whether she is angry with him, with herself or with the success of the rescue convoy, she does not know. People can cling to the roofs of trucks, she tells herself. And there is nothing miraculous in a spontaneous cure. It's just rare.

John Boy is sitting at the far end of the table, his arms folded, eyes looking up at the ceiling. He is tuning this out. The convoy succeeded, which is what matters. The rest is just static. Maybe there were fewer people in the camp than they had expected, or maybe they crammed in more people than the trucks could carry. Who gives a shit?

He doesn't need congratulating for the success of his convoy, but it would be nice if somebody said something.

"There's no way we can sanction another trip," says the director. He has just summarised the current political situation. The ex-president is believed to have fled the country. The new one has taken his place and the war is technically over. The shooting has officially stopped.

They can't risk another convoy. The director is firm on this point, sticking to it, even as his mind shies away from the uncomfortable truth that there is no longer any need for another convoy.

The director sees that Greg is smiling at him.

"How are we getting on with accommodation?" he asks quickly, before Greg can say anything.

The meeting settles into a detailed discussion of the capacity that could be made available in the event of a renewed flow of refugees across the border. The director breathes a silent sigh of relief.

At the end of the table, Greg puts out his foot and touches Maya lightly on the ankle. She feels his touch and knows he's looking at her, but at first she doesn't want to return his gaze. She stares at the table.

And then all of a sudden she realises that she is no longer angry. The refugees are saved, and if Greg wants to believe in some kind of divine intervention, that's his problem. They're safe. That's what matters.

She's not going to give him the satisfaction. But his foot touches hers again and she can feel that his eyes are still on her.

She looks at him now, meaning to tell him by a frown that he should leave her alone and stop being such a fool. But she feels the edge of her mouth twitch into a smile, betraying her.

Greg lays his hand on the table. As the discussion around them moves on from accommodation to food supplies, he slides his hand forward.

The tips of his fingers touch hers.

•

Again I am in broken darkness. There is no escape in this small room, nor ever silence. The external windows are covered by blackout blinds, but even this early in the morning, the brightness and muted noise of the corridor still penetrate the room.

Richard Hailey lies fully dressed on the fold-out bed, his eyes closed.

He has tried to sleep, but he is too conscious of the light and the noise from the corridor.

He will be needed again soon, a family has gathered, but he cannot attend until he is called.

So he has to wait.

Yet even with the opportunity to go back to sleep, he cannot.

Soon, he knows, he will fetch himself coffee from the machine down by the nurses' station. They will have news for him. It will be, he tells himself, sick as he is with frustration, the news he expects: no change; can't be long now; wait. Always wait. When they ask him whether he got any sleep, he will say that he did. He will thank them for the question.

One of them will say something about this coming so soon after Jamie Tout.

The room fills with the scent of woodland and wild flowers. Richard Hailey falls into a reverie that is part consciousness and part dream.

I appear in the room, my back to the door. Again I am the bright angel of his deepest belief, silent, radiating light as soft as candle-flame on the lids of his closed eyes. I raise my right hand and give him sleep. He is dreaming me.

"YOU ARE NOT ALONE, RICHARD."

In his dream, he wakes up. He swings his feet round and sits up, resting his elbows on his knees as he rubs sleep from his eyes.

"What time is it?" he asks.

In his dream, he has not yet opened his eyes to see me, nor has he heard me. He feels my presence, but believes that I am a nurse calling him to imminent death.

"Dawn," I say out loud. "You will soon be called."

In his dream, in one movement, he takes his hands from his eyes, stands up, and faces me.

"Oh!"

He stands motionless in the dream. He stares at me.

I look into his eyes and he looks into mine.

KNOW THAT YOU ARE NOT ALONE.

Then the door from the corridor opens. "Father?" He wakes up. He is still lying on the bed. There is a nurse in the doorway. Diana, her name is. She's one of the new ones, from eastern – central – Europe, he should know where.

"Yes?"

"Father, so sorry to wake you, but you are needed now."

She stands in the doorway until he has his feet on the floor and is clearly awake.

"Is the family asking for you. I'll be wait for you."

She leaves the door ajar.

He is alone in the room. He stands up.

He splashes his face with water from the basin and hurriedly brushes his teeth. Now he is ready. He leaves the room.

•

This is something that Maya doesn't do.

She doesn't do it with work colleagues.

She doesn't do it where there's hardly any privacy.

She doesn't do it when there are people who depend on her.

Nor when she is supposed to be getting up and working.

144

She doesn't do it at all.

And especially, she doesn't do it with big, ugly, stubborn men whose hearts are in the right place but who take stupid risks.

Big, ugly, stubborn, brave men.

Who wouldn't get anywhere with her parents.

Although she must have already mentioned him. They know his name and they have asked about him, so maybe ... maybe they might meet him one day.

"Mmm," she says, a long time later, when her breathing has settled, when she is calm again, watching her fingers draw up and curl a strand of the hair on Greg's chest. His heart is beating against her and she inhales his warmth.

He moves his head so that he can purse his lips and touch them very lightly to the crown of her head.

"Did I ever tell you that I nearly became a priest?" he asks.

"No," she says, astonished, raising her head to look at him.

But perhaps that does explain one thing. Maya had been surprised, very much surprised, to find that Greg had not done this before.

Neither had she. But they'd worked it out together.

Not the whole thing, but enough.

Greg smiles down at her and for a second she thinks: here it comes again. More talk about miracles.

But instead, he says, "I lost it. Decided I'd be a mechanic. Went and mended roads while I trained to mend cars."

"I never knew," she says, letting her head down again.

Then she tenses very slightly. "What religion?" she asks, thinking of her parents again. The word 'priest' gives her an answer. But she wants to hear it.

He laughs softly. "Religion is just a man-made thing, Maya."

She files the question away for another time. Perhaps it doesn't matter, certainly not now. But as they lie together in their private

warmth, as they settle together towards sleep, Maya begins to imagine
her father at ease with Greg in the front room of their home, perhaps
beginning to be convinced of the idea that in the matter of his
daughter's happiness, religion is not the central issue.

Maya sleeps.

And as Greg listens to her breathing, feels her warmth against
him, registers the precise fit of her body along the length of his, the
thought comes to him that this is his first opportunity to be alone.
This is the first moment he has had to himself since – whenever; he's
lost track of time. He needs to think. He needs to–

No he doesn't.

In the moments before he sleeps, Greg remembers the priest who
was once his mentor; the priest who once walked with him, listened
to him, discussed with him; the priest who first accepted his decision,
and in doing so, released him from the obligation to follow a vocation
that was no longer his.

Greg imagines telling Father Bernardi about everything that
has happened; imagines sharing with Father Bernardi his steady
conviction that he has found his life at last.

I shall tell him.

I shall share with him–

Greg sleeps.

•

In a kitchen on the derelict edge of the city where Greg once debated
faith and obligation, where Ben Rose now works, on a floor of torn
linoleum that sticks to the soles of his shoes, Father Bernardi, feeling
himself old now, meditates on the life he has lived: the ministry; the
teaching; the service. He remembers moments, faces, friends, and
as he works, his face reflects his memories. He smiles as a memory

comes to him of Greg Doyle, the young man so conflicted over his place in the world, but then, as he raises his eyes to the opaque wired-glass window in front of him, his face shades with regret. Where is Greg Doyle now?

Behind him there is water boiling and volunteers are brewing tea. When he has finished the washing-up he will go to wake the men. But he lingers, conspiring to break his own rule by giving them an extra five, possibly ten, minutes of sleep. In this hostel, at the priest's insistence, there is gentleness in the mornings.

I come to stand beside him and for a moment the rhythm of his work changes. His hands become slower and each mug is placed more carefully onto the drainer. But his mind turns to the men. Without speech, unconscious of my presence, he urges me to them.

I stand in the long dormitory. The space is physical with sleep. There are no curtains and the room is brightening, but nobody wakes. Men snore; one mutters in his sleep. There are dreams here, fragmented, full of regret, fear, despair. I raise my arms and bless this sanctuary.

The priest has his duty to perform. He opens the door of the room and reaches up to the light switches. The air is rank with sweat and long-worn dirt. The men should have washed last night, but he no longer fights them on this. Some have accepted clean clothes; others have refused and remained comfortable in their own familiar things. One has slept on the floor, or perhaps fallen out of bed and remained asleep. All hold their few possessions about them under their thin blankets.

The priest will clean before the cleaners, to remove anything that would not be there if he insisted on the rules of his own house.

"Good morning, gentlemen. It's a bright, sunny morning and there's hot tea and breakfast when you're ready for it. Showers, washing facilities, anything you need. For those of you who haven't been here before, we have a health check available after breakfast, and we're all here to listen if there's anything you'd like to share."

He knows immediately that not one of them has died in the night. This is an instinct he has developed. He also knows that today, none of them will come forward to talk to him. Those who offer the comfort of this house to these men, the priest understands, can be the least trusted by them. Better not to reach out, even in faith; better just to be open.

The priest wears a denim shirt, pinstripe trousers with a belt instead of braces, and trainers, all bought from a charity shop at which he volunteers when he has time and they are short-handed. He will say a prayer at the breaking of bread in the morning, but it will be silent. He will serve the men and then eat with them.

He remains in the background as the men prepare for the morning. Then, later, he sits alone at one of the bench seats, leaning forward over his mug of tea and his plate of sliced white bread and jam. The men sit in quiet groups and alone. Today, the old priest has met nobody's eye, not been beckoned to join a group, and he will not intrude.

I sit with him, unseen, waiting, giving him comfort. There are other presences in the room, but we are silent in our fellowship with the men and their helpers. The sun slants in through the tall high windows and the priest feels a freshness in the air. He thinks briefly of his niece, married to an architect in a large-windowed house among trees at the western end of another city. He thinks of her two tiny children, almost certainly awake by now, playing in their warm pyjamas in their twin cots. They sing to each other, he's heard it, a wordless, tuneless song that keeps them together. Like whale song, he thinks. He has never heard whale song, but he has the idea.

The men are beginning to leave now, and as they stand up from the tables, they take light with them. Some move away in silence,

148

unseen, while others hesitate, wave, speak briefly, clasp hands. Today, none linger. The old priest does not stand so close to the door that he cannot be avoided. He bows his head to each of the men as they leave, mostly singly, and his brief unspoken prayers shimmer in the air. One man grips his hand and others nod their heads to him, or murmur something.

And then the men are gone. The priest does not leave the dining room. He approaches a mess of plastic cutlery and plates at the end of a table. It is illuminated in a shaft of light from one of the high windows. He sits down at the table. From long habit, he shows nothing in his face. But he closes his eyes as he prays for the men in his care.

•

For Naseena, it is the straight lines. Standpipes are spaced at intervals along the pathways between the huts and tents. They run in straight lines. There are washing huts and latrine huts at intervals through the camp. No open ditches, but Naseena can see the lines of disturbed ground where pipes have been laid.

We are safe, she thinks. It is so different here. This camp was drawn on paper and then built from that paper. It was constructed for us and it was ready before we arrived.

Naseena is walking through the camp at Qasir. She is used to her small retinue of children, and she now believes that the way she is greeted, the way people reach out to touch her, even the men, is the same gesture of gratitude that all the relief workers receive. She smiles, bows, places her palms together in greeting, and passes on her journey through the camp. She has time off and nothing urgent with which to fill it.

Her freedom is unfamiliar, but she has learned to quash the sudden anxieties, like the anxieties of a dream, that she should be elsewhere, busy, answering a need. She smiles at a woman who touches her sleeve and recedes into a bow, but she does not stop.

Naseena sees a familiar face.

"Ali!" she calls, and Ali grins and waves. But he does not move. He is waiting his turn at a standpipe, holding a four-litre plastic bottle in each hand.

He will need help carrying those bottles when they are full. Naseena walks towards him. But then she stops. Suddenly, she has a cramp down her right side.

"Ow," she says, and then, "Ow!" again, more urgently. As she buckles forward she is aware that Ali has shouted and is running towards her.

Don't leave the bottles, she wants to say, as his face fills her vision.

And then the world swerves away from her, and she is clinging to the ground with her eyes tight shut.

•

In the men's refuge, Father Bernardi works. These are the hours of cleaning, when the house is made ready for the day and the coming night.

In the refectory the benches have been lifted onto the tables and the detritus of breakfast has been taken through to the kitchens. The floor is being washed. Father Bernardi walks through to the long dormitory. Here, the work has started early and he is therefore late. The beds are already stripped and the blankets have been removed.

"Happy Christmas, Father," says the young man with the wide-ended broom who turns to face the door as the priest enters. "I thought I would save you the trouble today."

It is not Christmas and the priest laughs. He is astonished. "Thank you, Tomas," he says. "What brought this on?"

The young man lowers his eyes. He is suddenly embarrassed. "I want to thank you, Father," he says.

The floor has only been cursorily swept, the priest notices. His attention fixes on the boy in front of him.

"What is the matter, Tomas?" he says, coming forward and taking hold of the broom. Tomas is thin, dark, bearded. He first came to this house as one of the homeless. He has been housed elsewhere now, but he is still one of the regular helpers. He is efficient, effective and willing. This is not how he sweeps a floor.

"Father, I wish to speak with you." Tomas is still not looking up. Father Bernardi leans the broom against a bed. He puts his hand on Tomas's shoulder and, following a sudden instinct, draws the younger man against his chest. He is fleetingly aware, as he does this, that he is a priest and an older man in an environment where physical contact is easily interpreted as abuse, but he dismisses this thought. Whatever problem he has, Tomas needs comfort.

Then Tomas is crying against his shoulder. Father Bernardi holds the boy away from him by his shoulders, stooping slightly to look into the still-averted face. "What is it, my boy? How can I help you?"

Tomas mumbles a sentence containing the word "confession", and the priest understands that a crime has been committed. Part of him relaxes: this is familiar territory, with familiar procedures to be gone through. But another part of him is suddenly afraid: what has Tomas done?

"Come with me," he says gently. "This is not the place."

He takes Tomas by the arm and leads him out of the dormitory. As he does so, the rhythm of prayer in his head firms into words: let nobody be hurt; let this be a small crime.

They do not go to the room Father Bernardi uses as a study when it is not occupied by the secretary. The priest knows Tomas. He is also conscious that he must honour Tomas's request. They go out onto the street and walk together in silence to the priest's church. I walk with them.

The church's doors are not locked; they never are. This is a point of principle with Father Bernardi, and over time, the local community has come to respect him for it. The windows are not broken and the altar remains intact. There is a rank smell of recent occupancy as the two men enter the dark space, but it contains nothing to suggest excrement or urine. All but one of the windows have been boarded over, and the last remaining stained-glass window is protected with steel mesh inside and out. Father Bernardi flicks switches to bring light to his church.

"Come, Tomas, we will pray first."

There is a great presence in this place, and I stand facing the altar as the priest and the young man pray.

Then it is time for Tomas's confession. Father Bernardi conceals himself behind the screen and the young man kneels.

"Father, forgive me, for I have sinned..."

I spread myself through them as the confession begins. I feel the jolt in Father Bernardi's heart as he understands what Tomas has done. I hold him as he understands the full extent of Tomas's deception: the younger man has volunteered at the home not to give thanks for the help he has received, but in an attempt to atone for what he did before leaving his home country.

I hold Tomas as the dam in his heart breaks and the confession pours out of him. I weep with Father Bernardi as the space left by the darkness in Tomas's heart is replaced with fear of the consequences of his confession. Tomas is not listening to Father Bernardi's words; he is not yet able to listen to such words.

Tomas steps away from the confessional before Father Bernardi has finished speaking. His mind is tangling itself into a knot of fear for his present self. His secret is known; he should not have confessed;

how could he have believed the priest would have absolved him and kept silent?

Tomas faces a time of trial. He is not alone as he stands knotted together, his arms wrapped around himself, still with fear. His aura is dark grey, heavy as imminent thunder, but there is light around him, and another angel with wings spread and arms open to hold him.

Father Bernardi steps down from the confessional, hasty, incomplete. There is more he wanted to say; there is more comfort he can give. He has not yet spoken his forgiveness for the part of Tomas's crime that hurts him.

"Tomas," he says. "Tomas, come here."

Tomas stands as stone, his back to the priest, closed up in darkness.

Father Bernardi approaches Tomas and raises his arm to place it across the young man's shoulders, to draw him in and give comfort. Tomas twists under him and Father Bernardi feels the knife pierce his diaphragm, just below his ribcage, and twist upwards as Tomas turns and thrusts forward and up, as he was long ago trained to do, driving Father Bernardi off balance so that he falls backwards onto the stone floor. As he goes down Father Bernardi sees, as if his mind takes a photograph, the candle I have lit for him in the sconce beyond the altar. "Uh!" His breath goes out of him as he hits the floor.

Tomas is kneeling on him now, crying, snivelling words that Father Bernardi can still hear as he falls into darkness. "I'm sorry, Father, I'm sorry."

Then, as Tomas stands and turns for the door, Father Bernardi focuses the last of himself on his attacker, and mouths the words, "I forgive you." He loses consciousness.

Then Tomas is gone. The door slams behind him. He will run at first, and then walk, remembering that he should act naturally. He has the presence of mind to run in the direction away from the home.

He will not return to the woman's flat either, he decides; he has money concealed elsewhere. Tomas has prepared for escape.

In the empty church, Father Bernardi begins to die.

•

Ben is sitting on the train. It's early again and he's got his coffee and the croissant that Hannah wrapped up for him that morning. He's watching the scenery begin to turn from fields and trees and occasional houses to concrete and buildings.

He woke up first today. Hannah was lying on her back next to him, and he had slid his hand across onto her breast and then down the gentle inward curve of her stomach to the discovery that her nightdress had worked its way up to her waist during the night and her legs were open already and she was ready for him.

"Mmmm…" she murmured, her eyes still closed, in response to his hand, and then he had felt her hand and moved himself towards her, so that, lying on their backs, they could turn their faces to each other and touch their mouths together, their lips and tongues.

I am so fucking turned on at the moment, thinks Ben on the train, feeling his body respond to the memory. What the hell is happening to me?

•

Father Bernardi's lung is pierced, as is his heart. His skull is fractured from his fall backwards onto stone. He is beginning to drown in his own blood.

It is his time.

Outside the church, a small dog, held on a lead by an elderly woman, suddenly barks and strains to escape. The lead is secure but there is a fault in the dog's collar. It snaps. The dog, a terrier, races up the steps of the church and throws itself at the doors. They open, as if they had not been properly closed by the last person to leave.

The dog's owner is embarrassed and angry and unwilling to enter the church. She stands on the top step, one hand clutching at the neck of her grey coat, hissing the dog's name through the gap, "Buster! Come here!" until she is interrupted by another elderly woman who comes up behind her.

"You can go inside, darling," says the second woman. "This is the house of God. You can't go in here, where can you go?"

She steps past the dog's owner.

The first thing she sees is the lit candle, burning with a steady flame at the far end of the church. This pleases her: the church should be used; people should light candles, if they have reason to do so. She goes inside, taking the step carefully; her old legs can no longer be trusted like they used to be.

Then she sees the fallen priest and the dog standing over him. There is light shining down from the stained-glass window, and it is given to her to understand immediately that the dog has not harmed the priest. She sees the blood spread on the stone.

"Oh Lord!" she says.

But she is not a woman given to panic. She turns around and pulls open the doors again.

She is lucky. Passing on the pavement outside is a group of young men.

"You boys! Wait now!" She speaks with authority. She has fostered boys like these.

But she doesn't allow them up the steps.

"Get down to the home there. You know it? Tell them to come straight away. The Father is hurt here. And be quick about it. Tell them to come."

She has a mobile phone. Her son gave it to her, for emergencies.

She never uses it, and she knows that the emergencies he had in mind involved her falling over, maybe breaking a leg.

But he has taught her to dial the emergency services, as if she needed to be taught that.

She uses the phone now, for the first time, and as she speaks to the calm voice, so insistent on the details it needs, she is surprised to learn, for the first time, reading the sign outside, the proper name of Father Bernardi's church.

She is surprised also when the phone is taken from her by the owner of the dog, who beckons her urgently inside.

"How good is the charge in this?"

The owner of the dog now kneels beside Father Bernardi, in the pool of blood, holding her own scarf to the wound below the priest's ribs.

"Good. It's good."

It's plugged in every night by my son, she wants to say. He's a good boy.

But the owner of the dog is already talking into the phone, and the woman does not need to be told that this old lady has medical experience.

"My name is Carey," the woman is saying. "Retired; I was a – yes, a stab wound, I think..."

•

Chandler Bishop, the boy from Megan's playgroup, is still asleep. He is a reliable little boy, regular in his sleeping patterns, and Sarah Bishop, his mother, who will become Hannah's friend, can count on having another half-hour to herself before he comes padding in to ask for a drink. The two older boys are with their father this week and the house is quiet.

156

It is dawn.

Sarah sits in an approximate lotus position with her back against the side of the bed and her behind on the big dictionary. She is facing the large bedroom window through which the sun is about to rise over the houses on the far side of the allotments. Her legs are crossed with her heels pulled back as close to the dictionary as she can get them and her hands are resting palm upwards on her knees. From where she sits, the window is full of sky but for the rooftops visible along its lower edge.

Sarah's eyes are closed and her breathing is barely perceptible by the time the sun's brightness crests the horizon and washes over her face. She feels the warmth on her skin but hardly registers the brightened colour through her eyelids. In her meditation the light is flowing down through her body from the place above her head where there is only light. Sarah breathes in energy, and on every out-breath, tensions and anxieties leave her.

Presently, her mind brings her the image of a bright figure, undefined, neither man nor woman, standing before her in an open space. She feels the welcome and walks forward, allowing the space to resolve itself into a green landscape of nature with blue sky above it.

In her mind, Sarah breathes in, although her body's breathing remains regular, and it seems to her that the figure is laughing, holding out its arms, shedding its brightness like a smouldering fire sheds smoke in a sudden breeze, until now she is facing a young man, arms tanned under the rolled-back sleeves of his shirt. He is dressed for hiking, with laced-up boots and a rucksack. He laughs, and as he does so, draws out her own laughter.

"Mummy?"

"Yes, darling?"

Off balance, seeing both the place beyond and her own Chandler, Sarah Bishop steadies herself with her hands, begins to unfold her legs, and then holds out her own arms to welcome her son. He comes to her, fuddled and soft, and settles into her. "Please may I have a drink?" he says. But he puts his thumb back into his mouth and settles against his mother and there is no hurry.

Sarah Bishop holds her son, rocking him slightly, and thinks: that was so clear. She's pleased with herself. Some days, it's all she can do to clear her mind. Her eyes are closed in the brightness and the sun is warm on her face.

A thought drops into her mind. Is it today that I'm visiting Chandler's friend's mum?

Megan? Hannah?

Must check the diary.

Go see her anyway, perhaps.

Just turn up.

After all, Sarah decides, she needn't limit herself to a life of making new friends by appointment.

That thought pleases her too, and she tips her head back against the bed, open to the moment, holding her son and seeing once again the open plains and the wide-open skies of her dream.

•

I ride in the ambulance with Father Bernardi. His condition has been stabilised, temporarily, but the hospital has been alerted and he will be taken immediately into emergency surgery.

BE AT PEACE, I whisper to him, and his mind settles. REST NOW.

Then, in the last mile of the journey to the hospital, his body falters. There is a new urgency in the voices on the radio and a crash team is scrambled to the A&E entrance.

I watch this with Father Bernardi and then he and I stand together in a white space. There is no time here, and we do not use words. I hold his hand, and we stand looking towards the light.

What of Tomas?

TOMAS IS LOVED.

What of the refuge?

THE REFUGE GOES ON.

What of me?

YOUR WORK IS DONE.

There is so much more that I could do.

IT IS YOUR TIME.

But he turns away from me. He knows that this is his time, but he does not want to go.

REST NOW.

In a bright room in which hours have passed, Father Bernardi opens his eyes. He gazes up at a ceiling that is made of square white panels, and presently he understands that the light source here is just a strip-light behind a frosted glass panel. There is a scent of flowers, and beneath that, a scent of ... cleaning?

He cannot move and he does not want to move. His body aches. His mouth is pulled out of shape and he can feel the discomfort of the tube in his throat.

Hearing returns and he becomes conscious of the machines around him. There is a nurse leaning into his field of vision and calling something and then she is gone.

He becomes aware that there is a brightness over him other than the brightness of the ceiling. He becomes aware that I am in the air above him. His eyes look into mine.

He sees the task I offer him.

There is so much more that I could do.

IT IS YOUR TIME.

Father Bernardi cannot smile. But his eyes show kindness.

I shall do that for him. And perhaps the good sister...
SHE WILL BE WELL.
Father Bernardi's eyes close. He sleeps.

•

Hannah Rose sits on the floor rug beside her daughter's bed, holding Megan's hand. Hannah has just cancelled playgroup – again – and I see that she is beginning to be frightened.

Megan is peaceful now, but she has been crying. Her cheeks are flushed and there is a dummy in her mouth that Hannah had not expected to need again. Megan's eyes look inward and she seems intent on the dummy, drawing on it in a fierce way that gives her mother a pang of recent memory.

Megan slept late, even slept through Ben's getting up and leaving, which Hannah had at first thought to be a good thing. But then Megan had woken up with a nagging headache, immediately crying, and now she has a temperature as well. The headache has not gone away, although it seems to have abated, and at one point she complained of aches in her arms. Hannah is thinking: not meningitis. Dear God, not meningitis.

She has called the doctor for a home visit and will call again if he doesn't come soon. Hannah is afraid and tired and beneath all that, in a deep place in her mind, there is another dread that goes beyond reason: could she possibly have caused this by her carelessness on Saturday?

I appear behind Hannah and make the sign of peace. In this room, in Megan's eyes, I am a white-robed angel and my great wings brush the floor.

Megan is not surprised. To her, it is natural that I should come. Pleasure shows in her face. To her mother, it is as if her daughter suddenly comes alive. Megan lifts herself up off the pillow onto her elbow and takes the dummy from her mouth.

"Chandler's here, Mummy. Hello, Chandler."

"Hello, Megan."

Her mother glances around. She cannot see me nor hear me. Shit, she's delirious, she thinks. So I spread my hands over her head and she is calmed. It's the imaginary friend again, she thinks. The dream-boy. Not the boy from the playgroup. The Chandler boy. Person. Whatever.

Hannah looks around again, but still sees nothing. She is exhausted.

I touch a blessing to her forehead, and as I do so, I feel the first, faintest pull of my own future.

Hannah and Megan both hear the doorbell ring.

"That'll be Dr Murison. Will you be all right while I let him in?"

Megan frowns. "Chandler's here, Mummy."

So Hannah Rose says to the room, "Oh, of course, yes, look after her, please, Chandler," before she leaves.

I kneel down by the bed. I am not bound by the dimensions of the room, and now the wings that Megan has given me extend down through the floor.

"Hello, Chandler."

"Hello, Megan." I put my hand on her forehead and the light connects us. Fleetingly, Megan sees the open plains and the winged horses.

"Will you tell me another story?" she says.

"Later."

"Your stories are special." I see in her mind the idea that she might bring me to her playgroup, to tell stories to all her friends.

She is peaceful now.

"You will sleep tonight," I tell her. "You will dream of the horses.

You know that the horses will come again when you call for them."

Megan puts the dummy back in her mouth and settles more cosily into the bed.

Hannah Rose and Dr Murison have been talking downstairs; there is a hush as they come within hearing-distance of the room. Hannah takes the last stairs two at a time, suddenly in a hurry, and Dr Murison follows a moment after. She stands back, and I do the same, to give him access to the bed.

"Here's the doctor!" she says, and thinks: I should have taken the dummy out before I went down.

"Hello Megan, I hear you're not very well again."

Tom Murison is a young man, the junior doctor in the practice, and he is sometimes teased by his wife that all the local women are in love with him. He crouches down by the bed, in the place vacated by Hannah, and begins his examination.

He has already diagnosed the extent of Hannah's anxiety, which has reminded him of an older doctor's saying that patients often know what's up, but don't know how to express it in medical jargon. As he looks at Megan he is alert and ready to be worried.

"Let's just take this out, shall we?" he says, removing the dummy and passing it back to Hannah Rose.

To Megan, Dr Murison is dry, cool hands and a nice voice.

In the time to come, she will cling to him and he will come to love her.

In the world as it is, he will remember her as his first defeat.

"Okay..." He checks her throat; slight inflammation. The patient is flushed, apparently listless according to the mother but alert enough now. Temperature, headache.

What weight to give to the mother's anxiety?

"Any tummy trouble?" he asks. He is holding Megan's hand. It's cool in his. The bedclothes are slightly damp, he notices; the patient

162

has recently overheated. But the air in the room is fresh.

"Not really. No. No, she's been eating well and ... fine. Nothing."

Hannah shrugs in desperation. She wants to say something that will make the doctor take this seriously.

I wink at Megan and she winks back at me. The doctor does not notice this but Hannah Rose does. She watches Megan lifting her pyjama jacket out of the way for Dr Murison to listen to her chest.

"Tell the doctor about your imaginary friend," she says, and immediately corrects herself. "Tell the doctor about Chandler."

Once, in his career so far, Dr Murison has been asked to provide reassurance about an imaginary friend. He knows what to expect: a girl, or a boy, or perhaps an animal, who is a good, albeit unseen, friend to a lonely child. Even digital television and computer games haven't put invisible friends out of business. "Yes, tell me about Chandler," he says, restoring his stethoscope to the inner pocket of his jacket.

"He's standing over there," Megan says. "He's smiling at me."

They both look in my direction.

"Hello, Chandler," says Dr Murison.

"Hello," I reply. But he does not see or hear me.

Megan has seen Dr Murison look at my waist. "Mummy can't see him," she says. "You can't see him."

"No, I can't," says Dr Murison. "But that doesn't mean he's not there."

"He's an angel," says Megan. "He takes me riding and he gives me dreams."

"Wow," says Dr Murison. "What does he look like?"

He is watching Megan and he sees that her eyes focus on me and track up and down. I smile at her and she smiles in return. He sees this too. It puzzles him.

"He's big and all white," says Megan. "And he's blue. He's got nice wings. He's got a rope instead of a belt and a knot instead of a buckle."

She frowns. "He's wearing a kind of dress thing. It's white and he hasn't got any shoes."

Both Dr Murison and Hannah Rose are taken by surprise by this. "Wow," says Dr Murison again. "What a lucky girl you are."

"Sometimes he's a daddy," says Megan, solving for herself the puzzle of my different appearance on the beach.

But as she speaks, Dr Murison goes back to his examination. "You lie down now, Megan. Have a rest." He draws the duvet up over her chest. "I expect Chandler will look after you," he concludes, surprising himself.

"Back in a moment, darling," Hannah Rose says from the door, and then she follows the doctor downstairs. As she crosses the landing, she hears Megan murmur, "Will you tell me a story now, Chandler?"

The doctor is waiting for her downstairs. "Well," he says, just fractionally drawing out the moment. "I don't think there's anything too serious wrong with her. If you pressed me, I'd say that she's probably brought something home from her playgroup. It's an age at which a child meets a lot of new infections."

As he is speaking, he is noticing that Hannah Rose is not reassured. This clinches it for him.

"But," he says, "and it's only a very small but, I'd like to make absolutely sure. I'd like to suggest a few tests, nothing serious, but I think you'll agree that it's much better to be sure with something like this." Now, as he speaks, he is aware of how powerfully relieved Hannah Rose is that he has not dismissed Megan's condition.

Parental anxiety is also a condition that deserves treatment.

He likes himself for this insight.

Maybe I really should do some tests.

So he gives her the standard explanation about making an appointment at the hospital, then explains what will happen at the appointment, how to prepare Megan, what to tell her, blah, blah, realising as he speaks that he's committed himself to ordering up "a few tests".

His big mouth. But better, now that he's said it, to answer those worries fully.

Although the possibility that Megan is seriously ill is remote.

She'll ring the surgery to ask about it tomorrow. Be a nuisance until she gets her tests.

At the door, Hannah Rose suddenly says, "What about Chandler? What about this ... hallucination?" She hates the word.

She hears the hesitation before he laughs. "Mrs Rose, you have a very, very imaginative daughter. I wouldn't worry about it at all. She's probably seen a picture somewhere, or you've been to church, and, well, it's just a very nice thought for her. I wouldn't worry."

Their eyes meet.

"We're not religious," Hannah says.

He shrugs, dropping his eyes: she must have picked it up somewhere.

"So just play along with it?"

He shrugs again, smiling as he regains her eyes. "If it makes her happy – and it seems to – why not?"

"I thought there might be something wrong in her mind."

Now he laughs. "Quite the opposite, believe me. You have to be pretty special to dream up something that detailed."

Hannah Rose closes the door. She stands for a second in the hall, as if listening. There is no sound to be heard. Then, swiftly, she crosses to the stairs.

Megan has fallen asleep. Her colour has improved and there is a smile on her face. In her dream, the horses have gathered to greet her at the white-painted fence, saddled and ready to ride. We run towards them, holding hands, both barefoot in the long grass. There are foals among them now, still unsteady on their feet. They are revealed as the horses shift apart. Megan cries out in delight as she sees them.

In the bedroom, Hannah Rose hears her daughter's happy cry. She stands for a long moment, a very long moment, watching Megan's face.

Then she says softly, "If you really exist, take care of her."

She closes the door.

•

"I could do more."

"You have enough to do, Chandrael."

In the world that is, Megan's illness will now become apparent to those around her, and they will suffer with her, and she will die.

"Megan could live a full, long life."

"Megan could live the life she has chosen."

We walk for a while in the clean air of the morning. Megan's dream fades around us. She will sleep more deeply now.

"It's begun, Chandrael. You feel it already."

"Hannah asked me–"

"–to care for her. And you will." She looks up at me. "But look to the future, Chandrael."

"This won't be easy."

"And yet it's your decision." Her hand takes mine. "If I can mend a radio..."

I return to the world.

•

Richard Hailey stands out on the narrow first-floor balcony of the hospital. He has requested a ten-minute cigarette break, although he does not smoke, as a way of making sure that all the nurses know where he is. They don't question 'fag break', and he doesn't think he could explain the real reason why he needs this time alone.

Richard Hailey is a trained counsellor as well as a priest, and knows he could do so much more than he does.

He runs a finger under the tight collar around his neck. In their eyes, he's just there to be an independent source of last-minute meaningless comfort to the children and their parents.

Comfort? Jamie Tout had been a brave little boy, so full of strength for his parents. Richard Hailey is suddenly full of indignation, seeing the small, bright child as he was so recently, intent on a plastic warrior figure, looking up to see the priest approaching, engaging instantly in his eagerness to explain the figure's powers.

Then the little face white on the sheet, sunken, empty of life; the parents.

"Father Hailey?"

He is startled. A nurse he doesn't recognise has cranked open the door onto the balcony. He hasn't heard the creak of the hinges. She either hasn't noticed, or chooses to ignore, his startled reaction.

"They told me you were out here." She tips her head in the direction of the children's ward. "A patient of mine is asking for you. He's very anxious to speak to you. I don't know if..." When he still doesn't speak, she adds, "I did ask."

He understands this to mean that she has already asked the children's-ward nurses whether they can spare him, and they've said yes without even thinking to check with him. A despairing irritability mixes with surprise that somebody in one of the adult wards should be asking for a priest.

But he is, after all, available on demand. That's the point.

"Somebody needs a priest?" he says. "Tell me."

But she is shaking her head. "Not that. You. He's asking for you by name. A friend of yours, apparently." She has to consult a note in her hand. "Robert Bernardi?" She looks at the note again. "Father Robert Bernardi? He's another..."

He registers her reluctance to say the word priest. But this is dwarfed by his surprise and a sudden, absolute happiness.

"Father Bernardi is here? Father Bernardi?"

"That's right, asking for you."

They haven't seen each other for...

"Where is he?"

He is expecting her to say: he's waiting with all the other visitors. But she says, "He's in the intensive care ward."

"What's he doing there?"

His mind is ahead of his voice. Even before the question is out, he has remembered that she said, "a patient of mine".

Father Bernardi is a patient, not a visitor.

She is answering the question she had expected him to ask. "He's stable. He's about to be moved. He was assaulted, but he's off the ventilator." She shrugs. "He's asking for you. Won't take no for an answer."

There is something in her voice as she says this, a faint affection, that confirms to Richard Hailey that his old mentor really is present in the intensive care ward. And asking for him.

For a second, Richard Hailey wonders how Father Bernardi knew he was here. But his work at the hospital is hardly a secret.

"Tell me what happened. How is he? How long has he been here?" They are walking now. Richard Hailey has been this way before, but never with this excitement, never with this nervous expectation.

He is unprepared for the white room, the lone bed, the murmur of machines, so like and yet so unlike the ward from which he has come.

Father Bernardi has shrunk, and for a second, Richard Hailey thinks he is dead. There are tubes emerging from beneath the thin blanket that outlines the body. But then the eyes open, and they are Father Bernardi's eyes, and all of a sudden, nothing has changed.

Richard Hailey reaches back and there is a chair under his hand that he draws up to the bed, conscious of nothing but his old mentor's eyes.

"I'm glad you came." The voice gathers strength as Father Bernardi speaks.

"What happened?"

Father Bernardi ignores the question. He says, "Tell me about your work."

Under the forgiving gaze of his old mentor, Richard Hailey begins to talk about the children's ward, about what he must do there, begins to talk about his own frustration, and then at last, as time slows and the room stills around him, he voices his greatest secret: his loss of faith, and of faith in himself.

He stops, feeling himself to be out of breath, and realises that he is afraid of Father Bernardi's reaction, as though he has given voice to a weakness beyond forgiving.

But Father Bernardi just says, "Tell me about the children."

Richard Hailey gathers his words and again begins to speak. Presently, he is telling Father Bernardi about all the lost children, their names, their special ways, their endings. At some point in the long confession, he begins to cry, and at some point, Father Bernardi's hand finds his. Richard Hailey speaks for a long time, and at the end, he simply stops, his face saturated, and says, "I'm sorry."

He has spoken fluently, and Father Bernardi has watched his face light up with love of the remembered children.

Father Bernardi trusts his instinct to wait.

"It's hard," says Richard Hailey eventually.

"Did you expect it to be easy?" asks Father Bernardi quietly, after another silence.

"It's not that." Richard Hailey is shaking his head. "It's just–" He is looking for the words. "I don't get any help, and I suppose I worry that I'm helping them as much as somebody else would if I–" he shrugs "–got out of the way."

Father Bernardi says the words that Richard Hailey will remember later. "If they need you, they will lean on you. Be there for that reason." He speaks softly. "Even your presence is comforting. I feel it myself."

But at this moment, Richard Hailey is still preoccupied with the tangle in his mind. "They need me now, and by being a priest, I can be with them when they most need me, when they're dying." He speaks as if he is explaining this to himself for the first time. "It's just that I need some kind of reassurance. Faith, I suppose, but something beyond that, some kind of sign." He shrugs again. "I'm committed to this work, Father, for the children and the families. I just need to–" He stops.

"Reassurance," says Father Bernardi softly, and chuckles at the question that drops into his head: would this boy recognise a sign if it came up and stood in front of him?

Richard Hailey mistakes the chuckle for a sound of pain. He has tired the old man out, although – he glances at his watch and is surprised – he has only been in here twenty minutes.

He begins to leave, but as he is promising to visit again, Father Bernardi interrupts him.

"Richard."

"Yes, Father."

"Will you get me a telephone?"

"A telephone? Of course. But–"

Richard Hailey has his switched-off mobile in his pocket. Would the hospital allow a phonecall from–

"I don't want to call anybody. But I would like to have a telephone in my room. Humour me."

The nurse is somewhere between amused and exasperated when Richard asks her for a telephone.

"He's been asking about that a lot. It's obviously bothering him."

Richard Hailey has remembered the big old Bakelite monstrosity in Father Bernardi's office. Replaced only on condition the replacement was black and had a rotary dial.

"I don't think he wants to make any calls."

"No. And he wouldn't get a line anyway." She considers. "There is an old spare handset that I could put on the table by the bed, if you think that might stop him worrying. It's a bit of a cheat, because he won't get a line, but..."

"He's an old man and he's got it into his mind that he wants a telephone. He's spent his life being available for anybody who calls."

The phone is big and rectangular, made of dull yellow plastic, with numbers on the front big enough for the partially sighted to see. The cord between the base and the handset is like a tangled spring. The thing is a museum piece.

"That'll do."

Father Bernardi is asleep when the old phone is placed on the unit by his bed.

"You've worn him out," the nurse says softly. "No visitors for a couple more days yet, I think."

"Am I his first visitor?"

She flashes him a sudden grin. "Oh, you don't count. You're staff. You're one of us, Father."

And then he is out in the corridor and she is gone back into the ward.

•

Doctor Murison is comfortable in his car. He has surgery, then paperwork, then another follow-up home visit later. The day is all mapped out.

I sit beside him, unseen, in the passenger seat of his second-hand, rusting people-carrier. He likes everything that this car tells him about his life. His children have made a den of blankets and cushions across the back seats. His wife has stored tissues, wrappers, lists, small toys and other essentials, including a mysteriously emptying bag of soft toffees, in the glove compartment. But the windscreen is clear, his briefcase fits neatly between the two front seats and his younger son has crayoned a portrait of him on the dashboard.

An imaginary friend who looks like an angel. There would be some interesting research to do on imaginary friends.

Maybe he should go online.

Although it's all common sense, really. A way of coping with anxiety that can't be expressed directly.

Which implies that Megan Rose is anxious, so maybe there's some tension at home?

Although the Roses don't present that way at the surgery.

Would I know?

And if I thought I did, would I be right?

Megan Rose goes to playgroup. She's coming up to school age, which is an anxious time for a small child.

Tom Murison slots the gearstick back into third and relaxes.

All white and blue, with nice wings. Wearing a kind of dress thing, but definitely a 'he'. Maybe it was a monk's habit, with the rope and the knot instead of a buckle.

That is one imaginative child.

Tom's attention is taken by the right turn onto the bypass. He makes the turn and tucks into the slow lane for the long, straight road home to the surgery.

His wife often tells him to speed up. Doctor, father, safe driver.

A flight of geese in V-formation, apparently navigating by the road, flies above and ahead of him for two miles before banking off to the left, into the afternoon sun. I wonder if angels fly in V-formation, he thinks, and smiles. Aren't angels always female, like ships?

Sheila and I could never go back to living in the city.

Into Tom's mind comes a picture of the region's main hospital. There's no logic to the association, except that living in a village and remembering the city equates to working in a small practice and remembering the hospital.

Tests. Yes, tests. Collect samples at the surgery, send them off to the lab, get the results. He smiles at the thought of the phonecall in which he tells Hannah Rose: all clear.

Then he frowns: the word she used was 'hallucination.'

Tom Murison parks in his reserved slot, reversing as usual to have an easy exit at the end of the day; handbrake, key, leave it in gear.

He is reasonably clear in his mind that little Megan is not hallucinating in any negative sense. Her imaginary friend puzzles him in some ways, but all of a sudden that is the secondary problem. The issue for him now is Hannah Rose.

Tom Murison remembers his strong sense of Mrs Rose's anxiety. There's the mental-health issue.

Get those tests done as soon as possible. Make that call: all clear. Release her from the anxiety.

He walks into the surgery, where immediately he engages with his life. There is a list of appointments and patients are already waiting. He goes into his consulting room and unpacks his bag. Take a blood sample here, urine, or do the full works at the hospital?

The hospital, he thinks. Just for once, the hospital.

He reaches forward to pick up the tiny dictating machine.

Then he puts it back down again and picks up the phone.

Without really thinking about it, he has reached a decision: Megan gets the full works, and he will make the arrangements himself.

•

Five minutes after Ben's arrival in the office that morning, a three-word email.

"Got a minute?"

So they are in Anthony's office.

Ben looks at Anthony again and his vision shifts, like one of those trick pictures, so that he's seeing a middle-aged man, balding, collar rucked up from hunching forward over his desk, fitted shirt tight enough to be already concertinaed where it creases. Anthony's eyes would be a composition of fine lines around dabs of colour.

Ben glances at the picture frame on the desk. She gets this man coming back into her life every evening, he thinks, looking at the woman's tiny smiling face in the left-hand oval. And so does the boy in the right-hand oval. He's in black and white. And come to think of it, surprisingly young. A grandchild, perhaps?

Anthony is still talking and Ben, who is pretty much on autopilot now, is leaning forward and nodding. But this isn't Anthony's usual talk. "It hasn't been announced yet, so keep it to yourself." Anthony is telling him about a major new marketing push, a strategic repositioning, rebranding, and Ben is suddenly scrabbling back in his mind for the stuff that he's already missed because he wasn't listening. The internet. Online marketing. Social media. Integrated virtual commerce.

Then suddenly they're talking about Ben.

"You don't want to end up doing what you're doing now, right?"

Ben, taken by surprise, nods in a way that could be construed as a love-my-job shake of the head.

"Maybe you took the job because thought you could shunt across to one of the creative desks?"

Ben nods ambiguously.

"I have a proposition for you. Not a company job, not yet anyway, but something you might want to do. Might give you a way out of that—" Anthony waves his hand "—crap on your desk."

"I've got the revised business-development target figures for—" Ben begins, but Anthony interrupts him.

"Sure. Don't spend time on it. Look."

He leans forward over the desk and Ben does the same.

"What if – we'll have to sort out the technology, but I think it's there – what if you weren't just interacting with a website or whatever, but interacting with real people, online? You're in your own office, but you're wearing some kind of headset, you know the things, VR, whatever, which means you're also in our studio, talking to one of our designers, who's maybe wearing a headset too. In his own office, I mean, his own studio." Anthony looks at Ben as though suddenly noticing something in his face. "This is my idea, right?"

"Of course, yes, definitely, yes," says Ben, nodding fervently.

"Okay ... well, in that case, why don't you go get your diary?"

Fear drenches Ben's insides. "My diary?"

"Yeah. You know. The one with the girl in it."

When Ben gets back, Anthony is leaning forward on his elbows on the inset fake-leather rectangle in the surface of his desk. It's this rectangle that signals Anthony's status in the company.

"May I see?"

There is no way Ben can say no. He bends the diary back on itself, almost breaking the spine, so that only the one drawing will lie open before Anthony. He slides the diary, open flat, across the desk.

"Thanks," says Anthony, pulling it towards him so that Ben can no longer reach to keep his fingers splayed to hold down the open pages.

Don't turn over, Ben thinks.

Don't turn over.

Oh fuck.

Anthony has looked at the woman and now he has raised the edge of a page and looked up to say: do you mind?

Ben nods.

Anthony turns the page and gazes at the week beginning three weeks ago. The moment stretches out into an endless piece of time. The caricature is not meant to be flattering.

Then Anthony drops a page and gazes at the week beginning two weeks ago. Then very quickly he flicks through the whole of the diary. Then he closes it and looks at Ben.

"I thought so," he says. "You can catch a likeness."

"...yes," says Ben.

"There's more to life than targets and spreadsheets and all that crap, don't you think?" Anthony says.

"...yyyyyy," says Ben, but not so clearly that he couldn't switch to "... nnnnn" in a microsecond.

"How fast can you work?" Anthony asks.

Ben knows an easy question when he hears one. He says, "Very fast."

"Rough sketches by," Anthony checks his watch. "Say, Thursday?"

Ben nods.

"Okay..." Anthony leans back. "The 3-D virtual-office experience. Virtual reality. Headsets. Whatever. The tech isn't the point. Draw what the client will see when we figure that out. Design studio first, make sure the creative guys are recognisable. With the women, none of the..." He moves his hands in front of his chest. "Hard-working people, all recognisable, all flattering, right? And if you can get a couple of the directors ... key thing is, this will be what the client sees when he puts on our headset, right?"

Ben understands, finally, what he is being asked to do. He feels a spark of excitement.

"I could talk to the guys in the studio..." he says, thinking aloud.

"Oh. No. No. Absolutely not. No. Don't mention it to anybody. This is our project. No." Anthony stops for breath. "Buy what you need. Bring me the receipts. I'll sign them and get them paid straight away. Just..." He runs out of words. "This is between us, okay?"

Ben says, "I'll get right on it." And shuts up.

"And get yourself another diary."

Alone again in his office, Anthony congratulates himself on how skilfully he handled Ben. This could work, he thinks. And: I like that boy. He deserves a chance.

With a sigh, he reaches out to the picture frame. He doesn't look at it, but his fingers lightly touch the glass.

•

I stand in front of a house that is now a convent. The house and its grounds are still enclosed by walls, but now the parkland and fields outside have been replaced by a shopping centre, a ring road, an estate of small houses with its own shopping centre, and within walking distance, the hospital.

There is a woman here. I watch her as she dead-heads roses. She is quick with her secateurs, and neat, catching the dropping heads with a practised movement in a wicker basket that she holds over her arm. But she finds no pleasure in the work. It should have been done properly by the appointed gardeners this morning, not piecemeal like this.

The woman wears her black habit as always, with waterproof boots and threadbare cotton gloves. It is cold today, but she does not wear her coat. She would be angry to know that one of the younger sisters, Sister Marie-Claude, has been detailed to watch her from an upstairs window. Her lips are pursed into a thin line as she snips irritably at the beautiful roses.

Sister Percy still thinks of herself as the head of her order. She has a reputation in the wider world that is founded on the contribution she made, as a younger nun, to the setting up of the convent's charitable trust and training school. The charity still funds much of the nearby hospital's research work into childhood illness, research work that has given it a national reputation, and the school still trains, provides, and where appropriate accommodates, volunteers to support the hospital's medical and research staff.

Some of the volunteers feel a vocation to join the order.

Most, these days, don't.

Sister Percy becomes aware that she is not alone. She looks up to see that there is a tall young man standing close to her. She is startled, and then irritated. Somebody must have left a gate open. Sloppy. Anybody could have got in – and now somebody has. There is a frown on her face as she looks up at me, but she can feel – she does not wonder how – that I am not dangerous.

"Hello, young man," she says.

"Hello," I reply.

"How did you get in?"

I look around. I shrug. "It's beautiful here."

"You know that this is a private place? It is a convent. Not for young men."

She speaks slowly. She has decided that I am mentally deficient in some way.

"Of course. I was admiring your roses."

"Are you a gardener?"

"A messenger, really," I say. "I love the beauty of it all."

She is a practical-minded woman and I am a mentally deficient young man who has found his way into the grounds of her convent. The priority is to get me out of here and then she will have a very firm word with somebody – everybody – about security.

"Hmm. Well. You can help me to keep these beautiful if you like."

The thought crosses her mind that she should offer me something – a drink, or a bite to eat. But she rejects it. This is a convent, after all. If this young man needs entertaining, he can look elsewhere.

"Perhaps we could walk now," I say.

The cheek of it.

"As you wish," she says, although the tone of her voice tells me clearly that it is not my place to lead.

We walk through the garden. Sister Percy begins to tell me the names of the roses, pointing out her favourites and describing her approach to their nurture.

"What's that?" I ask, pointing.

We have come to an ornate stone urn that stands five feet tall on its plinth in the middle of a formal garden. Sister Percy looks up and sees that a climbing rose, a mass of yellow blooms, has established itself in the earth inside the urn. It is beginning to spill over the rim.

"That's extraordinary."

She has not seen it before. Who could have planted it without her knowledge?

How long has it been there?

"Perhaps it's a miracle," I say.

She purses her lips. This suggestion is an impertinence at the very least, and possibly even a blasphemy. Sister Percy is on the brink of saying something. But the unexpected rose, the extraordinary rose, takes her attention. She stares at it, seeing its colour, its intricacy, the impossible profligacy of its growth. It must have been there for months, to have grown so much. How could she have failed to see it?

"Just open your heart to what comes," I tell her.

Sister Marie-Claude has come outside. She has followed at a distance. It is only now, as Sister Percy turns to chide me for this latest impertinence, that she notices her. Sister Percy understands in an instant that she has been watched since leaving the convent. Immediately she is angry; then, she curbs her anger. They watch me out of love, she reminds herself. It would be prideful to reject their concern. Her lips tighten. But it's got to stop.

She turns again and finds that I am already gone. This surprises her, but she is also relieved. Sister Marie-Claude is young.

She knows, but doesn't think to wonder how she knows, that I am gone and not still within the grounds.

As she takes the younger woman's arm, Sister Percy discovers that she is exhausted. "Bless you, dear," she says. "Perhaps we might sit down. That was an extraordinary young man."

Sister Marie-Claude frowns.

There is a round plastic table in a corner of the formal garden. Four matching chairs have been tipped forward against it to keep their seats dry. Not beautiful, but cheap and practical. Sister Marie-Claude helps Sister Percy to a chair and Sister Percy bites back the rebuke that she can sit down for herself, thank you. She closes her eyes, feeling the tensions ease in her body. She exhales.

Sister Marie-Claude has moved a chair to sit down next to her. There is concern in her eyes: how are they going to get back up to the house? Sister Marie-Claude's eyes dart back to the windows: will anybody see them and come to help?

"Thank you dear," says Sister Percy. She smiles, forgiving her companion for her attempts to help. The girl is young, after all. "I've just had the most extraordinary conversation with that young man. I've no idea what he was doing there, but he certainly knows his roses."

Sister Marie-Claude smiles in reply. But she is clearly nervous, sitting forward with her hands on her knees, and Sister Percy settles in her chair, relaxing to put the girl at her ease.

"He was standing there in the rose garden. Just standing there admiring the roses." Sister Percy laughs at the effrontery of it. "We spoke for a while. I showed him some of the roses, and then would you believe it, he started talking about miracles." Sister Percy shakes her head, smiling.

"What young man are you talking about?" says Sister Marie-Claude.

Straight out, just like that. No salutation, no respect.

But Sister Percy is too surprised to pick her up on it.

"The young man walking with me. You followed me. You saw him, of course."

She stares at Sister Marie-Claude. Is the girl an idiot?

But Sister Marie-Claude is frowning. "I didn't see a young man," she says. "You walked off on your own. That's why I came out after you."

Sister Percy is suddenly angry. "Do you expect me to believe..." she begins.

And then she is not angry. "Oh," she says. "Oh dear."

She's flipped, thinks Sister Marie-Claude.

"Reverend Mother, do you want me to get somebody?" she says, wishing above all that she was somewhere else.

But Sister Percy doesn't reply. "Oh dear," she is saying to herself. "Oh dear."

"I'll get help," says Sister Marie-Claude, and legs it back to the house before the crazy old bat can stop her.

•

These are only rough drawings, but Ben's pleased with them. There's one showing Anthony working on a design, ha ha, with the whole of the real design team looking out at the viewer from the other side of the table. Another is an overhead view of a meeting room, with – Ben is really pleased with this – a drawn-in cursor hovering over the seat at the head of the table.

They're in Anthony's office, and the sketches are spread out on the desk.

"They were talking about another agency doing the rebrand," Anthony is saying. He laughs. Ben does too. "But we're an agency, right? We've got the palm trees in the entrance and the fountain. We hire billboards and we sponsor TV shows nobody watches and those are our ads that get in the way when you're trying to watch stuff online."

Glancing aside, Ben sees the girl through the glass wall of the office. She's approaching from the door to the lifts on the far side of the room, walking past his desk, towards Anthony's office, with a bounce in her step like an ad for a new hair-colour range.

She sees him suddenly through the glass, across the open-plan distance, and it's as if the shock goes through her like a jolt of electricity. She tenses, losing her rhythm, and glances from Anthony's profile to him and back again. It's an over-reaction, but what strikes Ben is how quickly she gets over it.

She doesn't stop walking but swerves as though she wasn't heading for – him? Anthony? His desk? – after all, and goes on her way.

Wow, says Ben, thinking about what it must mean for her to react that way to seeing him unexpectedly.

He shifts in his chair, and with an effort, returns his attention to Anthony.

•

Sarah Bishop taps softly on her new friend Hannah Rose's front door.

She waits, but she hears nothing and can see no movement through the frosted-glass panel.

Nobody home. She checks the day, date, time on her phone. It was today. Half ten. Arranged a while ago, but – yes, today. She is five minutes late.

She steps back from the front door and stands on the path looking up at the house. The bedroom curtains are drawn shut.

What should I do now?

One more try.

She steps up to the door, and as she raises her hand, a blurred face appears in the glass. Hannah Rose opens the door.

"Oh."

"Hannah, are you all right?"

Hannah Rose is wearing no make-up and her hair is not brushed. She has obviously just woken up. But she is fully dressed. Instinctively Sarah steps forward and takes her by the arm, and as she does so, Hannah lets go of the door and steps back. Now they are both in the hallway.

"Hannah, what's the matter? Are you all right?"

Sarah is already moving Hannah towards what is obviously the kitchen.

"I'm fine, sorry, yes, I'm fine." Hannah is now sitting at the kitchen table, rubbing at her eyes. "I heard you knock. I must look terrible."

She stands up again. She is wearing jeans and the tee-shirt that she has so obviously just slept in. "Could you, do you think, kettle over there. I'll be–"

"But I should–"

"Oh, no, no. Stay, please."

"But I'm disturbing–"

It becomes clear to both of them that Hannah does want Sarah to stay.

"Just." says Hannah, waving her hand to indicate the kitchen and everything in it, and then she is gone.

When she gets back, changed into a denim skirt and a white blouse, sandals on her feet, face fixed and all fresh, she finds Sarah Bishop sitting at the kitchen table with two mugs of camomile tea. "All better now?" Sarah says, and they both laugh: like speaking to a child.

"I'm so sorry." Hannah opens a window. "We had the doctor here first thing this morning and everything else went out of my mind. Megan's asleep in my bed. I was up there with her." She laughs at herself. "Fell asleep."

"Nothing serious, I hope?"

An infinitesimal spasm crosses Hannah's face and then is gone.

"You know children," she says. "Sick one minute and fine the next." She smiles brightly. "Now. You've got – tea. What else do we need?"

Sarah Bishop is an observant woman.

"There's probably a bug going around," she says, looking down at the table.

It is not a question, but for a moment, between them, there is the gap where Hannah's reply should have been.

Then Hannah busies herself with a plate and the contents of a packet of the less childish biscuits – adding at the last moment a couple of the ones with jam in the middle. And a few broken-off squares of her personal bar of chocolate.

"I love this."

Hannah turns to find that Sarah has left the table and gone over to look at the art display on the door of the fridge. She is admiring one of Megan's old pictures, the one of the trees with their fat ochre trunks and round green balls of leaves.

"Oh, isn't that lovely?"

"She's quite an artist."

Hannah laughs. "So is Ben, actually."

Although there are no drawings by Ben on the fridge any more.

Hannah looks at her guest directly for the first time.

Sarah Bishop is a thin woman, naturally thin, tall with it, who wears a fitted white blouse over a heathery tartan skirt that Hannah recognises from a catalogue.

This is not what Sarah wears.

Hannah intuits that Sarah has dressed for the visit, and that these clothes indicate Sarah's assessment of Hannah.

Except for the luminous blue stones of the necklace and earrings.

"There's a programme on the television–" Sarah begins, turning away from the fridge.

"The art one? With that man?"

"Exactly. I've got a drawer ready to collect art materials."

"Meaning just about anything plus PVA glue to stick it all together."

They sit down at the table.

"Megan has an invisible friend," says Hannah abruptly.

"Invisible?"

"Imaginary. You know, an imaginary friend. She calls him Chandler, actually."

"Really? How fascinating. Is he–" Sarah adjusts her voice "–a naughty but lovable little boy, like mine?"

But Hannah doesn't laugh. "No. He's an angel. White, with wings. Also blue, somehow. A belt that's actually a rope with a knot in it. You know, the whole religious thing."

Again, there is a silence between them.

"In what circumstances," Sarah begins, looking down at her cup. "In what circumstances does this Chandler turn up?"

"Oh, at times when–" Hannah suddenly stops. "Times of–" She stops again. "Times of anxiety," she says finally.

That's when the telephone rings.

•

From the window where he stands, Greg can look across the flat ground at the window of Naseena's isolation room in the infirmary. Even though she has gone now, and the room is empty, a crowd remains outside the window, most of them settled on the ground as if they intend to stay. There is a soft murmur of singing.

"She couldn't have stayed." The director is standing behind him, also looking out at Naseena's window.

"She was heartbroken."

"Some things are just not negotiable. She had to be repatriated."

Naseena had been diagnosed with food poisoning and exhaustion. Nothing serious after all. But Ali and several others had been confined to the infirmary, no symptoms as yet but still under observation.

Greg sighs and turns away from the window.

"But she's on the mend," he says, repeating what they both know. "But she needed to go home, I agree," he adds, seeing the expression on the director's face.

Until recently, Greg was just amused by what he privately called the "cult of Naseena". He has changed his view now.

If she has to go home, all that commitment, all that drive, all that love will be wasted, he thinks to himself. If only I could come up with something for her.

He is not even slightly surprised when an idea drops into his head, fully formed and clear.

"I have a call to make," says Greg. There is a grin spreading across his face. "I think I might know somebody who can find her a worthwhile job, if she wants it."

"Nothing too physically demanding," says the director. "She'll need to convalesce."

"She's very good with children," says Greg, as though this is an answer. "Leave it to me. I'll make the call."

•

Ben's screen pings to tell him he's got a message. He looks up. It's from somebody called Shannah McKilvey. It reads, 'Meet in recep 10 mins :-)'

Ben thinks: I didn't even know her name until just now.

Damn.

He hesitates, then hits the Reply button.

He types, 'Can't today. Sorry. Sudden work crisis. No time.'

Hits Send.

His concentration is fucked. He needs a coffee.

He's just back to his desk when the screen pings again to tell him he's got another message. Ben moves the mouse to clear the screen saver.

It's another one from her.

It reads. 'Lets Do IT 2moro ;-)'

Ben stares at the screen for so long that the screen saver comes back.

He sits for a while in silence, his eyes reflecting the screen.

•

In the twilit room close to the nurses' station in the intensive care ward, Father Bernardi dozes. He is aware that he is half-awake, half-asleep, but for him, the dream is the more tangible of the two realities through which his consciousness drifts. There are trees, and water, and in the distance, it seems that there are mountains. In front of him is an open space of waving grass, and a pleasant sense of not being alone. Watching the grass, he feels the wind freshen the air.

At first, it seems to him that there are bells ringing – curious, flat bells like cow bells – and he looks around in his dream for whatever is approaching. But he is still alone, although not alone, and the cow bells translate themselves into the rusty, dust-impeded ringing of the old telephone that that has been placed on the bedside unit next to him.

Father Bernardi finds that he has the strength to lift up his hand and bring the receiver to his ear. The cord untangles itself as he does so.

"Good ... afternoon," he says, guessing at the time of day. "Who is this?"

"Father?"

"Yes?"

"It's Gregory Doyle. From..."

But Father Bernardi says, "Yes, Greg, of course." Father Bernardi remembers all his old pupils, of course, but today of all days, now that he is awake, there is no need for Greg Doyle to identify himself. "How are you, Greg? How is your work?"

Through the crackling on the line, Father Bernardi hears, "We've saved lives, Father. We've been lucky. It's ... miraculous ... wait to talk to you ... lot to say. But ... time ... lines aren't reliable. I need your help."

"Of course, Greg. What can I do for you?" Father Bernardi closes his eyes, straining to hear.

"...can't stay here. She's absolutely wonderful, a real asset, but ... just can't risk any spread ... well enough to fly her out ... very upset, wants to do more ... thought you might approach..." The line dies for a moment and then Greg's voice returns, oddly amplified. "...nurse ... given her ... number ... thought you might ... Sister Percy in advance ...

explain for me. She's worth it, Father. A good soul." The line crackles again.

Father Bernardi knows already what is being asked of him.

"Of course, Greg," he says, thinking that all souls are worth it, and Greg hears him.

"That's great, Father. She's already on a flight." The phone line is suddenly clear.

"How did you get through to me here, Greg?" Father Bernardi asks.

"Satellite phone." Greg laughs. "Worked out the time difference, guessed you'd be at the refuge, dialled the number and there you were. Miracle of technology. Why do you ask?"

But before Father Bernardi can reply, the phone goes dead. He holds the receiver in his hand for a moment and then reaches out to return it to its base. "Miracle of technology," he murmurs, and closes his eyes.

•

Ben works.

His idea has evolved. Now he wants to add a sequence of drawings – not to be part of the main presentation that Anthony will give, but as a handout – that will that work like one of those really old-style kiddie-cartoon drawing-things: you flick the pages and the drawings seem to move. Not a special effect; but a thing for a printer to do, a little booklet.

It's a gimmick, but it might be fun.

So he has shelved the main sketches for now and is working in a series of squares drawn on A4 sheets. He'll photocopy the sheets and cut out the squares. Something to play with while Anthony's making his presentation.

I am being paid to do this, Ben thinks. I am being paid to draw.

He decides to photocopy the top sheet as it is now, and cut up the copy so that he can overlay each frame to check how it's going to work. Not enough squares for a proper flick-through, he thinks, waiting for the photocopier to warm up, but enough to get the idea.

It's all happening for me. All at once.

•

"So what tests are they talking about?"

Hannah doesn't reply.

The call had come from the surgery.

A cancellation.

Megan can be fitted in at the hospital this afternoon.

"Tell me more about Megan's invisible friend," says Sarah, after an interval. Megan is still asleep upstairs.

"Imaginary," says Hannah. Then, "He was here this morning, when Dr Murison came."

"And she told the doctor about him?"

Hannah nods.

"Is that what he does? Turn up when she needs him?"

"I'm sorry. This is so silly."

"No..."

"He takes her riding, apparently. In her mind, obviously. He takes her riding and he tells her stories and they go flying off to Heaven together." Hannah stops abruptly.

Sick child. Angel. Flying off to Heaven.

"What a lucky girl," Sarah says quickly. "She must have an enormously powerful imagination. That's a wonderful thing."

Hannah is dabbing at her eyes. "I'm sorry," she says again. "I've been a bit worried, actually. Tired, I mean."

190

Sarah says, "If I could dream up an imaginary friend like an angel, I'd count myself lucky."

She puts just the slightest emphasis on the word "imaginary".

Hannah almost smiles.

Sarah reaches out and covers Hannah's hand with her own. She says, "How much have I told you about what I do?"

•

Sister Percy sits alone in her small office. Earlier, Sister Marie-Claude brought her a vase containing blooms of the new yellow rose. Coincidence that the girl chose that one, of course. Sister Percy first moved the vase to the top of the bookcase and then she brought it back to her desk. And now she sits here alone, weeping as she has not wept for years.

Open your heart to what comes, she says to herself.

And I told him he was trespassing.

What have I done?

The telephone rings.

Sister Percy is startled. She frowns at the thing, angry with it for disturbing her train of thought.

She picks it up. "Yes?" she says, perhaps too abruptly.

Then her face softens. "Father," she says. It has been a long time, but although the line is crackly and indistinct, she would always recognise that voice.

"Of course not," she says, glancing at the darkness outside the window. It is late, but it would never be too late to take a call from Father Bernardi.

She frowns. "Of course. If I can help, I would be delighted to do so."

As she listens, she pulls open a drawer and brings out a pad of paper and a pencil.

She writes, "Africa. repat cs ill. Qual? nurse. Doyle. Dante?! Danti."

"What is it that you want me to do, Father?" she asks.

She listens, and as she does so, she writes: "recup here then fnd nurs job!!! N or just caring. Train?"

"Is she a member of our church, Father?" she asks.

There is a silence and for a moment she thinks that the connection has broken. Then the crackling comes back, worse than before. She closes her eyes, concentrating, and then the crackling clears for a moment and she hears Father Bernardi's voice say clearly, "...came to me for help and I said..."

Sister Percy opens her eyes and sees that the yellow blooms in the vase are not, as she had first thought, new and just opening, but dying. A petal drops onto the desk.

Sister Percy leans forward over the desk. "Tell me more about this girl," she says, suddenly businesslike, and as the line clears, she begins to take notes in earnest.

•

"I don't think I can come tonight," says Hannah abruptly.

"Okay."

They are standing in the kitchen. It's time to go.

"You're sure you don't want me to come with you to the hospital?" Sarah says.

Hannah shakes her head.

"I'm at home for the rest of the day. If you do want to come round this evening, or you could phone any time."

Sarah is now late for pick-up time at the playgroup. But she is absolutely not going to mention that.

"Thank you for everything you said," says Hannah, but she is avoiding Sarah's eyes. "About the angel, and..."

"Oh," Sarah laughs, embarrassed suddenly but not sure why. "It's a way to relax," she says. "No big revelations. Not religious. Just, if you're stressed out – it's all in the mind."

"Mummy?"

Megan is in the doorway.

"Yes, darling?" Hannah now focuses exclusively on Megan, crouching down in front of her and putting her hands on her shoulders.

"Can Daddy put me to bed tonight?"

Sarah hears herself gasp. Megan looks up at her, a direct gaze that meets her eyes and lingers for a second while Hannah says automatically, "Of course you can, darling," and then catches up with the question and adds, "Do you mean, you want Daddy to read you a story?"

"No," says Megan. "I want Daddy to put me to bed. I want you to have a rest, Mummy." Abruptly self-conscious, Megan crosses her arms, turns round and stomps off.

Hannah straightens up, looking surprised.

"That doesn't happen very often?" Sarah asks.

"Never." Hannah is shaking her head.

Sarah is about to say something, when Hannah suddenly frowns, inhales sharply – a scent, fleeting, one that she recognises? No – and says, "Right. If Ben's taking over, I'd better do something for supper." She is suddenly very busy, starting the work of preparing Megan's supper with an opening of cupboards, pulling out of drawers, that is as clear to Sarah as the shutting of a door.

But at the last moment, just as she is about to close the door, Hannah says, "Tonight. I might just ... if it's still..."

Sarah saves her the trouble of completing a sentence. "Of course.

Come if you want to, and not to worry if you don't."
    Hannah closes the door quickly, as if she is about to cry.

The Path Ahead

We ride hard across open country, the wind slipstreaming our faces, the pounding of our wild progress taking the breath from our lungs, the ground loud with the urgent gallop of our need to be lost in wild movement. Onward we ride, driving onward, intent, our faces low over the pungent jumping manes of our wild golden horses, the herd galloping around us, breath and movement and urgency and cold air starting tears from our eyes, so many horses, so much need to focus, focus, focus in the moving country. We ride, we ride, our teeth clenched, and I hold her in my arms, my wings around us, my hands holding hers to the reins.

"There! Well done. All finished now."

"Oh my darling, well done, my darling."

Hannah takes Megan in her arms as the nurse who has taken the blood turns away, holding up the syringe to the light and tapping it with a fingernail. Megan, when Hannah loosens her hug and can see her face, is white with shock. Such a big needle, and nothing like this has ever happened to her before. In a moment, she is blinking, shaking her head, intent upon herself. But this is not her natural movement; she is still inside herself, transfixed with the shock of what has just happened.

"Oh my darling well done, we'll go home now and we'll have ice cream." Hannah is conscious that she's babbling, but her daughter's remote, pinched face draws anguish from her.

"We'll get these straight over to the lab, today I should think, and then if there's any need for a follow-up, I'm sure we'll call you," says the woman brightly.

Megan turns her face to mine. They hurt me, she says to me, without words.

But as she speaks, I see that in her face there is suddenly light.

This is where the horses are, she says. I've found them.

The horses gather around us, nuzzling at Megan's outstretched hand.

"Look at them, Mummy!" says Megan out loud suddenly, stretching up her arms, and Hannah, taken by surprise at this sudden apparent recovery, swings her daughter up and feels tight arms around her neck.

Sahasrael stands beside me as I watch Hannah carry Megan away down the white corridor.

"You rode too far," she says.

We stand together in a sea of horses.

"Tell her now, Chandrael," Sahasrael says, and then softly, "Tell her that we have come to a beginning."

And she is gone.

·

Ben comes home to find Hannah pulling on her coat.

He is elated with the drawings he has completed today, and wants to tell her all about Anthony's project and everything it will mean to him – to them. He has copies of the pictures he has already completed for Anthony, with one of the little flip-books he has made. He is sure that Anthony won't object to him using them, when the presentation is done and these drawings are no more than a filed-away detail of the company's history, as part of his application for a job as a creative artist.

Ben stands mute with the front door still open behind him, looking at her in shocked surprise. He is so full of his daydream that she'll be asking questions about his day and he'll be telling her about his future – and here she is on the point of walking out.

"I heard you coming," she says, as if this is a full explanation of why she is standing in the hallway shrugging her coat onto her shoulders and checking her bag for her keys. She can't meet his eyes.

This is when she should tell him about the tests.

But suddenly, she can't admit to him what she has done.

The hurt she caused their daughter this afternoon, the hurt she allowed to be inflicted on Megan, just to ease her own stupid anxiety, has woken up all the grief, all the guilt, of that disastrous beach. It is as if, despite her promise to Megan, she has done it again.

"Where are you going?" he says.

"Megan says she wants you to put her to bed tonight."

She still seems preoccupied with the contents of her bag.

"And I've got an invitation to meet a friend, so I thought: girls' night out."

She raises her head, tossing her hair back as she does so, and finally Ben gets to see her face.

"One of the playgroup mums. Nice woman. I think we're going to be friends."

She looks at him so directly then, with such a mixture of

confidence, challenge and facing him down, that he just nods. He understands now, or thinks he does. Girls' night out. Some kind of assertion of – whatever. Independence. A woman thing. No questions will be answered. Okay.

She's not leaving him.

"You'll come back safe?" he says.

"That's the plan."

"Megan's okay, is she? Anything I should know?"

Their eyes meet, and for a breath of a second there's that sense of teamwork around the baby, like it used to be in the early days, when they would hear Megan crying upstairs, and drop the argument – any argument. Megan first, always.

"She's had supper. She's had a story. She did want to stay up until you got home, but she's asleep." She glances back towards the kitchen. "There's some of her pasta still in the saucepan, or you can – oh, you know where the fridge is, you work it out."

They both hear the momentary not-quite-dislike in that sign-off. But then she comes up tall and kisses him goodbye. "It's okay," she whispers. "I just need..."

She doesn't know what she needs, but he stops her and says softly, "Have fun with your friends."

She slips away.

Ben stands in the familiar silence, feeling himself incongruous in his own home.

This is Hannah's space, he thinks.

This is what it's like for her when I'm not here.

"Daddy?" A faint call.

"I'm coming."

Upstairs, Megan is lying on her side in her bed, facing him.

"What's up?" Ben comes and kneels by the bed, level with her head, putting his hand up to stroke her hair.

"I don't feel very well."

"Oh no. What kind of not very well, Meggie?"

Ben leans closer just in time for a stream of half-digested shapes in a mostly red sauce to fly from her mouth and into his lap. Megan convulses a second time and the rest of her supper arrives on his shirt.

She relaxes back onto the pillow and begins to cry.

"Oh, baby," Ben is frozen with one hand stroking her hair and the other on her arm. His legs are tight together as he kneels and he hunches his body to make a bowl-shape for Megan's vomit. He can feel its sticky wetness cooling on his skin. But he doesn't move.

Damage limitation: so far, cleaning up means getting his clothes into the bath and rinsing them, then leaving them for Hannah. He can't let any of this get on the floor.

It occurs to him that he could call Hannah.

He won't do that.

He can do this.

She has missed the bed completely. It's clean. Nothing on the carpet – yet.

Ben realises that Megan has fallen back to sleep.

She is asleep. On her side.

Recovery position.

He watches her for a moment longer, then very carefully, very slowly, using his hands on the floor, the bed frame, the wall, he gets himself to his feet. Feeling himself hunched like a question mark, walking with his lower legs only, knees as tight together as they can be, he gets to the bathroom without spilling anything.

Ben sits on the side of the bath and kicks off his shoes. Then he swings himself around into the bath, knees together. He removes all his clothes – socks, pants and all.

Crouched naked in the bath, Ben listens to the silence of the house. He looks to see his towel on the back of the door, to wrap around his waist if Megan cries out and he needs to go to her.

He splashes cold water onto himself. Then he rinses his clothes, sluicing off the pasta shapes and ringing out shirt, trousers, then pants and socks, and arranging them on the side of the bath so that they will drip inwards and not onto the floor.

He crams the soggy pasta shapes through the plughole and rinses them away.

Then he puts his wet bundle of clothes in the basin and – going first to listen at Megan's door, briefly to watch her sleep, see her breathing – showers away the day, washing his hair, his body, every part of him.

Drying off, he wraps the damp towel around his waist, and – pausing again to check on Megan – he takes the bundle of wet clothes downstairs to the kitchen. He puts them in the sink and crouches down to look at the dials on the front of the washing machine.

Ben stands up, swearing under his breath. He moves over to the other side of the kitchen and pulls open Hannah's bottom drawer. He sorts through the receipts, guarantees, paperclips, postcards, loyalty cards, broken pens, screws, picture hooks, lengths of string, fuses, lids, small springs, wires, old shopping lists, ribbons, coupons off cereal packets, souvenirs of Megan and proof photographs of their wedding, until he finds the washing-machine instruction book.

He sits down at the kitchen table and opens the book at page one: Getting To Know Your Washing Machine.

•

Four women and one man sit in a circle of armchairs. There are greetings cards on the mantelpiece above the fireplace and strung across the walls. There has been a child's birthday. The room is informal and soft with cushions and fabrics in fire colours. The closed curtains are heavy, indigo.

Sarah Bishop sits in the upright chair beside the fireplace full of pine cones. This is her front room in her terraced house and this is her meditation group. Hannah sits in the comfortable chair facing her. Hannah is not quite sure what to expect, although Sarah did murmur to her, letting her in, "Just relax. Don't expect anything."

Sarah is serious about this, Hannah can now see, and there is something almost reassuring about finding people who take this kind of thing seriously.

Hannah starts to worry that she won't be able to keep her eyes closed and do the meditating thing without wanting to scratch or sneeze.

It's impossible to clear your mind of thoughts, isn't it? Even thinking about not thinking is thinking.

Oh shit, Hannah thinks, remembering the hospital. Oh my baby.

The elastic that connects her heart to her home tightens.

When Hannah stepped out of the house earlier on and heard the door close behind her, she closed her eyes and took a deep breath of night air and thought to herself: what the fuck am I doing?

She had almost turned back around and knocked for Ben to let her straight back in again.

Almost.

Megan will be safe with Ben.

Safer than with her.

Hannah closes her eyes. She is too miserable for this.

She will just sit here and not disturb anybody and leave as soon as she can.

It won't take long, Sarah had said earlier. The thing is, you might find it restful just to sit through the meditation, even drift off to sleep if you don't snore (Hannah had smiled), and then we can either talk or just sit together for a while. Nobody will know if you're not taking part. It's relaxing.

Hannah wills herself to sit still.

And then gradually, as she begins to listen to Sarah's voice directing them through a door and into a forest, she settles into a lucid dream in which she sees the path ahead of her, the slanting sun, the green sunlit leaves, the tall woman with long bright hair, the tall woman who is turning to look back at her, who is familiar somehow, who is looking back at her from the sunlit clearing, and the boy with her, the young boy with the rucksack, who is reaching out his hand to her.

"On the path ahead of you, in a shaft of sunlight, you will see what you have come here to find," Sarah's voice says. "It is a gift to you from your higher self. It is yours alone. Walk up to it and take it in your hands. This is yours alone. Give yourself time to study your gift, its weight, its colour, what meaning it might have for you."

Hannah opens her eyes and realises she has been asleep. She hears Sarah's voice say, "Now it is time to leave the forest. Take your gift and begin to walk back down the path the way you came."

Hannah stretches in her chair, and is relieved to see that all the others still have their eyes closed.

"Wow," says the man, Sunil. He is the first of the group to open his eyes. He sees Hannah looking at him. "That was deep, yeah?"

The woman next to him, Katie, is not quite returned, blinking, stretching in her chair like Hannah did. It is Deirdre who answers him, from across the room. "Did you get a gift?" she says. "What was it?"

"It was this big jug thing, like you might put flowers in."

"A vase."

"Yeah, right." Sunil is ready to talk about himself. "And the forest. Wow. Birds, you know? Trees, really clear. Really colourful. I had this really great path..."

Deirdre and Katie exchange the tiniest of smiles as Sunil, the only man in the room, begins to tell them all about his experience.

Sarah is watching Hannah. She did come with us, she thinks.

Don't ask her in front of the others.

"You got a vase?" Katie interrupts Sunil. She is back now.

"Yeah." He looks at her.

"My gift was a bunch of flowers. Uprooted, with their roots still on."

Sunil looks at Katie and of course Sarah, Deirdre and Katie all know immediately what he is thinking: vase; flowers. They are surprised that Sunil has got even this clear message so quickly.

Sarah says, "Is there a garden you want to nurture, Katie? Make it grow?"

But Sunil is already telling Katie that she can keep her flowers in his vase until she figures out a place to plant them. She seems to like the idea and he chances it. "Drink after?" he whispers, leaning slightly towards her.

She grins at him and nods her head. "Yeah. Okay."

So that's how it is.

Sarah looks at Hannah, who smiles back, oblivious. Hannah has seemed invisible to the others, in that they have not so much as paused to let her into the discussion, and Sarah is relieved.

She says her usual goodbye at the door, concluding with the reminder that always makes them smile as they leave. "You're all in the right place at the right time and doing the right thing." She comes back into the room. Hannah is still in her chair. Sarah sits in one of the comfortable chairs. "How did you get on?" she asks.

Hannah doesn't answer immediately. When she does, she stretches again, as if still waking up, and says, "That was lovely."

"How did you get on with the forest?"

Hannah says, "It really works, doesn't it? I feel so..." and illustrates how she feels by stretching her arms above her head.

Sarah thinks: something happened for you, didn't it?

Hannah is finally awake, and now she is getting ready to leave. Sarah can see that she is much more relaxed than she was when she arrived.

"No, thank you," says Hannah, to the offer of tea. "I think I'd better..."

And there it is: the anxiety is back.

The two women surprise themselves, and each other, by embracing: a quick, spontaneous hug.

Then Sarah is alone again inside her closed front door. She leans against the softness of her warm coat hanging on its hook. Not many tonight, but still, she is exhausted, drained. She returns to her chair by the fireplace.

Chandler appears in the doorway from the kitchen, blinking with sleep. He is wearing his pyjamas and holding something out in front of him. "I found this in the forest, Mummy," he says. "They said it was for you." It is a mug of tea, steaming in his hands.

"Careful you don't drop it, darling," she says, waking up. There is nobody in front of her. She must have fallen asleep and dreamed him.

Chandler is with his dad tonight, she remembers.

"Thank you for the tea," says Sarah Bishop out loud, laughing softly, and goes through to the kitchen to take the hint and get the kettle going.

•

When Hannah arrives home, Ben's suit trousers, shirt, socks, pants, handkerchief and bath towel are hanging on the fold-out drying rack in the kitchen. Three damp banknotes have been laid out flat on three separate sheets of kitchen towel. There's a pile of change, and Ben's season ticket.

Hannah stands by the kitchen table, where she has just put down her bag, and picks up the washing-machine instruction book. It's face down, still open at page one.

She looks around the kitchen. Plate and knife washed up. Breadboard out. Breadcrumbs and fragments of cheddar cheese on the breadboard, on the side around the breadboard, and on the table. Pickle on the plate and knife that he has at least put in the sink.

No disaster here, then. Was he trying to help? She sees that he has washed everything he was wearing as one load at 60 degrees. Cotton.

"Ben," she murmurs, looking at the crumpled suit trousers on the rack.

But she hasn't seen Megan yet. And where's Ben himself?

She doesn't call out. She goes upstairs and puts her head round Megan's door.

Megan is totally asleep, abandoned on her back with arms and legs wide. Ben is sitting against the bed, his own pillow behind his back, reading. He's wearing jeans and a tee-shirt. Bare feet.

"What's up?"

"She was sick. I thought I'd better sit with her."

"Sick? Why didn't you call me?"

She comes straight forward to her daughter, leaning close and feeling her forehead.

Whatever it was, there's nothing wrong with her now.

The tests? The anxiety? Shock?

Something she ate?

She still hasn't told Ben about the tests. But it's too late and too complicated now.

And she needs to think about the experience she's just had. Looking at Megan sleeping, she is reassured. The tests are history, not worth mentioning.

No news is good news. Anything else wouldn't be fair.

"I didn't want to disturb you," says Ben, giving her a lopsided smile. It's his irritating kooky-attractive look, as if he's expecting her to be impressed that he's just single-handedly cared for his own daughter.

"Well done for finding the washing machine at least," she says, plucking at the duvet to bring it forward over Megan, touching it into place.

This is going to have to change, she decides. He's not even part of his own family.

That job.

Ben moves out of her way, leaning sideways, still sat against the bed, looking up at her, watching the two of them, his wife and his child, and as he does so, a decision settles in his mind.

He loves them. He can feel it. This is where he lives.

The decision makes him feel good about himself.

"Let him find his own way, Chandra." We are silent in the room.

Ben decides that he will leave the job now. Build them the life they should be living.

"He has to find his own way."

Tomorrow, Ben thinks.

Tomorrow.

•

Night comes.

On the bedside table the digital clock counts away time as Hannah and Ben sleep. Hannah is silent, still, deeply asleep under a huddle of duvet. Ben is restless. I watch him as he rolls onto his back, throws open his arms, then closes up again, turning onto his side and drawing up his knees.

In his dream, Ben struggles in a tangled briar. There is a child's doll

206

caught on the thorns. Ben is naked but the thorns cause him no pain. Hannah is there – he knows Hannah is there, but he cannot see her.

I reach forward to release the briar. Ben jumps forward and runs barefoot through a softwood plantation of straight trees and slanting sunbeams. Colours flare around him. There are bright ribbons fluttering from the branches of the trees.

Ben stops running. He feels himself moving slightly as he comes to rest, and understands that he is weightless, yet secured to the ground. He has stopped in a clearing on the edge of a wide expanse of moving water. Ben sees that there is a boat nearby, tethered to a tree. He will remember the boat, but now he is studying the tree. It is neat, dark green, A-shaped, like a Christmas tree. Ben sees that the pine needles are in fact tightly curled-up leaves.

He touches a leaf, and as it begins to open for him, understands that he must not pluck it loose. Ben accepts this. He holds his hands out to the tree, and feels that he is at peace.

Ben's eyes open. He is instantly awake. He is lying on his back, his arms at his sides. His first move is to look at the clock: 01:37. Okay. He gazes at the ceiling, playing over the dream in his mind. Running. Ribbons. Tree.

I don't usually dream in colour, Ben thinks. Do I?

He'll forget the dream, he always does. But if he could tell it to Hannah, what interpretation...?

Trees, Ben thinks. There were trees.

Nature. Freedom.

He turns his head. Hannah is asleep facing him, her mouth pushed slightly out of shape by the pillow. As he looks at her, all of a sudden something shifts in his attention and he really looks at her. The familiar details of her face, brought up close to him, so familiar that he never really sees them. Her nose, her mouth, her hair; his wife has such fine hair.

Ben gazes at his wife's face, her natural face, undefended and open to him, and he is surprised by a sudden, deep warmth of feeling – love, tenderness, fear – welling up inside him. This is his girl. His girl, his own. Very gently, not to disturb her, he rolls onto his side and bunches up his pillow so that he can lie and look at his wife's face.

Where is it? he wonders. In the texture of her skin? The shape of her nose? The way her eyebrows…? Where is the beauty of this face?

He cannot find it, but it is there: he can see it in every feature. Ben rolls over onto his back and with the peculiar clarity of the deep night considers the life he now shares with the woman beside him – the soulmate, the partner, the stranger; the woman; the complete and distinct person. He is married to his wife. They have a child. They have built this life and together, they are – happy?

Ben pushes back the cover and swings his feet round to sit up on the side of the bed. He slides his feet into his slippers and stands up. He goes into the bathroom to fetch his dressing gown and then pads softly out of the room. Hannah is not disturbed.

In the kitchen Ben stands over the kettle as it boils. With the light on, he can see himself reflected in the dark window.

Hannah could still fit into those jeans she used to wear, Ben thinks, as he reaches up for a mug, and is briefly aroused by a memory of his wife shimmying herself out of those jeans, falling back on the bed, crying out in frustration when they snagged on her feet. She was so eager then, he thinks. He checks the time on the wall-clock.

And that clapped-out old Volvo. That time they couldn't wait, full-on, fighting out of their clothes, naked in an empty picnic area on a motorway. Ben smiles: what he remembers so fondly is the two of them scrambling back into their clothes afterwards, waking up to where they were. And then laughing so much they cried.

What the fuck do dreams mean?

Ben has made himself a mug-full of hot water. Forgot the teabag.

He goes to the sink to empty out the mug.

"This isn't enough," he murmurs.

Ben leaves the kitchen, and goes back upstairs.

•

And then, an ending.

"One of the things about being a dad, sweetie. You don't get a practice shot. I was never the dad of a fifteen-year-old girl before you came along. I know how to love you, and I think I can do that very well indeed, and I know something about being fifteen, although it was a long time ago. But the best I can tell you is, I love you very much and I'm going to do the best I can. I hope that's enough for now."

Bridget McCloud is in bed and Ken McCloud is sitting on the bed next to her. He has just read her a story, like he used to do ten, twelve years ago, and now he's saying goodnight – again. He was woken by her crying. In the time since Sally's death, Bridget seems to have gone back five years – more. She's been playing with old toys, reading battered old books. It's come naturally for Ken to read to her. This speech about being a dad has been building up for several days.

"I love you, Daddy."

"I love you too, sweetie."

Now he's at the bedroom door. He's turned out the bedside light and he's got his hand on the switch for the main room light.

"Daddy."

"Yes, darling."

"I think Mummy's watching over us."

He's straight back to the bed. He hears the echo – "watching over us" is a phrase from the funeral – but he recognises the need too.

"I'm sure she is, sweetie. I'm sure she is too." He pushes the hair back from her face. Then he starts a regular gentle stroking of her hair.

She doesn't say anything more and he doesn't prompt her. One of his wife's articles of wisdom, absorbed over all the years of being a dad, is that sleep is the true healer.

Bridget closes her eyes.

Ken McCloud watches his daughter's face, listening to her breathing change as she subsides into sleep.

We need a new beginning, he decides.

Sally McCloud comes from her place at the end of the bed to sit next to her husband. I stand in the doorway.

"I never really knew him in life," she says to me. "Not like this. He's so strong."

Before I can reply, she shakes her head and continues.

"Not strong. He's so tender." She smiles. "That thing he said just now about being a dad. He's such a mother." She laughs.

Bridget is asleep now. Ken takes his hand from her hair. He sits looking down at his daughter and Sally lays her head briefly against his shoulder.

He stands up and moves to the door. "Sleep well, sweetie," he murmurs. Then he adds, "If you are watching over us, I hope I'm doing okay."

Sally stares after him as he pulls the door nearly closed.

"I'm ready to go, Chandrael," she says.

Together, we rise into the sky.

Cheap Flowers Growing Wild

Ben has overslept. He's missed his train, so there's no point in hurrying. He comes out onto the platform a full hour later than he usually does, with his briefcase in one hand and no coffee in the other. No croissant either. He's late – not badly late, not really, but late enough for the coffee shop to be closed and the platform to be clear of commuters. Ben's not used to seeing the platform like this.

Hannah let him sleep. She woke him up before leaving with Megan for the playgroup. "You needed that," she said, and he's thankful, now, that he didn't immediately voice his irritation. He was annoyed – still is – but he's got a briefcase full of drawings and a project he's excited about, and now he thinks about it, he needs her in a good mood for when he tells his story of the future, which might be tonight.

He can tell Anthony that he worked at home on the presentation.

Ben checks his watch. Already the rush is over. Doesn't take long. One man is standing alone on the yellow line, as though he's positioning himself to be facing the door when the train stops, but the rest of the platform is clear.

Ben checks the board. Five minutes until the train comes, if it's on time.

He notices that the train times go down through the day: there's space now for more than just the commuter hour.

Ben starts to walk towards the end of the platform. On one side of the track, there's the beginning of some kind of industrial estate. On the other, trees sloping down a bank, and then the backs of houses. It's a terrace. All of them have dormer windows extended out of the rear slopes of their roofs. A view of the railway, Ben thinks. He imagines being asleep and half-waking to the rumble of an occasional train.

Or the constant rumble of commuter trains. Recorded announcements.

Ben turns and begins to walk back towards the other end of the platform. As he does so, the signal in the distance ahead of him turns green.

The train is a two-carriage local train, open-plan and bench seats, enough for the mid-morning lack of traffic, not the populated long commuter carriages that Ben is expecting.

He has to run to reach the train because it's so short and he's so far down the platform, and when he gets in through the last door, he sees that the other man is already sitting there, looking his way.

There's no way they can get out of speaking to each other. Ben nods, but the other man speaks.

"Looks like it's just us," he says.

Ben grunts something. He wants to open his briefcase and look at his drawings, but the only place he can sit without being too obviously rude is facing the man. He sits down on the other side of the aisle, and after a moment, both of them act as though they're busy.

The man has a brown briefcase, a large one that is so soft and old that it bends itself against him as he places it on the seat. Ben covets it. He sets his own fake-leather black box on the seat facing him and lifts the lid.

That's when the man laughs. He has taken out of his briefcase and laid beside him a newspaper, a bent A3 sketchpad, and a clutch of folded design drawings.

Ben has taken out of his briefcase and laid beside him an A4 sketchpad and his folded roughs of Anthony's idea.

"I'm an illustrator," says Ben. "A designer."

The man sticks out his hand. "Ken McCloud," he says.

•

No time like the present. The girl rang at nine sharp and Sister Percy suggested she come in immediately. Now she's here, fifteen minutes early for the agreed 10am appointment. "I shall be ready for her at ten," Sister Percy had told the face at the door firmly. But she had been by no means as irritable as she sounded. If punctuality cannot be achieved, and nowadays all the signs are that it can't, earliness is vastly preferable to lateness.

Sister Percy collects herself. She has been tired recently, perhaps a little overwrought, and in the fresh light of morning she feels very much restored.

Truth be told, Sister Percy is a little embarrassed at herself for her emotional outburst last night and yesterday. She must find a way to apologise to Sister Marie-Claude without losing her authority. To get so upset over a trespasser and an invasive, albeit welcome, yellow rose. Sister Percy frowns.

But she will do this as a personal favour to Father Bernardi. She has been asked for help, and she will provide it. She smiles for a moment. An old nun called upon by an elderly priest. Two old friends responding to a call for help. Hardly the stuff of miracles.

The yellow rose in the vase catches her eye. It is bright this morning, caught by a ray of sunlight.

Sister Percy frowns. She had forgotten the faith aspect. The girl is not a member of their church nor even of their religion – their faith. Sister Percy thinks of her fellow nuns. What would they think, if they knew...?

Sister Percy brings herself up short. Where are these thoughts coming from? She will do this for Father Bernardi.

When the girl is shown in, Sister Percy almost changes her mind. Brown skin, and black hair that looks as if it has been cut with garden shears. The girl is wearing trousers in a khaki material. Trousers. The shirt is of a similar material, but more faded. The girl is wiry and strong-looking but her face is sunken and thin; Sister Percy can see the signs of recent illness.

The girl's first words to her are, "Thank you." She speaks softly and there is something in her expression that rouses Sister Percy's heart.

"Do you have any experience of working with children?" she asks, relenting.

Sister Percy listens to the girl's story of nursing training, hospital experience and then a stint working as a classroom assistant in a primary school before volunteering for Africa. We haven't even introduced ourselves, she thinks. I haven't told her anything about our order.

Then she is reading the girl's CV and several letters. There is one from a woman called Brennan, all about the girl's willingness in medical matters. Reading between the lines, Sister Percy infers that the girl has experience of emptying bedpans.

As if that's enough.

"You were closely involved with the patients?" she says, and the girl begins to tell her about the parlous state of the camp in the final days.

Sister Percy looks up once, sharply, as the girl says, "Septicaemia had set in, so we had to..." and understands that the girl did more than deal with patients' basic bodily functions. She reads a letter from a primary-school teacher about the girl's "extraordinary aptitude with children".

This is almost too good to be true, Sister Percy thinks.

She picks up another letter, and as she does so, hears the girl's sharp intake of breath. Aha! she thinks. She looks up.

The girl is blushing. "I thought I had removed that one," she says.

It is another one from Africa. From a man, one Gregory Doyle. Sister Percy recognises the name. Father Bernardi's former pupil, the one who lost his faith and ended up doing voluntary work. In Africa, evidently. Still, any pupil of Father Bernardi's, even a lapsed one, would give an honest reference. Sister Percy's face remains expressionless as she begins to read the letter.

She stops reading and looks up.

"A miracle," she says.

The girl is blushing. "A boy who was thought to be dying," she says. "I was his friend." She shrugs.

Sister Percy says nothing. She returns her eyes to the letter.

A moment later she looks up again.

"Healed the entire camp," she says.

This time, the girl looks wretched. When she speaks, Sister Percy can only just hear what she says.

"That was nothing to do with me," the girl whispers.

A number of possible responses race themselves through Sister Percy's mind while her face remains expressionless. Was this man Gregory Doyle your lover? Was there really sickness before this supposed miracle cure? Is the man mad? Are you really claiming–?

But she isn't claiming, Sister Percy realises. She is denying any involvement.

Sister Percy lays the letters and the CV down flat on the desk in front of her and smooths them with her hands. She sits motionless in the sunlight, her face devoid of expression. She is the head of a religious order. She is an efficient administrator and a good leader. She is practical. An effective organiser. She is known and respected in her community.

Sister Percy gets up from her desk and crosses the room to the window. The sun has risen high enough in the sky to erase most of the shadows from the rose garden.

"As you know, we arrange palliative care – not full nursing care but voluntary support to the hospital's medical staff," Sister Percy begins, feeling her way to the limits of what she can offer. "We provide initial training and if necessary, accommodation and a modest amount of money…"

Sister Percy is suddenly aware that the heady, powerful scent of roses has blown all the way up into her office from the rose garden.

Through the closed windows.

Although that is of course imp–

Sister Percy discards her words.

She turns from the window.

Crosses the room.

Throws open her arms to the girl who has an extraordinary aptitude with children.

•

In a café by a river, I sit at a round table and wait. I am the young man with the rucksack again, adult now, present in the world, visible, alone, enjoying the sensations of the room. The man behind the counter is wondering about my accent. He takes me for an early tourist rather than a late commuter, but am I American? English? So far, I haven't asked him for directions, but he's pretty sure I'm not local.

I catch his eye across the room and raise my cup to him: good coffee.

Enjoy yourself, buddy, he thinks. Then he forgets me as he turns to his next customer.

Her again.

He sells her a milky coffee and a caramel square that he's betting she'll cut into quarters and then not eat.

"Okay..." he says, setting it all on a tray without being asked, and as she thanks him, Hannah tries to catch his eye. Today, she needs all the human contact she can get. Megan woke up perfectly well this morning and seemed healthy, but in the light of day, thinking about it, now that the tests have been done, she isn't going to stop worrying until she's got the results.

She's got the home phone diverted to her mobile.

They would have rung yesterday if there had been bad news.

The longer she has to wait, the better.

But still.

The café is scattered with solitary people, making it difficult to spot an empty table. Hannah brings the tray forward and is about to take the table next to mine when impulsively she changes her mind.

"Is this taken?"

"No, help yourself."

She sits down, facing me, and her first instinct is to protect her privacy. She busies herself unloading the tray, then slips the tray onto an empty chair. She notices the wilting flowers in the small vase between us, but they do not register in her mind: dead bluebells and an out-of-season, dying daffodil. She takes out the phone, checks it, and then comes to a stop.

She has chosen a table with a young man already sitting at it.

What if he...?

But I remind her of somebody. Has she seen me somewhere before?

When I look up and smile, she is surprised to find that she is not embarrassed any more. She returns the smile.

"I think he makes these himself," she says, excusing herself for the caramel slice. "I've just dropped my daughter off at playgroup," she adds, oddly compelled to supply the detail. "I'm on my way to..." She stops. Shrugs. We share a smile.

Then we return to silence. It's comfortable now.

"Excuse me," she says after a while. "But do I know you?"

"No," I say. After a second's pause I add, "You will one day."

But she is already saying, "I'm sorry, it's just that you seem familiar."

I smile at her. "People tell me that."

And then she waits for me to tell her who I am.

So I lean forward on my elbows and say, "Much of the time, I'm a messenger. I'm also a student, long-term." I can feel Sahasrael close to me. "And I suppose you could say I work in the caring professions."

There is a clatter of cutlery from the counter; it is a sound like happy laughter. For a brief moment the room is flooded with the scent of apples.

"So which of those are you doing now?"

"Messenger," I tell her.

"Do you have a bicycle or a motorbike?"

Our eyes meet and then I'm laughing and she's laughing too. "Sometimes, I even fly," I tell her. "Why the questions?"

"Sorry." She can't quite stop laughing. "Why not? I'm in a good mood. It's a good day." She stops. Suddenly, somehow, despite everything, it is. "Your turn to ask me."

It seems to her that I hesitate. "You've got a daughter," I say. I number off 'One' on a finger. "The daughter has a father." Two.

"Oh, you're good at this."

In a corner of her mind, she is surprised at how easily she's taking this. He's a stranger, and she shouldn't have sat at his table, let alone talked to him – but – yes – it's okay.

"You're married to him, he works, and you're thinking about whether to go back to work after all, or try for another child?"

She has splayed out her hand over the table so that we can both see her wedding ring.

She remembers that yes, until this latest worry with Megan she was beginning to think about having another child.

"How did you know?"

"She's your only daughter, isn't she?"

"Yes," she says.

"Hannah." She looks up and her eyes meet mine. I reach across the table and take her hand.

"I have something to tell you," I say.

Inside Hannah, as my hand touches hers, a spark finds its own spark and becomes alive. Time stops and we travel far from the café as I speak to her of the world that is and the world that could be. We pass through the door and into the forest and along the path to the clearing. And there we talk. I say to her, "I shall be with you."

Presently, Sahasrael says, "Enough. It is done."

Time begins again.

Hannah looks at me, sleepy-eyed.

I make a gesture with my hand that says: take the flowers; they're for you. She looks at them, cheap flowers probably picked from the wild, and the faint line of a frown appears between her eyes. What is it that she almost remembers?

But it is beginning to slip away. She remembers the accurate guess that she wants another baby. But after that – what? It is as if her attention wandered just as I said something crucial. But what? The question itself slips away.

Suddenly she is in a hurry to go. I remain seated as she stands up, pulling her things together. I reach out and slide the uneaten caramel slice across to my side of the table. She laughs.

"Bye," she says.

And that is all.

It is done.

·

In the darkened hospital room, Father Bernardi opens his eyes. I am unclear to him in the darkness, a figure in shadow.

"Thank you," I say.

I am present in the world.

He hears my voice and thinks I must be another nurse. His eyes take in the dark blinds and the switched-off lights. Today, between the nurses' frequent visits, he has been left to sleep.

"What time is it?" he asks.

"Morning," I tell him.

The light is close now, and I am beginning to be illuminated. But he is drowsing again. He thinks that I have checked his condition and will now leave him. He is thinking about the hostel. He has good people working for him. It can more or less run itself, and as long as he keeps in touch, Kieran can probably take on most of the day-to-day stuff. It's just–

He is about to become anxious. There is a question in his mind over Kieran's ability to keep the admin under control.

I touch him on the shoulder.

"Father."

He opens his eyes.

"Ah," he says.

Then, "Did it work?"

"I'll bring the children to him. They'll give him a sign he can't ignore."

Amusement shows in the corners of his eyes.

"Nobody else will see," I tell him. "If they do, they can believe what they want to believe."

"And the young woman? Was the good Sister able to help her?"

"She found it in her heart," I tell him, and he smiles.

"So the two of them will..."

"Enough questions, Father."

He sighs.

"Yes," he says.

And in that moment as his soul rises I am surrounded by all the brightness of the Heavens as the walls around us dissolve and the light flows up through the sky.

His voice calls a blessing that recedes into the wind as the whole of creation rises up into the one great light and I am cast back into nature, and left behind.

The Discovery of Self

Megan is standing at a waist-high red plastic table. Her sleeves are rolled back and she wears a yellow plastic apron tied at the back with ribbons. I kneel beside her. I am the bright angel, tall, with great wings that rise over all the children in the room.

"We're painting," she tells me.

"It's beautiful."

Her hands and wrists are covered with green and ochre paint. She is using her hands to paint trees with wide-based conical trunks and green balls of leaves. I watch as she scoops a finger-load of blue paint into the empty space that will be the sky.

"There."

Mrs Barnaby has been watching Megan today. The little girl has seemed preoccupied with something. Nothing specific, nothing to put a finger on, but not her usual self. Should she say something to Mrs Rose?

"It is your choice," I tell Megan now. "You chose this life. But I can change…"

Megan frowns at a sun that has become smudged with blue.

"Will it hurt?"

"I shall be with you."

She smiles suddenly. "Show me the horses."

The foal that comes forward is steady on its feet, a perfect horse, not yet full-grown.

"See?" says Megan.

"But you don't have to–" I begin, and then Sahasrael's quiet presence fills the room.

"Let it be, Chandra," she says. "She has chosen her life."

•

Ben is really just following her, like a piece of animated luggage, a suitcase on legs, answering when she speaks, nodding, agreeing, laughing, yes, no, let's, and all the while his heart is hammering at him with nerves and disbelief.

Today, she came past his desk to collect him, and he – just went with her.

He can feel everything unravelling behind him, all his decisions, all his commitments, and all for…

She leads him down the familiar street and then past the shops and the café and the sandwich outlets, and then they are in the tiny metal lift going up. Alone together, but neither of them speaks, they don't look at each other.

The flat is a cramped yellow corridor and then an open-plan space with a sofa and a low table and a television and a kitchen across a bar on the right. Through the floor-to-ceiling window Ben recognises London: trees, the river. They are high up.

"Do you want to set yourself up, then?" She drops her shoulder-bag on the table and goes through into the kitchen.

"Oh. Yeah. Sure."

Ben fumbles his bag, confused by dismay, or relief, that even now, he might have misread what they are doing here.

She comes back into the room with two clear brown drinks in flat-bottomed glasses, one in each hand, and stands in front of him while he frees a hand.

Then they are drinking whisky together.

"Cheers," she says, and her eyes over the rim of the glass are inspecting the room.

As though ... something's missing? Something might be out of place? Some clue left in the open?

Stupid. She's deciding where to pose.

"How about over there?" he says, gesturing at the sofa.

"This is really good of you," she says, and for a second he has the sense that she is teasing him.

She puts her hand on his chest and looks up into his eyes from directly below.

"It's a pleasure," he says, still confused, still hoping, dreading, hoping that they are here for him to draw a portrait of her.

She goes straight past him, scooping up her bag on the way, as though her attention has suddenly been caught by the far side of the room.

"How about the bedroom?" she says, pushing open a door he has seen but not yet acknowledged. "Let's be comfortable," she calls back.

It is another small, functional room with a large window. Rectangular bed, kidney-shaped dressing table with scale-model chair, bathroom through another door.

She sits down hard on the wide bed and plumps the two pillows into the middle. "Yeah. This is it." She bounces once and looks up at him. "If you get that little chair and put it here, and if I lie down like this." She swings her legs up and round onto the bed.

So now Ben is sitting by the head of the bed with his sketchbook on his knees and she is lying on her back on the pillows with one hand behind her head.

"Yeah? You think?"

But when Ben reaches down for his pencils she scrambles up again. "No, wait." She bounces off the bed and goes across the room to where her shoulder-bag has landed on the floor. "This is how I want it," she says over her shoulder, her back to him, and pulls her teeshirt off over her head.

"Sure," said Ben. No bra, long curve of her back, curve of her breast. She is pulling on a frilly, red – it is a nightdress, Ben understands, as she smooths it down over her jeans.

"Sorry," she says, giving him a conspiratorial smirk as she scrambles back onto the bed.

"Of course," says Ben, sounding really quite composed, considering.

So now she is lying on her back on the pillows with one hand behind her head and her nipples clearly visible through– "Oh wait." She gives him a mock-beseeching look. "It doesn't feel right. Ben, can you bear it if I–" And then her hips are up and she is pushing down her jeans – and a thong comes too, Ben notices – and then she is on her back again, stretching, raising one knee.

Ben, his sketch pad crammed into his lap, hovers in a moment of decision.

He can't. Mustn't.

He reaches out his hand and twitches down the edge of the nightdress over her breasts, just slightly, so that it covers the nipples and no more.

Their eyes meet.

It's Chandler's turn to come to the blue door today, and Hannah exchanges a quick smile with Sarah as he marches towards them up the corridor. Then she's inside, crouching down to pick up Megan, and Mrs Barnaby is standing beside her as she straightens again.

"We had such a happy day today, didn't we?" Mrs Barnaby is saying, looking to Megan for agreement. "Such a lovely picture."

It's on the wall, and Hannah has time to admire it. The usual blobby trees with fat trunks plus a white-mixed-with-other-colours thing in the foreground that could be a shopping trolley but is probably an animal.

"It's beautiful, darling," says Hannah, and Megan lays her head on her shoulder.

•

"Wait! Wait!"

So now she is naked and he is naked and they are hot together on the bed, kissing, all awareness in their mouths and hands. Ben moves forward, his hand between her legs, but now she pushes him back.

"Wait, will you?" He hears but brushes aside the faint irritation in her voice. He can't be deterred now. But he wills himself to let her climb herself over him and lies back as she steps down from the bed. She fishes a small bag out of her large bag and darts out of the room, naked. "Back in a sec."

Ben raises himself on his elbows and looks down at his erection. He daren't touch it. Another second and he might just have pushed her down and gone ahead anyway. Why the fuck did she have to wait until now, the stupid woman? Ben feels savage for a moment. Why the fuck now?

She's still gone. Ben watches his erection begin to subside. What the fuck does she think is happening here? Half time? The intermission? He laughs to himself. Might as well sell ice creams.

That's when he rolls onto his side, and, obeying no particular impulse, pulls open the drawer of the bedside table.

And sees the photograph frame. Double-sided, face-up. A colour picture of a woman and a black-and-white picture of a boy.

Just like–

This is Anthony's flat.

And she has the key because–

Ben is out of bed pulling on his pants, trousers, ripping his shirt.

I must have been fucking crazy. Hannah. Fuck. Oh my God, Hannah, no.

Megan.

She comes out of the bathroom, naked, bag in her hand, to find him standing in most of his suit, shoes shovelled onto his feet, trying to tie his tie with shaking hands.

For a split second she thinks it's a joke, or something kinky: she's perplexed; she can't see the game.

But then her face goes brick-coloured and hard. "Fuck you!"

"I'm sorry–" Ben begins, but she interrupts him.

"Fuck you! Fuck off!"

"I'm sorry, I can't–"

He's still conscious enough to grab his bag and look around for anything he's left, but she's still shouting at him as he opens the door and jumps out into the corridor.

·

This is not how they do things, but it's how they're going to do this thing.

Greg turns the key and the truck rattles into life.

"You're sure?" says the director, standing below the open window of the cab.

"The war's over," calls Maya from the passenger seat, as though that is an answer.

Greg, looking down from the driver's seat, meets John Boy's eye. John Boy and the director are standing together looking up at him.

"We'll give you twenty-four hours," says John Boy, "and then we're coming after you."

Greg cocks a finger at him. "I'll call you," he says, and the two men stand back to watch the truck roll forward onto the southbound road.

The war's over. It's safe. There's a camp to rebuild.

The first convoy is scheduled to start the drive south from Qasir to the camp tomorrow morning. When that arrives, within a few hours, the camp will be back in business. Smaller-scale than before, and oriented towards its original objective of providing medical services to local communities rather than aiding refugees. The war's over. Back to normal.

Greg Doyle and Maya Brennan don't actually need to take a truck and check the route in advance.

But he'll be running the new camp and she'll be in charge of its medical provision, and that's what they've decided to do.

•

Ben doesn't go back to the office. He walks. He has his bag with him, and that's all he needs from there. After tearing out and shredding the page on which he would have drawn the portrait, he – no, he doesn't tuck the rest of the big pad under his arm. He folds the whole thing in half, forcing it, and then, when it still won't fit into a rubbish bin, he stands in the street tearing pieces off it until it is all gone into the bin.

So all he has is the bag over his shoulder, containing the innocent art supplies.

He walks. He thinks. He imagines. He visits a public lavatory because his insides are totally fucked, but feels no better afterwards. In his mind the girl is shouting, "Fuck off!" and Hannah's eyes are filling with tears. "Why, Ben?" she is asking, not challenging him, not angry, just so very hurt, and Megan is saying, "What's wrong, Mummy?" She is beginning to cry too.

At some point in the afternoon, Ben thinks about ringing the office and resigning. He can never go back there. He imagines the girl telling Anthony.

He can't ring Anthony now. Ben thinks of the picture frame in the drawer.

Tomorrow.

"Why, Ben? Don't you find me attractive any more?"

Oh my sweetest love.

Ben does something that until this moment of absolute need, he would never have imagined he could do. He walks into a city gym and asks about temporary membership. Immediate temporary membership. How long do you want? Ben, who had been about to say, "One hour," hesitates. "Do you do trial memberships?" he asks. And it's his lucky day. Looking back on this moment, he'll be surprised at his luck. But in the moment, he pays by credit card for a month's trial membership, with the payment taken from his card after the first week if he doesn't cancel. After the first week. Ben thinks: I should have paid in cash. I've got a week to cancel it before it shows up on the card bill.

In the gym, Ben buys a towel from the shop and takes a shower. He stays in the water for half an hour, then he spends another half an hour drying himself and putting on the same dirty clothes before walking to the station.

"Let me understand this. You were in my flat with Ben Rose. He took you there and he raped you. This lunch hour. Today."

Shannah is sitting across from Anthony in his office. She came storming up the aisle between the cubicles, slammed the door hard enough to get everybody's attention, and then stood over him, hands on hips. "Your boy just raped me, Anthony! What are you going to do about it?"

In the face of her anger, Anthony can feel himself slowing down. This isn't right. She's not – what? Her clothes haven't been – what?

Anthony realises that he would be crucified if he objected that she couldn't have been raped because her clothes hadn't been torn.

Suddenly, he is glad of the witnesses through the glass in the main office. He is glad of the desk between them.

Maybe he's wrong.

But he isn't. Suddenly, he knows it.

He repeats her words. "My boy just raped you. You mean Ben Rose?"

"Yes. Your golden boy. The one you talk about. The artist."

"You went with him to my flat."

"Yes, and he–"

"Did you take him to the flat, or did you go with him?"

There's nothing in his voice, just the straight question, but she hesitates.

"He took me. He said he wanted to draw me. Then he wanted me to take my clothes off. He–"

"Ben doesn't know I've got a flat."

"He must do. He took me there. How can you be sure he doesn't know?"

"You're the only one who's got a key."

They look at each other.

The key had been a mistake. The flat had been a mistake.

Anthony's mind is suddenly clear. He comes forward to the desk, clasping his hands. He speaks gently. He does like her, and whatever the truth of this, she is genuinely upset.

"What I should do now is call personnel," he says. "I should have done that the moment you came in. But–" he raises his hand. "–they might want to bring in the police, and even if they didn't, this would become official. It would be known."

He adds, "If the police got involved, we'd have to make statements. There would have to be–" their eyes meet; he has no idea whether this is true, but he knows, he just knows "–a physical examination."

There is a minute change in the air between them that tells him he has guessed correctly. No physical evidence would be found.

"Or, if he ever comes back–" Anthony has been watching through the glass partition for Ben "–I could just fire him for you."

•

Ben arrives home convinced that Anthony has given Shannah his home number and she has called. And made it absolutely clear that it was all his fault. That can't have happened, Ben knows. But at the same time, he can't be sure.

He opens the door gently, as if they were all asleep upstairs. He closes it very carefully behind him, and as he turns, Hannah steps into the hallway in front of him.

"Hello," she says.

He speaks without thinking. "Don't go," he says.

She laughs. "I'm not going anywhere." She holds up Megan's discarded coat that she is about to return to its peg. "This is a nice surprise. What happened? You got off early?"

Ben understands that home has not changed. She doesn't know. This is the world as it was before he wrecked it.

"Oh, bad day," he says, lowering his eyes. "I just felt a bit out of it. Couldn't work, so came home."

"How do you feel now?"

But Hannah does not respond to Ben's illnesses in the way she does to Megan's. When he tells her he's fine, she nods and gets on with what she was doing, which now involves walking away from him into the house.

I have changed, thinks Ben, standing left-behind in the hallway, feeling himself to be an alien, a spy from some parallel world of betrayal and guilt. I am the shell of her husband, but I have changed utterly inside. This is the world I have lost.

Later, in a quiet, exhausted moment, Ben will reflect on this moment of misery. He will see the smallness of all their disappointments with each other over the years, and he will quietly, in the stillness of his mind, in a way that he will never adequately be able to express to her, with no expectation of her, nothing for himself, commit.

He will make a clear, hard decision. This is his life. This one. Its benefits outweigh–

He will never tell Hannah what he did. He will never rid himself entirely of guilt. But he will come to recognise how precious she is to him, how precious is his clear conscience to him, as the stain fades; he will see how deeply he betrayed the whole of his life, how close he came to disaster.

"He is ready enough, Chandrael. Let it come."

As she walks away from him, Ben follows Hannah through the house and into the kitchen.

"So," she says, crossing to the counter and turning to face him. "You want tea? Coffee?"

He looks at her. All of a sudden, he sees that she too has something on her mind.

"What's up?" he says, changing gear, feeling dread.

She can't know about today; no – seeing her face – she doesn't know.

But he can see that she is building up to telling him something. He steps forward and takes – no, stopping himself – just touches her arm.

"So what is it?" he says softly.

She smiles at her own nervousness and relaxes.

"I think it's time for another one," she says.

His mind goes blank.

"A baby," she adds, although they both know he understood.

"Well okay," he says. Then corrects himself: "Well, okay," he repeats, more positive this time, like he's waking up to the idea and likes it.

But she doesn't respond. She doesn't look up.

He thinks: there's something else.

She thinks: I still haven't told him.

Not about the pregnancy-testing kit she bought this afternoon.

Nor that she thinks she might be…

He thinks: is she–

"Daddy, Daddy!" Megan runs into the kitchen and instinctively he drops into a crouch and opens his arms. "Daddy!" she hugs him tightly, face buried in his shoulder.

"Hey," he says, half-laughing, putting out a hand to regain his balance. "What brought this on?"

Hannah thinks: Ben just naturally goes down to her level. He's a natural father.

I still haven't told him about the tests at the hospital, either.

The phone rings.

234

Hannah fails to notice the look that crosses Ben's face.

She picks up the phone and her voice is warm as she says, "Hello?"

"Mrs Rose? Hannah?"

"Yes?"

Ben looks up. He hears the sudden anxiety in her voice.

"It's Tom Murison. Dr Murison."

He's on a mobile.

Something catches in Hannah's throat as she says, "Yes, doctor."

"Hannah, I've had a call from the hospital. They've got the results through. They were wondering–" His voice breaks off for a second and then he tries again. But in the tone of his voice, he's told her. "They were wondering if you'd be free to go in to discuss them." Again, she hears a break in his voice, and then he says, soberly, as though he has regained control, "Now."

"Doctor, what–"

"I don't have the results myself. They rang me first. It's a–" she can sense him shaking his head at the insignificance of the detail he is giving her "–a formality. A thing, you know? I'm on the way to the hospital now. I'll meet you there."

"Doctor," says Hannah, although she has no idea what she is going to say next.

"There'll be a nurse to look after Megan, a crèche, I don't imagine at this short notice–"

"My husband is here. He can–" With her free hand she has pulled her bag towards her and now she is rifling it for car keys. The contents spill out onto the worktop. The unopened box of the testing kit is knocked onto the floor.

"That's very good news. Bring your husband with you."

Whether Dr Murison ends the call then, or they are cut off, she never knows. She drops the phone onto the worktop. "Fuck." She can't find the fucking car keys. She throws her tablet aside, her old

Filofax. "Fuck this bloody bag." She upends it on the worktop.

Ben, who has watched his wife's face drain from its natural paleness to the colour of bone, has the presence of mind to whisper to Megan, "Go see what's on TV. I need to talk to Mummy. Quickly, darling."

Megan recedes, her eyes wide.

Then he stands up and grips his wife by the arm.

"Tell me."

Their eyes meet.

"I took her to the hospital. Tests. They want us to go in and discuss the results. He said now. Now. Both of us."

Everything else falls away.

"What about Megan?"

"Bring her with us." Ben can see that Hannah is about to break down. "That was Dr Murison. He's going to meet us there. Do you understand?" Her eyes are wide open and he can see right down into her fear. "He's going to meet–"

"Got it," he says, gripping her by the upper arms. "I absolutely have got it."

He is suddenly very focused. "We'll go in my car."

Crazy thing to say. They only have one car.

"Get Megan ready. Books and toys."

He snatches up the car keys.

"But–"

He doesn't give her time to protest. "I'll be back in a second."

He runs, actually runs, out of the kitchen. He grabs his briefcase and then he is running up the stairs. He empties his briefcase out on the landing – he doesn't want Hannah to see him with a suitcase and he doesn't want her to have to do this – and then he is in Megan's room, picking up night things, underwear, whatever else he can fit into the briefcase. In the bathroom he shoves his daughter's toothbrush and the tube of toothpaste into his trouser pocket.

236

His head is as clear as it was that night Megan was born, when Hannah woke him to say that her waters had broken.

On the stairs back down, he stops for a second: what about Hannah's night things?

No – he can sort that out later.

Hannah is already outside. She is buckling Megan into the car seat.

He loves her.

Loves both of them.

She doesn't see the briefcase that he throws into the boot, doesn't ask as he straightens up and says, "I'll drive. Come on, get in."

And then they are in the car and he is driving them to the hospital. In the back, Megan is talking. He can't quite make it out but apparently some friend of hers called Chandler is coming to play or came to play or something like that, and they're going riding.

"That's lovely, darling," he says.

Hannah is a big chunk of silence carved out of the air beside him. Her face is turned away, but when he reaches across to hold her hand, she suddenly holds him tightly. He realises she is crying and trying to hide it.

He holds her hand, and drives.

The Last "Should"

I have one task yet to complete. The children are gathered and waiting.

I am the young man with the rucksack once more, walking down a long, empty hospital corridor, a visitor here, an outsider. There are framed children's drawings on the wall to my left, group photographs of surgical and medical and administrative teams to my right. A sign on a closed door reads Bereavement Counselling and gives times of opening. Rectangular lights pass above my head. The air in this corridor traps sound.

A group of four young men in pale scrub suits approaches me; they are intent on whatever it is that has amused them. As they pass me, one bumps my arm. He swings round as he walks, "Hey, man, sorry," and raises his hand as if for a high-five, and then moves on.

The sensations of the physical world flow through me, so close now.

I come to a conjunction of three corridors, a wide space where people meet. There is a reception desk, ranks of chairs, a rack of magazines and hospital literature. Along the side of one corridor there are glass doors that give access to the outside air. Recessed into the side of another corridor is a deep rectangular space that has been populated with high tables and stools. This is a coffee shop, a brief rest-stop for visitors and hospital staff. Across a corner there is a counter, glass-topped, showing wrapped buns and brownies, and behind the counter, there is a coffee machine.

I stand in the short queue. The young woman behind the counter is no longer new to this job, although she is still happy with the novelty-feeling of generosity she gets from selling comfort foods and coffee, hot chocolate and tea, and she will not stay for much longer. This morning, she applied for the job that she correctly believes will determine her future. She's sure she'll get it, but when she thinks about it, she doubts herself. She trained and has worked as a teacher, but become disillusioned with teaching in this country, and the job is at an international school in Europe, high among mountains.

My turn. She smiles at me. "What would you like?"

In her mind, she is playing a game: she guesses that I will ask for double espresso, splash of hot milk, nothing to eat. She makes her guesses detailed, so that if she is right, she is entitled to the chocolate brownie she awards herself as a prize. She never eats it, goes outside for her break and just breathes the air, but she likes to know that she could.

"Could I go for a double espresso, splash of hot milk, nothing else?"

Our eyes meet and it seems to her that she recognises me as a regular. "How's it going today?" she asks as she turns to the coffee machine.

"Oh, it's a good day," I say. "You?"

"Oh," she shrugs, and the gesture takes in the coffee machine, the counter, the hospital. "Living the dream, right?"

As I take my coffee, my hand touches hers. As I turn away, I say something to her that she does not quite hear.

"Excuse me?"

But I have turned away and the queue is too long for her to call me back.

Did I really say, "You're happier than that"?

No matter. She smiles for her next customer, and as she does so, something clicks in her mind; this time, she really smiles.

I carry my coffee across the space to the table in the other corner, away from the counter, away from the occupied tables. One of the two stools at the table is free.

On the other stool sits Richard Hailey.

In the eyes of the customers who have noticed him, he is a thin, black-haired man, solitary, not to be approached. The young woman at the counter knows who he is, but in this space he is off duty and she gives him privacy. Today he has not acknowledged her. There is a circle of emptiness around him like the dust around something that has fallen hard to the ground.

Another child has died.

I place my coffee on his table and sit down on the stool opposite him. He is aware of me but he does not look up.

His open-necked white shirt is not fresh and his black suit is crumpled. He has tried to sleep in these clothes.

He becomes aware that I am watching him. At last, he looks up at me. "Yes?" he says.

I meet his gaze.

"Hello, Richard," I say.

With that he sits back and says, "Do I know you?"

"I think you do."

He shifts in his chair. "I don't think so," he begins to say, and then he stops.

"You're a hard man to reach."

He looks at my shoulders, my shirt, the straps of my rucksack, my hands and forearms, all the physical details, not at my face. He sees that I am a young man. He sees that I am wearing a blue checked shirt, open at the neck, the collar frayed, sleeves rolled back at the cuff. I am wearing a rucksack, for goodness' sake. I might be a hiker, or a tourist, or a student. Heck, I am younger than he is, he thinks, relieved.

I smile at this. He smiles too.

"Come on," he says, indulgent now that he has dismissed me. "Stop messing me around. I'm busy here."

"Do you remember that night I brought two children to your office?"

My voice sounds so real, so ordinary to his ears.

"And when you were asleep? Do you remember?"

I look into his eyes and he looks into mine.

"Richard, you asked Father Bernardi for a sign."

I reach forward, and take his hand.

He does not see the children enter the café. They stand in the doorway, a tight-knit group, holding each other's hands for courage, looking around for us. For Richard Hailey, they have returned as he knew them in life, although they remain unseen in the room. They are shone through with light. They are all here.

Jamie Tout sees us and points. The children wave to us, although Richard has still not seen them yet. I have hold of both of his hands now.

The children come running across the room, their chatter and laughter unheard to everybody else, racing between the tables, and they flock around Richard, pulling at him, calling up for his attention, calling out stories of Heaven, calling his name, tugging at his sleeves, a waist-high tide of children whom he had thought lost.

"Won't you let them thank you?"

I release Richard's hands as he understands what he is seeing. "Oh!" His face opens and then he is off the chair and crouching, tears filling his eyes. "Oh my boy," he says, putting his arm around the shoulders of a small boy who is telling him excitedly that there are aeroplanes in Heaven, and cars. He looks up at me and then down again as a girl puts her arms around his head and kisses him on the cheek, nearly knocking him off balance.

I raise my hands and spread my wings, and in the café, nobody glances at the man in the black suit who seems to have crouched down to retrieve something from the floor.

Only a baby, propped up in a pram, laughs and claps her hands at something her parents do not see.

It is done.

I leave Father Richard Hailey in the care of the children.

•

At the hospital, waiting at the main reception desk, Hannah and Ben and Megan are met by Dr Murison. He will guide them.

"This place is a maze if you're not used to it. There is a logic, but you need to study the floor plan to understand it."

Ben says something about unravelling a ball of wool and Dr Murison says, "Yes, we find people who have been here for days," and then they have run out of things to say to each other.

Hannah feels that she is having to half-run to keep up. It is as if the two men are hurrying to get away from her.

Ben is focused tightly on getting them to their destination. He doesn't want to think, and although he is not conscious of doing it, Hannah is right, he is running away from hearing what she might say. If he takes the lid off his mind, he fears that a huge bubble of emotion will force itself up from the depths, displacing everything on the way to the surface, and then, he will lose control utterly.

Tom Murison now knows the diagnosis that they are about to hear. He is afraid for them and for his own competence.

Watching Megan run ahead of them, her hand up as if she is holding an invisible balloon, Dr Murison thinks: what if I had not bothered with the tests?

The card they were given directs them to room TC36. This turns out to be an empty waiting room with a hatch in the wall. Dr Murison waves them to a line of chairs and they stand irresolute as he goes to the hatch and calls out, "Hello?"

Then there is a woman in a blue uniform who is expecting them. She emerges from a door next to the hatch in the wall, and her presence washes over them. Hannah and Ben start to follow her as she takes Megan to a corner full of old-looking toys.

Megan looks up and gives her mother a small wave that Hannah will remember for the rest of her life. It is an odd wave, as if Megan already understands that she must wait for them here.

Then there is a man in an open-fronted white coat, old-style, waiting for them outside another open door. Tom Murison is standing back to let them go ahead of him and for a moment their arrival in the room is just like any arrival in any room.

Then they are arranging chairs so that Hannah sits in the middle with the man in the white coat facing her across the desk, upon which he has arranged papers.

His name is Mr Trenchard and he begins to tell her that he is a consultant in childhood – but his words abruptly cease to have meaning. Hannah watches him speak, aware that he is describing tests and results, aware that these numbers and these counts and this science have come together to threaten – but it is only in the summary, when she hears the word "aggressive" followed by "rapidly" and then "hope", that Hannah makes contact with what she is being told.

244

"Are you trying to tell me my daughter is dying?" she interrupts.

It is as if the sudden question, spoken aloud, heard for the first time even by Hannah, becomes its own answer.

For the first time, Mr Trenchard looks up, and for the first time, she meets his fugitive grey eyes.

The shock delivers itself all at once. Hannah's eyes cram shut and she convulses forward into herself, keening a low sound of pain.

Mr Trenchard looks at Dr Murison and the look that passes between them says: that didn't go well.

Ben is still staring at the two doctors.

"So what's... So she's..." he says.

Then he gets it. He clutches Hannah to him urgently and awkwardly across the two chairs. The two of them fix together into a tight stillness.

Mr Trenchard gazes down at his papers. Dr Murison's hand wavers in the air, unable to find a landing place on the combination of Hannah and Ben.

Then Mr Trenchard is speaking again.

Megan can be admitted tonight for a course of treatment that could start tomorrow morning, unless they want time to discuss...?

Suddenly Hannah is electric with the need to be with her daughter. The room disrupts itself as Hannah rises from her chair and steps past Tom Murison's clumsy attempt to get out of her way and snatches at the door. She has left the room before the doctor's chair, as Tom Murison half-stands, hits the grit-coloured carpet tiles.

Then Ben, following her, slows his pace as he watches Megan rise from her toys and open her arms to her mother, as though the situation is reversed and the daughter comforts the mother.

Hannah goes down onto her knees and the world slows down around the two of them, mother and daughter, as they hold each other in their own shut silence. No words pass between them in this moment, but when Hannah rises to her feet, both mother and daughter wear the same intent expression, as if one hard emotion that they have shared lingers in their separate minds.

Then the night unfolds itself into their lives.

They are taken to find the ward and the bed made ready behind its curtains.

They meet the kind nurse who doesn't need to be told, whose welcome seems so focused on Megan until she puts a spontaneous hand on Ben's arm as his face, at last, begins to crack.

They meet the other nurse on the shift.

And the Childcare Support Assistant.

And the trainee.

They hear the ward and glimpse equipment that one day they know they might need. Most of the children are asleep, but there is one tired mother holding a waking child's hand. There are other parents too, they realise, sitting silent in the gloom. There are no set visiting hours here, they are told. Ben and Hannah try not to look at the other children, the drips on their stands, the transparent tubes secured to faces.

This armchair is comfortable and there are blankets and pillows and more if you want them; I'll show you where.

Hannah realises that there is no bed here for her, nor ever will be. But she draws a comfort from this: the ward is in the rumpled care of nurses, kind nurses, and support assistants, not doctors like – she has forgotten the grey man's name.

Hannah looks with an affection born of dependency upon the Childcare Support Assistant, who tells her, again, patiently, that her name is Marie-Claude.

"Might go home tomorrow," Marie-Claude is telling Megan, who is excited with the adventure of her bed in a tent of curtains and having Mummy sleeping in the chair beside her.

246

"Where will you be, Daddy?" Megan asks, and for a moment Ben doesn't know.

"You can stay here," says the Childcare Support Assistant softly, and Ben hears two things in her voice: first, that he can stay here; secondly, that the role of the second parent is to go home.

We need to work out a shift system. One of us here at all times, the other looking after everything else. Both of us here for the treatment.

"I'll come back in the morning and hear how you got on in the night," he tells Megan. "You and Mummy stay here, and I'll go and look after our house."

Then it's teamwork. Hannah is settling Megan down – it's only nine, he's surprised to discover, although the whole ward seems to have been asleep for hours – and he is up at the nurse's station finding out that Megan has a treatment already scheduled for 14:00 tomorrow, after which they're free to go home, although Megan will certainly feel tired and might feel queasy and they can certainly stay, and then the second treatment in the sequence is scheduled ... Ben doesn't understand what he finds comforting in this sequence of dates, and it is only much later, days later, that he works it out: these are the dates, stretching out into the future, on which the hospital assumes that Megan will be alive.

Looking for a toothbrush for Hannah under white strip-lights at an all-night franchise in the hospital's main reception area, Ben realises that Dr Murison left them soon after they arrived at the ward. Now, thinking back, he can remember Dr Murison giving him a card – here it is now, in his pocket, and one for Hannah – with all his numbers. Did I say goodbye?

He catches the eye of a tall, healthy-looking woman in a dressing gown who is browsing the magazine rack, and that reminds him of something else.

He pays for his small bag of groceries – two bananas, apple, sweets for Megan if the nil-by-mouth thing doesn't kick in until morning, bottled water, toothbrush for Hannah, toothpaste because he can't remember whether he packed it, new caterpillar toothbrush for Megan, magazine, comic, cuddly blue pony with big eyes – and walks out to the hospital car park.

The sky is clear, black, with stars. Ben reaches into his pocket with his free hand and finds his mobile. Without thinking, he thumbs in the number of the gym he visited this afternoon. It does not, and will not ever, occur to him that he does not know the number he has just entered into his phone.

I stand beside him, silent in the darkness, as he tells the gym's voicemail that he has decided to cancel the trial membership he took out this afternoon.

Ben switches off his mobile again and stands for a moment looking at a row of empty parking spaces. He walks to the pay machine and finds out what it will cost him to park here tomorrow.

Then he returns to his family.

•

Hannah Rose tries to pray. It is 03.57 by the clock she can see through the gap in the curtains. Megan is deeply asleep. Hannah has risked leaving her daughter twice now, once necessarily to use the bathroom and wash and clean her teeth, and once because the Childcare Support Assistant offered her tea and Hannah felt she should go and talk to the woman while she was making it.

That was the last "should" in Hannah's life. Megan was awake when Hannah returned. The trainee was there, looking up and smiling and getting up from her place on the edge of the bed, but Hannah can't bear the thought of Megan waking up alone again in the night and not knowing where she is.

248

Hannah feels that she will never leave this bedside again.

She sits in the armchair, comfortable except that the blankets have made her sweaty under her jeans while her top half is cold, and her head feels that if these horrible, scrambly thoughts ever stop, they'll only be making room for the nasty, caffeiney headache that is just waiting in the background.

She must have dozed, and once or twice she has caught herself in a reverie of forgetting, but now Hannah looks out through her eyes with the desolate clarity of exhaustion.

Hannah closes her eyes and hears herself beginning her prayer with words she last heard at her own wedding. "...please let my baby be all right," she continues, switching from the familiar words as she engages with what she is saying. "Please let my baby be all right." The tears run down warm onto her cheeks. "Our Father, let her be well again, I don't want her to die. Please don't let my baby die."

A hand touches her knee. Startled, Hannah opens her eyes. There is a man kneeling in front of her. He is young, wearing a black suit and an open-necked shirt. Immediately, Hannah panics. "I'm so sorry, I–" Her hands are scrabbling for a hankie to wipe her eyes, pulling the blanket around her shoulders, trying to do ... something.

But there is nothing she can do and she gives up trying. Hannah is too exhausted for anything to form properly in her mind, even embarrassment. She sits limp in the chair, blinking at the man through wet eyes.

There is an expression on his face that is not exactly a smile and nor is it exactly sadness but it is comforting and Hannah is comforted. The silent moment between them extends into measurable time and he says softly, "Would you like me to pray with you?"

"Yes," says Hannah, her voice as soft as a child's.

For a long while he says no words and they sit together in the gentle, breathing silence, holding their hands and together. And then

when the moment arrives that they are both ready, Richard Hailey
begins to speak, softly, and as Hannah listens to the rhythm of his
words, the comfort of sleep spreads in her and she is transported away
into rest.

Against The Hours

In the soft reaches of Heaven there are many countries and many cities, many gardens and forests and many wild spaces. There are trees and there are harmonies, and in the distances always there are high gold places filled with light and angels. In Heaven there are light skies and many realities under the truth. We are all of us inside Heaven and some of us rise to find it within ourselves. Our hearts tell us of Heaven while our minds still search.

In the darkened ward, Richard Hailey wakes from his vivid dream to see that the mother is asleep. Gently, he releases her hands. She does not stir as he reaches forward to raise the blanket around her. He gets to his feet and stands for a moment looking down at the little girl. She is asleep too.

Richard Hailey touches the tip of his fingers to his lips and reaches forward to transfer the kiss to the little girl's forehead. She stirs slightly and he stands motionless with his hand extended over her head until she settles again.

He steps back from the bed and turns to leave. The trainee is standing outside the tent's curtains, watching him. She holds out the mug of tea in her hands and he takes it from her.

"Thank you," he says softly.

The tea has had time to cool, but it is the expression in her eyes that tells him how long she has watched him.

•

Morning. The phone rings. Anthony picks up the phone. He is alone in his office. There is nothing on the desk in front of him. No distractions. Two chairs facing him. It's all set up. But Ben Rose hasn't showed up yet, and Anthony is disconcerted by this. He had intended to call Ben straight into his office first thing with the HR guy and get it done. Redundancy, not dismissal. Quick and no argument. But now the whole morning is shot to pieces. Anthony can't start anything until he's dealt with Ben.

The human-resources goon is also standing by the phone in his own office, waiting to come when Anthony calls. But he probably doesn't have anything else to do, the creep. He exists because policy says meetings like this one need a trained witness and a formal record. Anthony isn't happy with it, but that's the way the rules say it is.

"Anthony, it's Ben."

"Where are you?" says Anthony automatically.

"I'm at home. Look, Anthony, I'm not going to make it in today."

Anthony's immediate reaction is to think: good move, kid.

But Ben is still talking.

"I'll be in tomorrow, but look, Anthony, I've been thinking and I want to talk to you. I need time off certainly, but I think I'm going to have to leave the company."

"You think – wait a minute, you need time off?"

252

"We had to go to the hospital last night. My daughter's – we've had a shock – You know we've got a daughter, four, Megan?"

"Yes," says Anthony. But what he's really heard is Ben's tone of voice. Anthony's hand goes to the drawer and brings out the double picture frame. It lies open on the desk in front of him, the two small faces, the colour face of his wife and the black-and-white face of his son.

"Oh, Ben," says Anthony, leaning forward over the desk, enclosing himself around the phone call as he listens to the young man's voice telling him of last night's catastrophe.

"Forget about us," Anthony says, cutting across Ben's assurance that he will come in tomorrow. "I'll set up a compassionate leave of absence. You're entitled to it, it's in your contract–" Anthony doesn't say why he has been reading Ben's contract "–and the good news is, it's indefinite. I'll send you – no, listen – I'll send you my home numbers if there is anything I can do to help, but right now I'll handle everything this end. Don't make any big decisions and just stay with your family." Anthony adds, without meaning to, "You'll regret it if you don't."

He can feel Ben's surprise at this speech.

"Good luck, boy," Anthony says softly.

When he puts down the phone, he is surprised to find that his heart is beating hard in his chest. He sits in silence for a moment before closing the picture frame and returning it to the drawer.

He picks up the phone to tell the HR guy to go fuck himself, and when his wife answers, realises that he has speed-dialled his own home number instead.

"Darling," he says, and they can both hear the pain in his voice, the pain of old loss.

"Why don't you come home?" she says.

And Anthony, holding the phone to his ear, realises that he is now, in the middle of his morning, going to go home.

Both Hannah and Megan were asleep when Ben arrived, first thing, with a full suitcase for Hannah. He left a message with the new nurse on duty before going out to explore the hospital and then going off again to drink coffee because they were both still asleep when he got back.

Then he went outside to call Anthony on his mobile from the car park.

The call ends. Ben stares at the lightening sky.

"Stay with your family," Anthony had said.

"Good luck, boy," Anthony had said.

Ben is standing in the same place as he stood last night, which is not far from where his car is now parked. He thinks: if we get through this, I will find something worthwhile to do.

He thinks of the man he met on the train. Ken McCloud's business card is still in his wallet. Ben rubs it between his fingers and thinks: as soon as we get through this, I'll call him.

Ben walks back into the hospital.

He will make it right.

But he can't deal with that now.

At the nurse's suggestion, he brings Hannah a mug of tea and finds her waking, just ready to receive it. She opens her eyes and at first seems to be looking round for somebody else. Then she wakes up, taking the mug of tea from him and holding it in both hands to blow on it as he crouches awkwardly in front of her.

"I slept so well," she says softly. Megan is still asleep.

He slept well, too. He is full of energy. He tells her about the ward's shower room, which actually they did see last night, and about the shop and the small enclosed garden with the bench. "Best fresh air's in the car park, though. It's windier."

She lets him talk for a while as she drinks her tea, and then asks, "What about the office?"

"I called them. It's fine. I've got the day off and if I need longer." He hesitates. "I'll go in tomorrow when we're more sorted and talk to Anthony."

"Ben, you can't just not go to work," she says.

That is a conversation they are not going to have now. Megan suddenly rolls over and says, "Hello Daddy."

Then it's Hannah and Ben against the hours. Megan is hungry and restless and the ward isn't geared to such a lively child. But they get through it. Hannah manages to grab a shower and a sandwich and Ben has brought her a change of clothes. He disappears for half an hour and comes back with a handheld electronic device preloaded with games. It's pink, and Megan finds a game with dogs in it. Hannah has always banned such things from the house, but in the circumstances, she nods, accepting the need.

Then Ben starts drawing. Reluctantly at first, on whatever paper he can find. But when Hannah comes back from the shop with a proper sketchpad and some pastels, he's sitting up against the pillows with Megan beside him, saying, "And then Sleepy gets up on Pugh's back, but he's so sleepy he's going to fall off, see, and then Horsely..." Ben glances up, seeing her, and goes back to his drawing.

They are visited, during the morning, and they are briefed on what is scheduled to happen. There is a course of treatment booked, so they're in the system, but it is likely that it will end up shorter, or longer, or just different, as Megan's needs become clearer. Once, Hannah begins to ask Ben, as he reports back on another step-away-from-the-bed conversation with a new face, "Did he say anything about how quickly she's going to..."

But she falters, and as Megan calls, "Come on, Mummy!" they exchange a look that acknowledges how much cannot be said as well as everything that can be said, and they return to their daughter.

•

"So you're not going to fire him."

"He's not coming back."

"But you're not going to fire him."

"I can't. He's gone already."

She doesn't like that. But she doesn't say anything.

Anthony adds, "His baby's really sick. He found out last night."

"That's convenient."

Anthony raises his eyes and looks at her.

A minute passes.

Then she makes a jerky, convulsive movement of her hand and the key lands on the desk in front of him.

"Fuck you too, Anthony," she says.

He finds out later that after she left his office, she went straight to her desk and picked up her bag. When somebody spoke to her, she did not reply. She punched through the double doors, leaving them to swing behind her, and then downstairs she is reported to have gone straight out past reception and into the street.

HR will send her two letters, neither of which is answered, and the balance of her salary is paid into her bank account. Anthony will write her a reference – a good one – and send it to the last address he has in his personal book for her. That, too, will not be acknowledged.

And then one day, five years hence, switching on the TV in a hotel room in northern England, Anthony will look at the face of the woman presenting the local news, and think: I know her from somewhere.

Then he will laugh softly, shaking his head, and say something to Janey about how strangely life turns out sometimes.

It turns out that what's happening today is more tests as well as the first treatment.

They've had the initial blood tests, the results of which were bad enough to get them admitted straight away, but now there needs to be a bone-marrow test as well, and something else. Chemotherapy, radiation, bone marrow. Hannah, struggling with the tangled-up confusion of all this desperately important, changing information, finally succeeds in reducing it all to a simple set of manageable facts.

Today, at 2pm this afternoon, Megan will be lightly anaesthetised. A sample of her bone marrow fluid will then be drawn from her hip by injection. The sample will be taken away for immediate analysis. When the results of that analysis are known, final decisions will be made about the composition of Megan's drug treatment. That will be administered orally at this stage, although it could also be administered – "No," says Hannah – by injection.

Ongoing treatment will be subject to test results, but may include radiotherapy as well as further chemotherapy. It may be necessary at some stage to administer treatment by injection into Megan's sp– but Hannah's mind shuts down at that knowledge.

Ben is using the sketch pad to write down as many of the medical terms as he can, interrupting doctors to get them to spell words that sometimes, even they can't spell without looking down at their notes. By the end of today, Ben will know everything the hospital and the internet can tell him about Megan's illness.

A man in a black suit puts his hand lightly on Hannah's arm and she smiles to recognise him. "This is my husband," she says, and Ben, too, finds himself comforted by the man's presence. He looks across and sees that Megan is playing on her bed with the trainee they met last night.

Megan may experience some discomfort from the bone-marrow injection, they are told, and they would like to keep her in for observation for at least a few hours after treatment and ideally overnight.

She may be tired and feel sick, perhaps, but no, it is very, very unlikely, that there will be any hair loss from a single treatment.

Hannah closes her eyes.

Should they, perhaps, get on? 2pm is fast approaching, and unless there are any more questions...?

•

Night comes.

Now they are like the other families in the ward. They are no longer fearful, they are exhausted.

Now Megan is like the other children in the ward. She is no longer lively. There is even a plastic tube taped to her arm.

But she was so brave, so brave.

Hannah is weak and tired and her whole face is trembling and wet with tears. Ben is asleep in another armchair they have found for him and put on the other side of the bed. The curtain is pushed out around his chair, invading the space of the empty bed next to them. In Hannah's lap, held in her hands but forgotten, there is a mug of lukewarm, sugary tea that the trainee brought to her an hour before.

Megan opens her eyes. "Mummy," she whispers, and Hannah, in a single fluid movement that somehow also includes finding the mug and lifting it unspilt to the floor, brings herself up and forward over the bed.

"I'm here, my darling," she whispers, taking her daughter's hand and leaning forward into Megan's line of sight so that she doesn't have to move her head. "I'm here, my love."

"Hello Mummy," Megan breathes.

Her eyes are glassy and unfocused and for a moment Hannah thinks that she is sinking straight back into her pain-relieved sleep.

Hannah gently holds her daughter's hand and moves back so that her tears will fall harmlessly on the pink blanket.

But then Megan's eyes open again.

"Mummy," she says, staring at the empty ceiling, her voice suddenly charged with panic, and Hannah moves straight back into her view, stabbed by the split second in which Megan could not see her and was afraid.

"I'm here, my darling, I'm here."

"Mummy."

Hannah can feel Megan relax. She wants to say, "Don't be afraid." But she can't mention fear. "I'm always here, darling," she says, committing herself on the instant to a permanent vigil.

"Mummy, look after Chandler."

"Of course, darling," says Hannah automatically. Chandler? "Of course I will."

"There are horses. And he's going to be..."

But Megan's voice fades before Hannah can hear what Chandler is going to be.

"I will, darling," Hannah whispers, watching her daughter subside back into sleep. "I will." Already, Hannah has perfected the art of crying in absolute silence. "Oh my God," she whispers. "Please."

Ben wakes suddenly. Her jerks forward and Hannah hears his intake of breath. She watches him remember where they are. He looks round and sees that she is awake.

"You go home," she says softly.

But he is studying her face across the bed, seeing the tears and the exhaustion.

"I don't think so," he says.

He looks at her for a moment longer and then he checks his watch. Then he gets to his feet and stretches.

She feels, rather than hears, the moment of decision.

He says, "I'm going to find out whether they need us here any longer." He comes round the bed and leans down to kiss her on the forehead. "If anybody's going home, we're all going home."

And before Hannah can say anything, he is gone.

•

And then time passes. So much time, so quickly. They go home. They travel between the hospital and home. Other things happen. People come. The supermarket. There are messages and cards. Shifts are organised. Sarah Bishop. Even Mrs Barnaby. Hannah lives at the hospital, comes home and sleeps. Ben is always at home or at the hospital. Teamwork around Megan. He is going to leave his job. He thinks he has a new job but the old job is still paying him although he hasn't been in so he can't stop – Hannah can't take it in. Megan, Megan, Megan.

So many doctors talking in low, slow voices. So many explanations. So many facts and numbers. So much pain.

Megan, Megan.

And then it ends.

The grey doctors are satisfied.

The treatment is complete.

The prognosis is good.

Megan can come home and stay there.

Hannah accepts the card with the check-up appointment and tries to be happy. But she is too tired to celebrate.

Instead, she sleeps.

Preparations

Another day.

Megan is drawing. She is sitting at the kitchen table with her colouring book and her crayons. Hannah is preparing vegetables at the counter. There are bars of sunshine slanting in through the glass panels of the French windows. Later this morning, it may be warm enough to take a rug and the toys out into the garden.

Hannah is working from a recipe in a cookery book about healthy eating. There are no toxins in the house now. The water is filtered, and all three of them have become near-vegetarians, except for oily fish and other sources of Omega 3, minerals and vitamins. The bathroom cabinet has been cleaned out; they use perfume-free, hypo-allergenic products to wash and prepare themselves for the day. Near Megan is a ceramic bowl containing bananas, organic apples and thoroughly rinsed organic seedless grapes.

Her mobile buzzes in her bag. Ben.

"Hello, darling."

"Hello Ben. How did it go?"

"We really liked each other, I think. Fantastic office. His daughter was there." His voice cracks. "I'll tell you later. All well?"

"Yes."

Hannah slices carrots lengthwise. She will give them in a bowl to Megan, who might eat a few. Celery goes down well, too. Megan really is very good.

Plums for pudding, stoned, with bio-yoghurt.

"Mummy?"

"Yes, darling?"

"Can we have sausages for lunch today?"

Hannah turns and looks at her daughter.

She has become accustomed to Megan's lack of hair.

"Sausages for lunch? I'm doing you a bowl of special crunchies, darling."

Megan goes back to her drawing.

It is this passive acceptance that most unnerves Hannah, like treading on empty space. She so much wants her daughter to argue, cry, whine.

Be healthy.

There are still a couple of packs of chipolatas in the freezer.

"We can have sausages if you like, darling."

Megan brightens up. "Hooray!"

But Hannah just hears the weakness in her daughter's voice.

"Come on, darling," she says, bustling suddenly. "I'll get the sausages and you clear the table for me, will you?"

She'll microwave them, dammit. Just one big treat can't do any harm. And maybe – no. Hannah catches herself. There is an unopened bottle of tomato ketchup in the cupboard, but maybe that should stay out of the way. Past its sell-by, probably.

Megan begins to pack her crayons away and Hannah hears the

request that hasn't been spoken.

"I'd love to look at your pictures, darling."

So mother and daughter sit together at the kitchen table and Hannah sifts through the pictures Megan has drawn. There's one of them in the kitchen now – Megan has become much more self-aware lately – with Hannah slicing big orange carrots and the fridge for some reason transposed to beside Megan, a big white shape, and there's one of the house, with the front walls transparent to show them all in their beds. Megan has filled her own room with blobs and shapes for furniture, but the other rooms are empty and Hannah's and Ben's bed is just a rectangle.

"They're lovely, darling. We must put them up." Hannah picks up the next picture. "What's this one?"

"That's me and Chandler going riding, Mummy."

Hannah is taken by surprise. Chandler again, she thinks. Stubborn, bloody Chandler who won't ever get out of my daughter's head.

Then something gives in her mind, and she leans forward to look more closely at the picture.

There's a lot of blue for the sky and a lot of green for the ground, and in the middle of the picture, there are shapes that remind Hannah of those long party balloons that get twisted into dog shapes. Knowing what the picture is, Hannah can separate out the two horses and the small pink stick-figure that is her daughter. Chandler is represented by stick-figure legs and a round head without features. But his arms are drawn as ovals, so that they billow out behind him as though he was wearing very loose, light sleeves. Megan is riding ahead of him in the picture, and although it's pretty much one of Megan's typical four-year-old pictures, Hannah gets a sense of perspective, as though Megan and her invisible friend are riding away from her, into the white space at the top right-hand corner of the picture.

"Chandler says I'm a very good rider, Mummy."

To Hannah's certain knowledge, Megan has never been near a horse in her life.

"That's kind of him," says Hannah automatically, staring at the picture.

"I'm going to get a horse when I'm–"

Megan suddenly stops herself, as though she has thought better of the word that comes next.

Hannah's heart stops.

Megan looks off to one side, as though she's heard something, and then says to her mother, "If I'm allowed. Can I get a horse when I'm allowed, Mummy?"

Hannah stands up abruptly.

"Let's stick them on the wall, shall we? Then Daddy can see them when he comes home. We could go outside this afternoon."

"Would you like me to draw Chandler, Mummy?"

Hannah stops.

"Yes, darling," she says. "I think I would like you to draw Chandler. I would like you to do that very much."

"What do you want him to look like, Mummy?"

Hannah doesn't understand the question.

Megan huffs impatiently. "With wings, or like a daddy?"

It takes a moment for Hannah to muster up an answer.

"With wings," she says.

"Oh good," says Megan, and Hannah watches her as she glances to her right and begins to draw. She glances to her right again and to Hannah suddenly it seems that – it seems that–

Then it all comes rushing in on her. "Can you see–" she begins, before her mouth shuts up tight, biting off the question.

She clutches at her head, feeling the downy stubble where she has shaved off her hair to be like her daughter.

Megan is concentrating on her drawing.

Hannah stands rigid in front of her.

Then Hannah lowers her hands carefully to her sides.

She will not lose control.

She takes a long, slow breath, stilling herself, quelling the tears that have started to her eyes.

It is a delusion. A side-effect of the treatment that they will be able to address when–

When Megan is fully healed.

So for now–

"I'd love to meet Chandler one day," she says, in a jollying-along, upbeat-mummy voice that sounds false even to her.

Megan looks up at her, clearly surprised. Then she looks to her right, looks at her again and then again to her right, exactly as though she has begun to reply but been interrupted.

"You have met him, Mummy," she says, and there is perplexity in her voice. She glances to her right again. Then her face clears, as though she has just understood something funny.

"Have I? When?"

"At the beach."

"I've met Chandler at the beach," and Hannah can't keep the hysterical note out of her voice.

"When I was with the cousins. Remember? I fell over in the water and Chandler came and saved me because I was drowning." Megan pronounces 'drowning' in a doomy, child-solemn voice, as though she doesn't understand the word but knows it's serious.

"That man was Chandler?"

"Yes, and the lady was..." Megan hesitates "...Sassrail?" she says. Then, as if she's getting it from dictation, "Sar has rail, Mummy, Sah has ray ell. She's going to be your friend."

"The lady on the beach is going to be my friend," says Hannah, holding down the bubble of hysteria. "Is she going to be Daddy's friend?"

She is surprised when Megan shakes her head.

"Chandler says Daddy isn't ready yet," Megan says, gazing directly at her mother. She pauses, and then says, "Chandler says to tell you..." again, she hesitates "...you are beloved of Heaven. You mustn't worry. That's nice," she says, glancing to the right. "Really?"

It's so convincing that for a second Hannah even thinks she sees a white figure crouching next to Megan, speaking these things softly into her ear.

"Beloved of Heaven," she says.

Megan suddenly giggles.

"Is there any ice cream, Mummy?"

"Ice cream," repeats Hannah, and turns like an automaton to the freezer.

There is none. But on the top of the fridge, there is a not-quite-empty box of chocolates that Hannah has forgotten. She upends the box on the table.

"Daddy does love you," says Megan. Again, she glances aside. "Find himself?" she says. "What does that mean?"

That is when Hannah abruptly leaves the kitchen and goes upstairs to lie on her back on her bed with her eyes closed. Tears stream down from the outer corners of her eyes and are diverted by her ears onto her neck, from which they fall to make a damp patch on the pillow.

She leaves Megan finishing a drawing that in the world as it is now, will spend a month Blu-Tacked to the fridge and forgotten; that will then be remembered and taken down carefully to be placed among Hannah's sacred things.

She lies on her back with her eyes closed, and when Megan finds her, she raises her arms without opening her eyes, so that her daughter can come forward and lie with her, listening to her heart.

Beloved of Heaven.

"You're going to have a baby, Mummy," says Megan, her voice muffled against Hannah's chest.

·

They are in the hospital again. They have come suddenly. Megan woke up this morning and her face–

Her face was–

Yellow. Ochre. What? A wrong colour from the paintbox.

Hannah feels that she is barely in control. She cannot catch up with what is happening. It is all happening too fast. She cannot catch up with her own panic.

They were met at the entrance and Megan was settled in a wheelchair. It has a table and a headrest and is clearly designed for a disabled child. "Look Mummy," she said, "My chair's got wheels." Megan has seen wheelchairs before. They follow along the familiar corridors, Megan's retinue of two parents, two nurses and one trainee.

It was the trainee who somehow knew their car and waved them to the reserved space near the entrance. It was the trainee who had brought the card to put on the dashboard to say that they were allowed to park there.

Naseena, her name. Naseena, Naseena, remember the name. Hurrying beside the wheelchair, Hannah notices that Megan has reached out and is now holding Naseena's hand.

There will be no going home now. Megan will have to be admitted so that they can treat whatever new threat lies behind this sudden ghastly change in her skin. Hannah is sick with dread now. This is a setback. Neither nurse has spoken to her yet. Only Naseena has looked across and given her a brief, precious, sad smile.

Hannah's face feels as though it is leaking out like rotten sawdust from behind the expression of bright confidence that she has so far been able to maintain.

One nurse is pushing the wheelchair and the other is carrying a folder of papers. Hannah guesses that these are Megan's notes, those too immediate to be kept in electronic form. They have to be kept close to her now, Hannah tells herself, so that they can be consulted by the many doctors who will come to deal with this present crisis. Certainly more than one doctor will come because skin is a separate – thing, and – Hannah's thoughts keep spiralling off and she has to keep reining them back in to where they are now.

They are in the ward, at the familiar bed, and the familiar faces by the other beds, and now here is the black-suited man from the night so long ago, offering tea, taking the small suitcase from Ben – Ben brought a suitcase? Hannah hadn't noticed – and then gently taking her aside as the trainee yields to the two new men, one in a white coat, familiar, impersonal, the other in blue, and there are tests to be done, and Megan touches her hand, and the trainee goes with Megan, and then Hannah, who is somehow now in a small office, subsides onto a sofa and weeps.

Ben is there, and so is the gentle man.

"I need to be with my daughter," Hannah is saying.

"Just for a moment," the man is saying. "Just for this moment. Megan is safe."

"This is bad, isn't it?" Ben says, and his words puncture Hannah's cocoon. She hears in them Ben's effort to stand upright in the face of this catastrophe, to gain control of himself and what is happening; his effort not to cry.

The man doesn't speak and Hannah opens her eyes. Not hearing an answer, she is desperate for one.

She sees the man holding Ben, hugging him like they're reunited brothers, and she realises that Ben is now, at last, crying.

She comes to her feet and the man yields to her, stepping aside

268

as she takes back her husband. Then there are paper hankies in her hand and her face and Ben's are no distance apart. They are weeping together, sharing, drying each other's eyes, and she is saying things like, "We've got to help each other," and, "Come on, we need to be strong now." And they are not exactly laughing nor is Ben exactly embarrassed to be crying, but it is as if a clouded space between them has cleared and they are together.

There is a tap on the door and a voice tells the man that Megan is back in her bed.

In the corridor, Hannah sees that her daughter is settled against white pillows and nodding at something the trainee – Naseena, that's it – has said. Naseena is sitting on the bed, talking to Megan, now listening, now talking, now holding her hand. They are both clearly absorbed in the conversation and Hannah stops, raising her arm to stop Ben too.

The two of them walk forward more slowly, not wanting to interrupt such an obviously happy moment in such a place.

•

"Tell me about Ali. Was he really naughty?"

"No, he was a good boy. He carried water for his family. He ran errands for his father."

"He came with you too."

"Yes. He was kind. When it was my job to look after the children, he would translate for me, tell them what I meant when I didn't know the words in their language. I suppose he was naughty sometimes." Naseena smiles at a memory.

"Say some words in Ali's language."

Naseena does so, and Megan repeats them. Naseena teaches Megan the words for 'Mummy', 'Daddy', 'yes', 'no', 'please', 'thank you' in Ali's language. Megan seems to have forgotten the syringe already. Naseena is relieved; she hadn't wanted to step in, but the mother had been so clearly on the point of collapse.

"Was Ali sick like me?" Megan asks.

Naseena knows enough about children not to be surprised by the question. As she answers, she wonders how much Megan has understood about her own condition.

"I thought he was sick, but he was not very sick. One day he woke up from a sleep and he was better."

Naseena watches Megan think for a moment about going to sleep and waking up better. Then Megan smiles suddenly.

"Chandler says Ali was naughty sometimes."

"Really? Who is Chandler?"

"Chandler saved Ali from the soldiers. Chandler told Ali you must leave."

Naseena remembers Ali's talk about meeting an angel. When did I tell you about that? she wonders, looking at the little girl.

Megan makes a small movement forwards. "Ali went looking for water among the trees," she confides, her eyes wide with the seriousness of it. "There were soldiers hiding there, but Ali didn't see them. He saw Chandler instead. Chandler told him to go back to the camp."

Naseena is nodding slowly, like a parent concerned to indicate that she is taking a child's wisdom seriously. She is thinking: I didn't tell you any of this.

Megan suddenly waves. "Hello Mummy! Hello Daddy!"

Naseena realises that she has forgotten to stop nodding. She stands up off the bed to give Mr and Mrs Rose access to their daughter.

•

Time passes and the Rose family does not go home. They are waiting for a doctor to come to them with an explanation of what has happened to their daughter's skin. They have been told that the analysis of this morning's tests will not take long. Megan has been dozing since the trainee left them with her. There is a sour-sweet, off-milk smell around the bed.

Hannah cannot tell whether she is dreading the explanation, or impatient. When the moment comes for them to be told, she finds that she is at least partly insulated from it, as though the shock of it is so great that it cannot be lived all at once.

First, Naseena returns to be with Megan.

Then, Hannah and Ben are led down long corridors of featureless perspective to the white door that is the entrance to room TC36. Here, once again, they meet Mr Trenchard. Doctor Murison is also waiting in the room, half-rising as they enter, but his presence barely touches Hannah's mind.

Megan's count is significantly lower than Mr Trenchard would have expected. It seems that her condition has metastasised. Now she has suffered a significant renal failure.

"What does significant mean?" Ben asks.

Mr Trenchard isn't looking at them.

"What do you do about that?" Hannah asks him.

Finally, Mr Trenchard looks at her, directly, in the eye.

"We can keep her comfortable," he says. Then once again he is referring to the papers on his desk.

"I meant, what treatment?" Hannah falters.

Mr Trenchard looks up and his gaze slides off Hannah's.

"I'm afraid I think that you should begin to prepare yourselves," he says.

And then he is sitting at his desk and not looking at them and they are staring at him.

"Prepare ourselves for what?" says Ben.

Hannah raises her hand.

"Tell us what to do," she says, her voice as fragile as the truth. "Realistically," she adds.

Colin Trenchard looks across his desk at the mother of his terminally ill patient and is suddenly able to speak. They are past the news. Now that he has told her. The mothers are always so much stronger.

"We can resume treatment if you wish," he tells her. "But it causes her discomfort. And I have to tell you that it may be better – for her – if we focused on making her comfortable." He becomes conscious that he is speaking in short lumps of sentence. He pauses. "I think that you should prepare yourselves to say goodbye."

Ben is waiting for the man to start telling them about the small hope that still remains. That if only they – just – something, Megan may still pull through. There's a miracle cure that might, just might work. There's a miracle. But the man has stopped on the bit about saying goodbye. Ben doesn't get it. "When can we expect..." he begins.

"How long?" says Hannah next to him.

The doctor looks at her again over his clasped hands and elbows leaning on his papers.

"Perhaps weeks," he says. Then, a short time later, he continues in a slower voice. "It's impossible to be accurate, of course, but I should certainly think you have a week." He is about to say something else, but Hannah interrupts him.

"Is she in pain?"

"Oh no, that's one thing you certainly don't have to worry about."

The doctor is babbling on about pain relief now.

"Can't we look after her at home?" Hannah says, interrupting the man.

Of course they could, but with her condition this far advanced...

"Can we stay here with her?" Hannah no longer has time for the niceties.

Yes, they certainly can, and Megan will be able to have all her familiar toys...

There's more, but the key fact is, they're going to get Megan now, and then go over and find Megan's bed, and while they're settling her in, they will be shown, one at a time, how to operate whatever it is they're being given for the pain.

Ben suddenly catches up with what Hannah and the doctor are discussing. The doctor is describing the key stages, the indications, the progression in terms of visible symptoms and impact on vital organs. They'll know when the end is near. Hannah is nodding like she's being told for the first time how to change a nappy.

Megan is dying. It's a progressive thing. She will go on dying and then she will be dead. That's what the doctor meant by giving them a week.

Ben suddenly interrupts the discussion by howling with grief and clutching at his head.

•

Megan opens her eyes. She smiles to see Naseena sitting on the side of the bed once again.

"Hello," she says.

"You were asleep," says Naseena.

"I was..." Megan closes her eyes again. "Lovely dream," she says. There is a fresh drip attached to her arm.

Naseena is holding Megan's hand in her lap. She reaches out her free hand to brush Megan's hair back off her forehead.

But as she does so, Megan's eyes open abruptly. "No," she says.

Naseena withdraws her hand. "I'm sorry I startled you," she says.

"Chandler told me what you did for Ali," Megan murmurs; Naseena has to lean forward to hear her clearly.

"What did he tell you?" she asks automatically, not really engaging with the words. She speaks in a soft voice intended to reassure by its tone.

Then she realises what Megan has just said. Megan looks at her.

"I'm going to the horses now," Megan tells her.

Naseena's mouth opens, then closes, then opens again. "I don't–" she begins.

Megan smiles faintly. "Chandler says you do," she says.

Then her eyes close and she is asleep again.

There is suddenly a presence beside Naseena. A hand touches her shoulder. She looks up into the eyes of Richard Hailey.

"Come on," he says. "I think you and I need to talk."

•

"No doubts, Chandrael?"

Sahasrael and I walk together on the dry floor of a green forest. There is music in the soft air, and the sound of bees. Open-winged butterflies hang like mandalas on sunlit leaves.

"Even now, I could heal her."

"You could," says Sahasrael.

"Perhaps I will ask you for a miracle one day."

Sahasrael laughs softly. "If you do, my love, it will be freely given."

And she is gone.

In The World That Will Be

Megan has been moved to a small room of her own near the nurses' station. Sahasrael and I have spoken in this room. But now there is a switched-off television and the teddy bears and other toys that the nurses have brought from the ward's collection. Pugh and Sleepy are on the pillow. There are colourful books and the TV remote on the cabinet beside the bed, with a jug of pale fruit squash and a small posy of flowers, in a glass, that Hannah picked a week ago. The flowers have not died.

The patient has been left alone with her parents. The diagnostic trolley has been pushed to the side of the room. Megan still has the cannula in her arm, because it would discomfort her more to remove it, and there are pads taped to her chest that lead to a heart monitor. This has been turned to the wall with the volume down; the only sound the machine makes in the room is a faint electronic pulse that cannot be switched off.

Hannah Rose is seated on the right-hand side of the bed. Ben

Rose is seated on the left. They are both leaning forwards. Each holds one of Megan's hands and they are holding each other's hands across the bed, making a circle. Their clasped hands do not touch the sheet; they do not want their child to be hurt by the pressure. But they must hold each other.

I acknowledge the higher presences in the room. When Hannah and Ben think back on this moment, each of them will remember a brightness in the clean air. The chrome and white furniture, and the pale wood panels, will seem to shine with a warmth that in their world, the room does not contain.

Megan opens her eyes.

"Hello, Mummy," she whispers.

"Hello, darling." Megan's mother leans forward, letting go of her husband to put her hand at Megan's cheek. She rises out of her chair to kiss Megan's forehead, so gently, so gently. She tells herself that she must be stone. She must show no tears. She must not cry. "Hello, my darling," she whispers again, her voice breaking.

"Don't cry, Mummy," says Megan.

But her mother falls back in her chair. For this moment, she cannot speak.

"Darling." Nor can her father speak for the pressure of tears. He goes forward onto his knees beside the bed, kneeling upright so that his upper body is close to his daughter. Now he takes her hand in both of his. "Darling," he repeats. He cannot stop his tears.

"I love you, Daddy," says Megan.

Her father's face falls forward onto the sheet beside her. For a second, he cannot stifle the sound of his sobbing. He has forgotten to keep his weight off the bed, but Megan is beyond discomfort.

Megan sees me.

"Hello, Chandler," she says, her voice briefly strong again.

Her mother raises her face from her hand. Her face is smeared with weeping.

"Hello, Megan," I reply.

Only Megan hears me.

But Megan's mother's face is suddenly blank with shock.

"Chandler," she says.

Then suddenly she is urgent, pressing forward for an answer. "Darling, is Chandler here? Tell me, is he here?"

Ben is staring at her. She shakes her head at him: she'll explain later.

"Don't take her," Hannah says to the air. "Please. Don't take her."

Ben reaches for her across the bed.

Megan is close to death. She sees the bright presences around the bed.

She says, "No, Mummy."

Her voice is soft again. Both parents stoop to hear her. "Daddy, Chandler's here," she says. She tries to lift her arm, to point, and for a second Ben thinks he sees something: for him, I am a refraction of the light against the curtain.

"Daddy," Megan whispers. "He's going to tell me a story."

"And we're going to play," I say.

"We're going to play in Heaven," she whispers, and I know that both of them hear her.

"Look after her," her father says to the air around me.

Later, it will comfort Hannah to believe that he saw me. He will describe me to her in the terms she needs: a brightness, a presence, a figure of light. He will sometimes doubt that he did see ... anything, but he will never admit this doubt to his wife.

Megan sleeps. I wait. Hours pass. Nurses and a doctor come and go in the room. Measurements are taken of Megan's physical condition. In the world, the day fades into night but the light remains in the room.

Sahasrael comes to me. She places her hand on my arm.

"Now, Chandra," she says.

I move forward over the bed so that Megan and her parents are enclosed in light.

Megan dies.

In the distance, her parents hear the faint sound of a bell. It is an alarm, sounding at the nurses' station as the signal of Megan's heart ceasing. In their own hearts, Hannah and Ben feel the impact of her passing. It is as if the air releases her. "Oh my darling," Hannah cries, her eyes closing with tears as she falls forward.

And then Megan stands beside me at the end of the bed. I see that she is silver in her innocence, risen into light.

"Did you think such an experience would be chosen by a young soul?" Sahasrael asks me.

Megan looks around at the presences, calm, quiet, and then she recognises me.

"Hello, Chandler," she says.

She is still in her human consciousness.

"Welcome, Megan," I say.

She looks down at herself, raises her hands and looks around. She wears her own white night-dress and she has given herself the shimmer of wings. Her eyes are bright blue.

"Is this Heaven?" she says.

Now we are surrounded by fields of long green grass rippling in a silent breeze. Faintly in the light the horses are visible, tossing manes the colour of honey and stamping in their impatience to be gone across the plains. They nuzzle each other, watching Megan.

She is watching them. "Am I dead now?" she says.

"There is no death here, beloved," I tell her. "There is only the path to the divine."

"What about Mummy?"

"Tell your mother not to cry," I tell her.

Once again we are at the foot of the hospital bed where her parents weep. I move my right hand and we are visible in the room. Megan's mother raises her head and sees her daughter. Megan laughs in delight and raises her hand to wave. Behind us the horses are visible too, gathered at the white fence.

Hannah's eyes meet mine. "Chandler," she breathes. I see in her mind that she remembers me now from the beach and the café. I bow my head to her and she bows hers in return.

ACCEPT FROM US THE TRUTH THAT ALL IS WELL, I tell her, and for a moment she hears her daughter's voice. "Mummy, we're going riding!" And then the light fades and the room is silent again.

Richard Hailey, who has seen all of this from his place by the door, comes forward into the room.

It is done.

•

I ride with Megan Rose and then we are the horses as their colours merge together with the speed of our passing. The galloping of the horses and the rising and the falling of their backs around us blend into the one river flowing, and as they do so, the pounding of their hooves becomes the rushing of bright waters over washed stones and for a brief eternity we are gone into the harmony together, the green fields dissolving into glass, the river flowing and the silver water open to receive her, and then she travels onward into the mystery, and I am left behind.

I stand with Sahasrael in the wake of Megan's passing. We are on hard, flat ground scattered with rocks. She touches me on the shoulder, but still, for the first time in this endless place, I feel alone.

"I want to help them."

"Then go to them, my love," she says.

•

In the beginning, the world is nowhere, and there is nothing. I float in an absence of otherness that is neither light nor dark. It is infinite and I am One.

Then there is movement, and in movement there is a beginning. I am. I am moved. I am contained in space and time.

There is only Is. And now there is Will Be.

My companion passes behind the veil. I am alone. Stillness is acceptance.

Movement sparks movement. I move. I swim upwards through the old seas of creation towards fins, and a tail, and then legs, and arms; my tail and fins disappear. Gradually, my spine straightens. I have feather-light fingers and toes, and I can open my eyes. In my warm sea, I still swim.

My mother feels me for the first time and I can feel her. I hear voices. Movement is my speech.

I am scanned. In the outer world, my father watches a screen. He says, "That's his head! Did you see his face? God, isn't he beautiful?" and cries.

My mother, who carries secretly in her purse the print of Megan's scan and her first photograph, will cry later, alone. Megan, my older sister who died before I was born. And now here is another tiny soul coming into her care.

Then my mother and I, and sometimes my father, sing. I hear my mother's voice in a certain tone and I move in invitation and she sings to me. The songs have no meanings; they come to me as waves to fit into my ocean, my boundless, endless ocean, and I feel held and loved, as though this is Heaven. It seems to me that this is the world into which I have been born.

I am serene. Serenity is acceptance.

Then the world comes for me. The ocean convulses and is gone. There is wetness, cold, heat, pushing, touch, pain. I am held in a tight space, tight, falling; pain; I am heavy; I can no longer float. Beached. I learn fear. I learn self. Fear is self.

Then the world splinters into light and cold and noise and space and broken sound. I swerve upwards through the light and hard-edged things fix themselves into my sky: there is up, down; there is a lightness, a darkness, a plane of grey. I am shocked: I open my mouth to draw it all up into me and then expel it all in one shriek of grief.

And there is my mother's voice, louder now, clearer, and I am held tight again in a second ocean of warmth and lullaby. A picture prints itself in my brain: my mother's face, overlaid with the sound, the smell, and I nuzzle forward and feed.

I am ended and I am begun. I am.

•

Mrs Rose. As I said on the phone this morning, I thought you might want to see this rather than I put it up on the wall with the picture. The assignment was "Write about yourself" and usually this age group stops with name, age and possibly pets and family – in the same way that the picture is usually just the family group! He is such a lovely, bright little boy and please, nothing to worry about. You have my number, any time, you know. Muriel B

•

My nam is Michael Chandler Rose. Chandler is my midle nam. Mummy says it is a speshal nam. I had a sister but she did before I was born. Her nam was Megan. I am forna haf.

my frend is cald Sahasrael. I can spel it. mummy cant see Sahasrael but she taks to her. Sahasrael tels me storys and we play gams. Sahasrael can fly.

I drad a picher of Sahasrael for Mrs Barnaby said thats lovly darling.

Love from Michael Chandler Rose XXX

William Essex is author of the novel *Escape Mutation -
A Journal of the Plague Years* and the short-story collection
God - The Interview and other stories. His other titles include
*Ten Steps to a Bedtime Story - how to get a lively toddler to sleep
before the supper goes cold* and *The Book of Fake Futures*.

William Essex lives in Falmouth, Cornwall.